Readers Love K.L. Hiers

Acsquidentally in Love

"Hiers rolls worldbuilding mythology, delicious flirting, erotic scenes, and detective work into a breezy and sensual LGBTQ paranormal romance."

—*Library Journal*

Kraken My Heart

"This is a really good series. It is one that is worth reading over again, just for the fun of it."

—Love Bytes Book Reviews

Just Calamarried

"Sloane and Loch are so crazy in love that you can feel it."

—Virginia Lee Book Reviews

Our Shellfish Desires

"It's a really lovely use of the romantic triad idea…four stars."

—Paranormal Romance Guild

By K.L. Hiers

SUCKER FOR LOVE MYSTERIES
Acsquidentally In Love
Kraken My Heart
Head Over Tentacles
Nautilus Than Perfect
Just Calamarried
Our Shellfish Desires
Insquidious Devotion
Ollie's Octrageously Official Omnibus
An Inkredible Love

Published by Dreamspinner Press
www.dreamspinnerpress.com

AN INKREDIBLE
LOVE

K.L. HIERS

REAMSPINNER
PRESS

CHAPTER 1.

ONE YEAR AGO....

FRED WILDER decided the most frustrating thing about being a ghoul was not being able to eat.

Despite the lack of appetite or need for any sustenance, he still often found himself hovering in front of his empty fridge. He didn't keep anything there for guests because he never had any over, and whatever he bought would have been wasted since he couldn't eat it.

He missed cake, chocolate in particular, and the mere memory made his mouth want to water. But he could not eat food now any more than he could drool over it.

Fred was a ghoul, a member of the only slightly undead. He'd suffered severe burns in a fire five years ago, and the doctors said he would not survive his injuries.

His best friend's sister, Lynnette Fields, refused to accept that prognosis and broke out the family grimoire. After some very rough translating, she was able to bind Fred's soul to a wooden spoon before he died and then later created a copy of his body to complete the ritual. His soul now bound to the ghoul vessel, Fred had cheated death. Like all forms of the forbidden art of necromancy, it came with a heavy cost.

High up on the list was the frustration of not being able to eat any damn chocolate cake.

Fred also couldn't feel much of anything, emotional or otherwise, except pain. Being a ghoul meant constant and unavoidable anguish as his body continually tried to rot. All of his prayers to the old gods went unheard, and there was nothing he could do except rely on magic.

Magic could be a bitch. It was heavily regulated in modern times, including the necessity of rigorous testing to determine specific disciplines and an annual state license to use it legally.

Being a Sage and a rogue witch, Fred's death certificate said unregistered.

Sages were followers of the Sagittarian faith, witches who worshipped a pantheon of gods that roamed the earth long ago. Gone into the dreaming, an eternal state of sleep, the gods had left their mortal followers and allowed a new monotheistic religion to take root in the form of the Lord of Light.

Most people considered the ancient ways to be nothing more than a joke and gave into the Lucian system willingly.

But not Sages.

They had their children at home, resisted testing that they thought was unnecessary, and though few in number, some lived proudly as rogue witches. They could be fined, arrested, or even jailed, but at least these witches were free of what they saw as an oppressive system.

If Fred had allowed himself to be registered, his discipline would have been fire. Lucians were fine with that, but that made no sense to Sages. Fire wasn't just fire. It could be warm and comforting like Shartorath's hearth, or it could be simmering and hot like Merikath's embers.

Or like Fred, who had Baub's rage, it could be wildly destructive and lethal.

The Sages believed that the gods would return one day. They would no longer have to fight, and they would be able to practice their religion and culture freely. Fred was pretty sure of it too.

After all, Fred knew the gods were alive and well because it was one such being who had solved his best friend's murder. It was also a god who had done the murdering.

Lochlain Fields had been killed almost a month ago by Tollmathan, the god of poetry and plagues, over a piece of a mystical totem that had the power to wake up Salgumel, the god of dreams and sleep. Salgumel was said to have gone mad in his dreaming and waking him would end the world.

That was Tollmathan's plan anyway, but Lochlain happened to be the favorite of Azaethoth the Lesser. The patron god of thieves himself took over Lochlain's body and found a private investigator named Sloane Beaumont to avenge Lochlain's death.

They solved the crime, destroyed the totem, and during a fierce battle, Sloane was gifted a sword of pure starlight by Great Azaethoth himself to kill Tollmathan and become a Starkiller, a slayer of gods.

As if that wasn't spectacular enough, Great Azaethoth gave them another miracle: Lochlain came back from the dead, completely restored and alive again.

Lynnette made a ghoul copy of Lochlain's body for Azaethoth the Lesser to inhabit to continue his romance with Sloane, and they didn't have to worry about the usual pitfalls as Azaethoth's godly essence kept the body from decomposing. Their mutual friend Robert Edwards finally confessed his secret love to Lochlain, and Lynnette was getting ready to move in with her boyfriend, a geeky forensic guy named Milo.

It was a happy ending for everyone all around.

Except Fred.

Each day for him was more of the same, and it sucked.

As a ghoul, he wasn't supposed to have any emotions. He was supposed to be disconnected from them and feel nothing except constant physical pain. But Fred was becoming aware that he felt something else, a hollowness that had transformed into an ache that often rivaled his physical agony.

He was lonely.

Since Lochlain had begun his new relationship with Robert, Fred rarely saw him. They hadn't gone out on a job all month, leaving Fred to work on his own. He still had rent to pay, ghoul doctors were expensive, and like Lochlain, Fred was a thief.

He'd just returned from a heist, breaking into a warehouse to jack some old ugly paintings for some very enthusiastic collectors. The job was easy enough, security was light, and he would make the drop tomorrow night.

That left Fred with all of this evening and most of tomorrow to amuse himself, and standing in front of his empty fridge had lost its charm.

He didn't bother calling Lochlain because no doubt he was busy fawning over Robert. Lynnette was either waitressing or packing up to move in with Milo. He briefly considered calling Sloane or Azaethoth, but he didn't think it wise to disturb a god and his mate, no matter how chummy they were.

Everyone had someone now, and while he wanted to be happy for them, he was resentful. He wanted someone of his own to spend time with, to watch television with or to cook for even if he couldn't eat it, someone he could read to, a person to laugh with.

He wanted a friend who had time for him, maybe more than a friend.

Romance wasn't unheard of between ghouls and the living, but they had to be pretty fresh for anything to be palatable. Fred had been rotting for years, and outside of his own decomposition, he couldn't feel much. A hug was distant pressure and shaking someone's hand was a cold tease of sensation.

He couldn't imagine trying to physically be with anyone now, but he still longed for company. Even if he couldn't feel it, the mere idea of holding someone eased his discomfort and made his anger vanish.

Fat chance of that ever fuckin' happening.

Fred slammed the fridge door closed harder than he should have, and a new stab of pain lit up his arm. A giant rotten sore that had been festering was starting to leak.

"Shit."

Quickly bandaging it up with a dish towel, he stalked across his apartment to find his phone. He scrolled through his contacts, found the entry titled "Doc," and hit Send.

It rang a few times before a sleepy woman's voice answered, "Hello…?"

"Hey, Doc," Fred grunted. "It's me."

"I know who it is," Doctor York replied with a grumpy yawn. "What's wrong?"

"That spot you fixed ain't fixed no more. Need help."

"On your arm?" Doc sounded concerned. "Fred, I've tried to heal you three times now."

"So, do it four times."

"It doesn't work that way. I've told you. Ghouls are not forever. You're gonna keep rotting."

"Four times. Let's go." Fred refused to accept this dismal prognosis. "Come on, I'm good for it. I'm getting paid tomorrow."

"It's not about the money. It's just… I don't think I can help you. Your rot is getting worse."

"What about a new body?"

"No, your rate of decomposition will only increase."

There was the sound of a door opening and shutting noisily through the phone, and Fred could hear the jingle of the fancy wind chime Doc kept on her front porch. A lighter clicked, and then she inhaled, coughing on the smoke from her cigarette.

"If you try to jump ship and transfer your soul," she continued, "your new body will rot even faster than the one you're in right now."

Fred sat down and tried not to get angry. Anger was always so easy. "So, what the fuck do I do?"

"I know another ghoul doctor who might be able to help," Doc soothed. "He only takes patients by direct referral, and I don't know what he charges these days."

"Already said money don't matter."

"He's local," Doc said. "I'll get in touch and find out how soon he can see you."

"How soon?"

Doc sighed. "I'll call him right now, okay? I'll tell him it's an emergency."

"Thanks, Doc."

"Be good, Fred. I'll let you know as soon as I can."

"Okay. Bye."

Fred hung up and set his phone down on the coffee table. He didn't need to sleep, so the only option left to him was to wait.

He had given up trying to pass the time with television. Even commercials made him angry because of the sheer volume of smiling faces. Oh sure, they might be frowning over a drain being clogged or excess belly fat, but once the miracle product was introduced, they were happy again.

There was no magical switch for Fred, so screw that.

Reading was equally irritating, and he could only get through a few paragraphs before he'd lose focus. He wasn't sure if that was a side effect of being a ghoul or not, but it was maddening. He could read out loud without much bother, but it seemed pointless to read to himself without anyone to hear him.

Screw that too.

The only thing that ever seemed to pacify his sour temperament was popping in an old VHS tape with some episodes of his favorite television show, *Legends of Darkness*. It was a fantasy about a young man named Trip who went off to a magical land full of goblins and unicorns and had the most incredible adventures. Although it was easily over thirty years old, the special effects atrocious, and the quality of the footage was abysmal since he'd recorded it off his TV, nothing else brought him any level of comfort.

It reminded him of a simpler time, being a kid with Lochlain when they'd watch it together for hours on end. They'd act out their favorite scenes, make up new stories, and play until they passed out.

That was ages ago now, but watching the show still eased that bothersome ache inside Fred. In thirty-minute increments, he could submerge himself in the magical world of the show and escape the cruel reality of his constant suffering.

At least until the end of the episode anyway.

He'd just made it to the second episode when his phone rang.

"Hey, Doc," he answered. "Gimme some good news, please."

"Hey," Doc said, sounding more awake than before. "Good news. He's agreed to meet you, but he's got some conditions."

"Which are?"

"You don't ever give out his name, where he lives, or what he does for you."

"Sure." All typical rules for ghoul doctors.

"Also. You don't question his age, his scar, or anything else about him."

"Okay." A little more unusual, but fine.

"Try not to be weird if he gets really handsy. It's just how his magic works, so don't be freaked out. Good? Good."

"Okay. How much?"

"He doesn't actually want a cash payment. You'll have to go shopping for him," Doc said, and it sounded like she was smiling. "I'm going to text you his address and a list of things he needs."

"Things? Like what?"

"Just get whatever is on the list if you want him to help you. Look, he doesn't get out much. Do it and be there tomorrow before noon."

"Fine." Fred tried not to sound agitated and failed. He took a deep breath, trying again when he said, "Thank you, Doc."

"Take care of yourself, Fred."

Fred ended the call and waited for the list to come through. He preferred dealing in cash, but if a simple shopping trip would settle the debt, that was fine too.

When the text popped up, Fred quickly realized there was nothing simple about it.

"A fuckin' faucet?" He blinked, continuing to read out loud. "Bread, but not white, the brown kind with crumbled oats on top. A trash can, small enough for a bathroom and any color except green, but blue would be really good. Body lotion, cucumber melon if you can find it, but the pinkie orange kind is okay too. Can't remember what it's called, but the bottle is pink with orange stripes. Donuts with sprinkles, but if there are no donuts with sprinkles, please get strawberry poofies instead." He scoffed. "What the fuck is a poofie?"

He checked the address to make sure it was legit, and he found it was a tiny speck in the middle of the forest almost forty-five minutes out of town.

Guess the guy really liked his privacy.

The rest of the list was full of more weirdly specific items. All of it was food except the faucet, trash can, and lotion. There were a few twenty-four-hour markets a short drive away. As long as he was going to be up, he might as well get the shopping done. He got up to leave, touching the Tauri shrine to his parents on his way out.

Tauri was another ancient religion that revered the old gods, though they called them by different names and believed in a cycle of multiple lives. While the ways of the Sages had faded to time, the Tauri faith remained in dominant practice in certain parts of the world like India and eastern Africa. Fred's mother's family had been from India, and she converted to the Sagittarian faith when she married his father.

They kept up with a lot of Tauri traditions like ancestor shrines and morning prayers, and his mother never cut her hair and only cooked vegetarian meals. She had also chosen to honor her father by passing his name on to her son.

She named him Farrokh.

They died when Fred was a teenager, both from complications of heart disease, and Fred became an honorary member of the Fields family with Lynnette and Lochlain. Though he embraced the Sagittarian religion, he never forgot his mother's faith, and he honored her by maintaining the shrine.

He honored his father by taking care of his old truck.

It always took a few cranks to get it going, and the engine sputtered and groaned the whole drive over to the store, but Fred wouldn't trade it for anything in the world. He could remember being too small to see over the dashboard, wedged in between his parents as they drove along, going grocery shopping just like he was now.

Damn, that ache was back again.

Fred ignored it, parked, and went inside the store.

It was surprising how much could be learned from doing someone else's grocery shopping.

Fred picked up on his new doctor having quite the sweet tooth, enviously dropping several types of cookies and sugary treats into the cart as he went along the aisles.

He gleaned that the doctor also drank a lot of tea, as there were at least four varieties on the list to pick up. It was clear he didn't cook much since there were also at least a dozen varieties of frozen dinners, and the lotion spoke of loneliness to Fred.

Or perhaps the doctor really liked to be moisturized.

Maybe he was just projecting, Fred thought glumly. He stared down at his bursting shopping cart and felt a wicked stab of jealousy. He couldn't even remember the last time he'd gone grocery shopping. Probably when he was still alive.

There had been times since his death that Lynnette had asked him to go to the store for tampons or pads, a seemingly squeamish task for mortal men. Fred was always happy to remind her that he was perfectly willing to go even when he had a pulse, and the guys she'd been seeing were just trash.

He also remembered to get chocolate, even if it made him more than a bit jealous he couldn't eat it.

Somehow, that had played into her relationship with Milo. There was a story about him already having a box of tampons from a busted nose and him pledging to buy all the feminine products she would ever need.

Fred thought it was sweet. He liked Milo, and he made Lynnette happy.

Looking into his shopping cart, he wished he was buying these groceries for someone he cared about.

But that wasn't possible.

He'd had his chance to find love while he was alive, and hell, he didn't even know if he could feel those kinds of emotions now. He knew he cared about his friends, but he often wondered how much of that was real and not an echo from his life before.

He cared for Sloane and Azaethoth, he reasoned, and he had met them as a ghoul. It couldn't be impossible, but it felt so far out of reach. After all, who would be interested in dating a big rotten guy? How could they even be together?

Thinking that way led to a lot of fuckin' misery.

Miserable enough to end it all.

He'd heard about other ghouls doing it. They would get so tired of the pain and the rot that they would stop healing and let themselves wither away. It could take weeks for the act to happen naturally, and Fred couldn't imagine that kind of agony.

Being lonely still sucked, though.

He finished shopping and loaded up his truck with the groceries to return home so he could refrigerate what needed to be cold. He was able to find pretty much everything except the faucet. He liked having food in his fridge again, even if it was inside the bags from the grocery store.

It made his apartment feel less empty somehow.

Back to the couch he went, sitting down and turning the TV back on. He let his mind drift, zoning out and trying to relax with a few more episodes of *Legends of Darkness*. When the tape was over, he would wait for it to rewind itself so he could play it again. This was as close to sleep as he could get, and he listened to the familiar creaks and thumps from his neighbors when morning finally rolled around.

The guy on the left would hang around in the kitchen, fighting with their coffee maker for the next twenty minutes before taking a very long shower. The lady on his right had kids, and there was always a rush of loud cartoons and screaming. The people upstairs clomped around like horses, and he never heard a peep from the neighbor below him.

The ache in Fred's arm was getting worse, and the pain made him want to punch something. He needed to move to distract himself from the discomfort. He got up and paced absently around his couch.

Doc had told him to be at the new doctor's house before noon. Maybe he could show up early. The pain was making it hard to concentrate, and he stopped suddenly, staring at the carpet beneath his boots.

He hadn't realized it before, but he'd done this so often that he was leaving a trail of wear in the carpet.

Time to go.

Fred gathered the groceries back up and headed down to his truck. He had to step around a pack of small children as their mother herded them off into the elevator. He whispered their names as he heard the mother patiently fussing at them to hurry along.

"Eleanor, Elizabeth, Vincent."

He could still remember when he used to hear them crying at all hours of the night and was thankful he didn't need to sleep. The corners of his mouth twitched up in a smile when he saw them swearing to their mother that they had done their homework just as the elevator doors were closing.

Fred knew damn well that was a lie because he'd heard the familiar blips of their latest video game when it was supposed to be bedtime.

He opted to take the stairs. It was a little quicker, and he didn't want to scare the kids.

At his size, he was already intimidating. His mother had told him he was built like the mighty god Theros, an amalgamation of the Sagittarian gods Salgumel and Bestrath, who was known for his broad build and big belly. The smell didn't help, and Lynnette had told him he had a serious case of resting bitch face.

Whatever.

Once he got the truck loaded, he punched in the new doctor's address and drove his sputtering truck along. It was definitely a haul, and he took his time navigating through traffic. He was already going to be a few hours early as it was.

Outside the city, the strain of cars eased, and Fred eventually pulled up to a small cottage a few minutes after nine. There wasn't shit out here except old fences, fields, and trees, and he was instantly wary.

The place looked like it had fallen off a country postcard right down to the lush flower boxes hanging outside the front windows and the white trellis framing the stone path up to the door. He was surprised to see flowers blooming like that so late in autumn, and he wondered if they were fake.

It was too perfect, too quaint, and Fred hated it immediately.

Fred had to duck and turn sideways to step through the trellis on his way to the front door. He knocked a few times. There wasn't an immediate answer, so he tried again.

He heard a noise, a loud grunting, and was immediately on guard.

"*Ignis*," he murmured, summoning a small ball of fire as he slowly crept toward the sound. It was coming from the back of the house, and he stepped around the corner, ready to fight any potential enemy.

What he saw was a skinny half-naked young man digging in the dirt and wrestling with a tree root. He was blond, filthy, and had ear buds in. The music was so loud he could hear the bass thumping through, and the young man hadn't noticed him yet.

Fred dismissed the fire, and he watched for a few moments.

Doc had said this guy was young, but this person looked like he was barely out of high school. His body was lean and steaming in the chilly air. The vision of sweaty pale skin might have been quite appealing when Fred was alive, and maybe it still was, but he didn't think much about it.

He was here on business.

"Hey," he tried.

The young man kept digging, fighting with the stubborn root as he murmured under his breath. He was singing along with whatever was pumping into his ears and remained completely oblivious to Fred's presence.

"Hey!" Fred roared, a bone-shattering shout guaranteed to get some attention.

"Oh!" The boy whirled around, quickly pulling the buds out of his ears. "Sorry! I must have lost track of the time!" His smile was bright, punctuated with a crooked canine, and Fred spotted a long scar across his throat that snaked up to his left ear.

"You the doc?"

"Are you Farrokh?"

"Call me Fred."

"Hi, Fred!" the young man eagerly offered his hand to shake. "Elliam Sturm! Just Ell is fine. It's so nice to meet you!"

"Yeah," Fred said, accepting the gesture. As he shook Ell's hand, he found that he didn't want to let go. "Thanks for seeing me."

Huh.

Weird.

Ell's hand actually felt warm.

CHAPTER 2.

"YOU CAN let go of my hand now," Ell whispered loudly.

"Right. Sorry." Fred jerked away.

That couldn't have been real. He hadn't felt anything like that as a ghoul. Then again, he could swear there was still a tingle of lingering warmth clinging to his fingers. "Your stuff is in my truck."

"Great!" Ell smiled. "I'll meet you at the front door, okay?"

"Yeah." Fred watched Ell disappear through the back, and then he walked around to his truck. He opened the tailgate, grabbed the groceries, and headed to the house.

Ell came outside to hold the front door open for him, waving for him to go on inside. He gawked at all the bags hanging off Fred's arms. "Gosh! You didn't have to try and make it all in one trip. I would have helped you!"

"It's fine."

"Right. Heh. Ghoul strength perk, yeah?"

"Where do you want them?"

"Kitchen, straight ahead!"

The inside of the cottage was just as cute and quaint as the outside. It was clean and smelled like old earth and spicy cinnamon. The living room furniture was upholstered in faded floral prints with colorful mismatched pillows, the worn wooden floor creaked with every step, and the kitchen was absolutely packed with plants.

Some were in pots, others were hanging in dried bunches across the window, and more were stacked up in old coffee mugs on the counter next to a mortar and pestle. Fred had to assume the plants outside really were alive if these were any indication of Ell's green thumb.

There were also a few crystals lining the windowsill, and Fred recognized them as healing totems.

Ell was right behind him, taking some of the bags and setting them up on the counter. He was already eagerly diving in to start unpacking the food. "Thank you so much! Ah, you found the poofies!"

"Got everything you asked for." Fred set the rest of the groceries on a small table, frowning as it tilted to one side with the added weight. "Well, everything except for the faucet."

"Oh, that's okay. Uh. Hmm. No problem. I'll figure it out." Ell zipped around the kitchen as he put everything away. "I really appreciate this. I don't have a car, so it's not exactly easy to go into town and get what I need."

Fred sat at the table, watching it wobble as Ell relieved the presence of the food. He was not very impressed so far, but he told himself to give the kid a chance. Doc had recommended him after all, and she hadn't steered him wrong yet.

Ell disappeared briefly to put away the lotion, no doubt in his bedroom, and he came back with a clean shirt on. "Okay! Are you ready to get started?"

"Yes, please." Fred's arm throbbed.

"So." Ell washed his hands in the kitchen sink. "How long have you been a ghoul?"

"Five years," Fred replied. "I trust you're going to be discreet. I don't want any trouble with the law."

"I promise," Ell assured him. "I don't believe people should be illegal, Fred. It's not your fault you're a ghoul, you know? I'm happy to help and to help very quietly."

"Good." Fred watched Ell dry his hands off with a towel and then approach him.

"Where's the worst of it?" Ell looked Fred over. "We should probably start there and get that out of the way."

Rolling his sleeve up, Fred replied, "This. Doc York has healed it plenty, but it keeps coming back."

"Doesn't look real great." Ell frowned. "Did you… did you die in a fire?" He peered over the bubbled sore.

"Yeah?" Fred couldn't hide his surprise.

"Sometimes ghouls show wounds from their deaths," Ell explained. "It's some super crazy psychosomatic reaction, you know? I had one guy who was shot to death, and his bullet holes kept coming back. This looks like a burn, but I wasn't really sure—"

"Can you fix it?"

"Oh, right." Ell turned a very lovely shade of pink. "Sorry. I don't get much company out here, and I guess I tend to talk a lot because I basically spend all of my time talking to my plants. They say that's good for them, but uh. Crap, I'm doing it again. Right. May I touch you?"

"Go right ahead," Fred said immediately, though there was a small part of him that was eerily unsure.

Maybe what happened before was just a freak accident.

Maybe he'd imagined it.

Ell's fingers gently pressed around the edges of the wound, and Fred knew it was real. He could feel firm pressure, the warmth of Ell's touch, and he greedily wanted to feel more. He had to fight the urge to arch up into Ell's hand like a damn cat, and it was difficult because it had been so long since he'd experienced anything even close to this.

Well, at least not since that one time Azaethoth the Lesser touched him, but that was with tentacles and at a very upsetting time in Fred's life.

After all, Fred had thought his best friend was dead.

"Uh, I might need you...." Ell was trying to look at the whole wound, but Fred's sleeve wasn't up far enough. "Can you...."

"What?"

Ell was blushing. "Could you please take your shirt off?"

Fred moved to comply without hesitation. This body was nothing but a vessel, and he certainly didn't care who saw it unless they were going to snitch on him for being a ghoul.

His broad chest and arms were covered in large bubbled-up scars from being healed before. There were a few fresh spots of decomposition down by his hip, his thick round belly, and on his legs, but those weren't bothering him like the giant sore on his arm was.

Ell sucked in a quick breath, scanning over Fred's wounds with a very concerned frown. "You've been, uh, rotting pretty bad for a while, haven't you?"

"Yeah," Fred said simply. "Can I put my shirt back on now?"

"No." Ell cleared his throat. "I mean, you need to leave it off so I can heal you."

"Not using totems?"

"No, I don't need them."

Fred was surprised again. Healing ghouls was tough work, and most witches needed a totem or some kind of other focus to concentrate their magic to even make a dent. "Okay, so, what do you do? Doc said it might be... touchy."

"This." Ell placed his hand over the sore on Fred's arm and smiled. "It may tickle."

Fred was about to argue that he probably wasn't going to feel a damn thing, but there was such a sudden surge of warmth that he jerked in surprise. He could feel heat, some itching, an intense and weird sensation that was overwhelming because he was actually *feeling* something.

The rotten flesh knitted back together in seconds, and not even a scar was left behind. It was smooth, flawless skin, and Fred wanted to sob. Ell's touch made him ache deep inside in the most wonderful way, and for the first time since his death, he didn't feel any pain.

Ell's eyes fluttered, his body swaying a little where he stood. His grip on Fred's arm tightened. "Mmm, how's that?"

"How the fuck did you do that?" Fred blurted out.

"Magic, silly!" Ell laughed, sliding his palm up Fred's arm to an old spot of rot. Just as before, the scarring faded and only left perfectly healed skin in its place.

Fred looked over Ell with a brand-new sense of respect. He'd never heard of anyone being able to heal ghouls like this before, and he suddenly didn't think buying groceries was nearly enough to pay for this quality of work.

Ell was inspecting the area on Fred's hip and laid his hands there next, flooding Fred with another rush of heat. He was wobbling a little more, closing his eyes as he said, "I'm going to finish this, and then I have to sit down."

Fred saw Ell starting to lean too far and instinctively reached for him. He grabbed his arms before he could tip over. "Hey. Easy, little one."

Pitching forward, Ell braced himself against Fred's chest. His expression was hazy as if he was dizzy, and he blinked up at Fred. "Wow. You have, like, crazy long eyelashes. They're really pretty."

Fred had no idea what to say to a compliment, so he ignored it. "Are you okay?"

"What? Oh! Shit, I'm sorry. I should have stopped."

"What happened?" Fred held Ell close, frowning down at him with concern. He was alarmed that he could feel Ell so vividly in his arms—his warmth, the soft fabric of his shirt, and how hard he was shaking.

Fred could have sworn Ell's eyes were blue, but they were a vivid shade of purple.

"Too much…." Ell pulled away and promptly collapsed into the closet chair at the table. "I tried to heal way too much."

Fred took the other seat next to Ell, and he missed his touch immediately. The familiar bite of pain was on its way back, but whatever Ell had done seemed to have at least knocked a few of its teeth out. "You gonna be okay?"

"Oh yeah," Ell promised with a weary grin. "Totally. It drains me. Healing. It always has. I'll be totally fine by tomorrow. Just need to rest. Try to eat something. I get weak and cranky, and then all I want to do is nap and watch television. It's like I have to recharge my magic batteries. Sorry, sort of rambling again."

"You don't have a television," Fred said flatly, sliding his shirt back on to cover himself up.

"I do in my bedroom!"

Fred thought of the lotion and smirked. "I bet you do."

"Huh?" Ell was a little slow to catch the insinuation. When he did, his jaw dropped. "No! Not for that! I just, it's, it's—!" He covered his face with his hands. "It's for normal television watching!"

Fred chuckled, enjoying the way Ell was trying to hide his blush. "It's okay, kid. You're only human."

"I like watching documentaries about animals," Ell protested. "That's it. Totally normal, not what you're thinking about things."

"Sure about that?"

"Anything else, well, that's, that's just none of your beeswax."

Fred laughed. He couldn't help it. It was funny. He couldn't remember the last time he'd laughed like this. Being around Ell was refreshing, positively revitalizing, and the world didn't seem as bleak all of a sudden.

"You're so gross," Ell teased, peeking through his fingers at Fred. "And gross because you're dirty, not ghoul gross, just to be clear."

"Feeling better?" Fred smiled.

"Yes, thank you." Ell dropped his hands on the table. "Tired, but I don't feel as dizzy."

"Is this why you don't take a bunch of patients?"

"Yeah," Ell replied, picking at his nails with a sigh. "I wish I could help everyone, but I can't. I'm not strong enough."

"I really appreciate you helping me," Fred said earnestly, again surprised by how much he meant that. He was smiling and laughing and wow....

It was almost like being alive again, however fleeting.

"Doctor York told me how bad off you were," Ell said with a note of sympathy. "I know you've been hurting for a long time. But hey, just give me a few months, be patient, and you'll be fine."

"Fine?" Fred echoed.

"After I'm done healing you, you won't need to come back. The ghouls I've helped stop rotting when I'm done."

"Bullshit." Fred couldn't help it. He'd never heard of any ghoul being able to beat the rot. Then again, he'd never met a healer like Ell before either.

"You just wait, Freddie," Ell challenged playfully. "I'll make a believer out of you."

"Hmmph." Fred was still skeptical. "We'll see. How soon can I come back?"

"Oh, you can come by anytime!" Ell exclaimed. "I never have anybody over except ghouls. Not that there's anything wrong with ghouls, of course, and you seem really nice."

"You don't know me that well, little one." Fred snorted.

"That's what all crusty on the outside and gooey on the inside people say. I'm willing to bet you have a very soft, sweet, squishy center."

"You gotta buy me dinner first if you wanna get at my squishy bits." Fred winked, surprising himself that he was flirting.

Even more surprising was that Ell seemed to like it.

"Would a frozen chicken nugget dinner be enough?" Ell grinned. "I know you can't eat it, but you can still totally have one."

"I'll have to think about it. I think I'm worth at least a meatloaf."

"Oh yeah?" Ell laughed. "I'll bet you are." He suddenly grimaced. "I mean, I'm sure that you're super nice. I didn't mean, like, betting you are in a weird pervy way. I really cannot stop the stupid things from coming out of my mouth right now."

"Don't worry about it, little one." Fred was enjoying the teasing, but there was a nagging voice in his head telling him it was best to stop now before he got too carried away. "How about tomorrow?"

"For the meatloaf?" Ell's eyes widened.

"For healing."

"Oh! Yeah. Got it. Healing. Right." Ell dragged his fingers through his hair, fiddling with a piece on the side. "You can come by again tomorrow. I'll be feeling better then."

"Need anything else from the store?"

"I don't need any more food, but could you please try to bring me a faucet?"

"What kind?"

"The kind that gives… water?"

"What kinda sink is it for?" Fred clarified. "Where in the house?"

"Oh." Ell tried to stand up, wobbled, and sat right back down. "It's the faucet in my bathroom. It's leaking real bad, and it's driving me crazy."

"I could take a look if you want," Fred offered. "May not need a new faucet, might just need to tighten up somethin'." He stood. "Where is it at?"

"It's through there," Ell said, pointing to the hall that led off from the kitchen into the back of the house.

"Lemme go see."

"Wait!" Ell pleaded, holding up his hand and grabbing Fred's arm as he walked by.

"What?" Fred flinched, finding that Ell's hand was still eerily warm through the fabric of his shirt.

"Don't go in there," Ell protested.

"Why?"

Ell looked mortified. "It's messy."

Fred snorted. "I'm sure I've seen lots fuckin' worse. I need to look at the sink to see what's wrong, okay?"

"Okay," Ell conceded. "Just…. Just don't look in the bathtub."

"I won't," Fred promised, leaving Ell behind as he lumbered off into the bedroom.

There was a canopy bed off of which several plants were hanging, a small television on a dresser, and more books than Fred had seen at some libraries. The shelves next to the window were packed, and the overflow was everywhere. Books by the dozens were stacked all over the room, against the wall and across the floor.

The bathroom was small with a large clawfoot tub that ate up every inch of free space. The afflicted sink was clean, and the toiletries stacked around it were tidy.

He didn't know what was so bad back here that Ell could be concerned about except the amount of books being a potential fire hazard. Although he was curious, he decided not to look in the tub as Ell had requested.

The sink was definitely dripping, and jiggling the handles didn't do anything. Fred figured it could be something as simple as a worn-out O-ring or a corroded washer. Without tools, though, he wouldn't be able to tell.

Fred came back out of the bedroom, finding Ell still sitting at the table and dozing off. He gently nudged Ell's shoulder. "Hey."

"Hey." Ell lifted his head, sleepily staring up at Fred. "Mmm, sorry. Did you fix it?"

Ell's eyes were a deep shade of blue, not violet. Maybe Fred was seeing things.

"Need tools," Fred replied. "You got any?"

"Gardening tools?" Ell grinned sheepishly.

"Right. I'll bring some tomorrow when I come back. You need anything else from the store? You want some cash?"

"No. I'm okay." Ell shook his head quickly. "What you brought should last me for a while, and I don't need any money."

"You realize I've paid thousands of dollars for docs that can't heal a fraction as good as you?"

"Really?"

"Uh-huh."

"Well, I guess I just don't need it," Ell said with a shrug. "Keep your money."

"Don't feel right," Fred said firmly.

"Well." Ell glanced around the house. "Are you good at fixing stuff?"

"I know my way around tools, yeah." Fred resisted the urge to pursue the obvious innuendo. "What is it you need?"

"I love this place, but it's old and it needs some work to keep it from falling apart. I don't know how to do any of that stuff, so you can help me fix stuff in exchange for healing you."

"I can handle that. Tomorrow, then?"

"Yeah!" Ell stood and immediately swayed. He held on to the edge of the table to steady himself. "That sounds great."

Fred almost reached for him again but stopped. He suddenly felt awkward, and he didn't know what to say.

Ell was smiling at him in such a sweet way, and there was something about him....

Fred needed to get out of here before he made a fool out of himself.

"Tomorrow."

"See you then!" Ell waved. "Bye, Freddie!"

Fred turned around and showed himself out. He didn't mean to, but he kicked up a bunch of dirt and gravel as he sped out of Ell's yard. He had the sudden urge to get away as quickly as possible, like he was on a job and cops were closing in on him.

The last of the warmth he'd experienced from Ell's touch had faded. The pain was back, but it was certainly duller than it had once been. He rolled up his sleeve so he could check out the healed skin again.

It was perfect.

Much like little Ell, his brain unhelpfully supplied.

He squashed the invading thought, though he couldn't deny how at ease he'd felt back there. He had laughed for the first time in ages, and hell, he'd even flirted.

Fred hadn't had an inkling of attraction to another person since becoming breathing challenged, but he had definitely felt *something* when he was with Ell. Fred wasn't sure what to do with it except pretend it didn't exist.

Was probably some side effect of the healing, he reasoned, nothing more.

Back home, he went ahead and loaded his toolbox in the back of his truck. After some consideration, he put his drill in too. There was no telling what kinds of things Ell might need repaired in that old house.

He returned to his apartment, soon finding himself sitting back on his couch and staring at his phone.

There were several hours left before he was due to meet with his clients. He had the paintings stored beneath the floorboards in his bedroom for safe keeping, and he hadn't looked at them since he stole them. He didn't have any desire to.

They were a product, that was it, and he would deliver them as promised. He didn't usually take jobs like this, stealing something directly for a client. Usually, he and Lochlain worked with a fence who would serve as a go-between and sell off whatever they stole.

Their usual guy was Robert Edwards, the man who had waited until after Lochlain had died to confess his love for him. Thanks to Great Azaethoth's miracle, however, he got another chance, and it had worked out for them quite well.

But Robert hadn't been pushing product like he used to since he was busy with Lochlain, and Fred didn't want to steal anything he couldn't pass off in a timely manner.

Fred had reached out for work through some old contacts and immediately was offered this job. The pay was good, not too much, not too little, and the target was a cinch.

Now all he had to do was wait so he could get paid.

His phone beeped, and it was a text message from a number he didn't recognize.

Hey! This is Ell! Hope you're doing great! I got your phone number from Doctor York. I hope that's okay!

The corner of Fred's mouth tugged up, and he kept reading.

I'm sorry to bother you but when you come over tomorrow do you think you could also help me with fixing a light switch in my living room? I've tried changing the bulbs and it still doesn't work.

Good thing he packed the drill. He began to text back, smiling as he thought about Ell waiting for his reply inside that ridiculous little cottage.

no prob

Fred frowned, deleting the message. That didn't sound very friendly. He thought about it and then tried again.

no prob :)

That was better, right?

Fred didn't give himself too much time to overthink it, pressing Send and putting his phone back down. He wasn't expecting another reply. It didn't matter.

Ell was his ghoul doctor. They'd just met. They were confirming negotiations. Nothing more.

Wait, was that another text?

Fred flinched as he scrambled to answer his phone, swearing he could feel his heart pounding. He was practically giddy, and he couldn't wait to see what Ell's next message said.

Except it wasn't Ell this time, it was Lochlain.

Groaning in annoyance, he opened up the new message.

Hey, buddy. Robert and I were gonna go out tonight. Wanna come with?

"And watch the two of you suck face all night?" Fred mumbled. "Hard pass."

no thanks working

He didn't even bother reading the reply. He already knew what Lochlain was going to say, and he shouldn't have gotten his hopes up that it would be Ell. That was ridiculous.

Frozen on the couch, Fred did everything he could do to ignore his phone. It was almost time to get ready for work. He needed to focus on the task ahead of him. The drop was this evening at eight o'clock, he was to come alone, he would knock three times, and then—

The phone beeped, and Fred lurched forward to snatch it up from the table.

Can't wait :D

It was Ell.

Fred stared at his phone.

That was a big smiley face.

That had to be good. Ell was saying he couldn't wait to see him. That was definitely good, but Fred didn't know what to write now. It was stupid. There was nothing else to say, but it still felt like he needed to type something back.

But what?

Ask him about meatloaf?

So long was Fred caught up in gawking at his phone that he didn't even realize what time it was until his alarm went off. He often set them to help him keep track of the hours, and now it was time to leave to meet his clients.

He would deal with replying or not replying to Ell later.

He had to work.

After retrieving the paintings from the compartment beneath his bed, he hurried downstairs to his truck. It was dark now, quiet, and he loaded up fast to get going.

But shouldn't he text Ell back? Would it be rude not to reply? Was a meatloaf joke dumb?

Dammit.

He really needed to focus on the task at hand, but it was hard when his mind kept retreating to the fresh memories of warm hands, bright eyes, and a crooked smile.

Once Fred arrived at the meeting spot inside the back room of a seedy bar, he would later blame being distracted by his new and strange infatuation for what happened next.

After all, if he wasn't so caught up thinking about the merits of a smiley face versus a winky face, maybe he would have noticed the gun being pointed at the back of his head before it went off.

Well, fu—

CHAPTER 3.

EVERYTHING ABOUT this meeting was supposed to be simple.

Show up to the bar, hand over the paintings, get paid, leave.

Nothing about it had been right from the start.

The men at the door were too light-handed with the frisk for starters. They didn't bother to check for any weapons or wards. In fact, they were rushing Fred inside without any care at all.

That should have been the first clue.

The second came when he stepped into the back room and no one asked to see the product he was carrying. The four paintings were tucked under his arms, wrapped up in old brown paper, and not a single person in that room asked to see what he had brought.

Bang.

The bullet rocked his skull, and he distantly felt what was left of his eye dripping down his cheek as he collapsed to the ground.

Well, that was annoying.

"Why did you do that?" one of the clients squealed hysterically in a squeaky voice. "We could have just paid him!"

"We need the money," the gruff shooter behind him argued.

"Yeah, and now we have a body to dispose of, Jeff!" said another deep voice. "Idiot!"

The paintings were wrestled from Fred's arms, and he made no movement to indicate he was alive. He was a ghoul. It would take a lot more than a shot to the head to kill him, but now he was just pissed.

Anger was so easy.

He could feel it burning inside of him like a volcano about to erupt, robbing him of his senses and any clear thoughts. He was a fool. This shouldn't have gone down this way. He had been too busy worrying about fuckin' emojis instead of staying focused on the job.

It wasn't Ell's fault, not exactly, but Fred couldn't explain why else he felt so unlike himself. The only variable was being healed earlier today, and the unusual swirl of emotions he was experiencing: joy, happiness, longing, hope....

Oh, hope was dangerous.

He didn't deserve to hope for anything with Ell. No one in their right mind, least of all a miracle worker like that cute little blond, would ever fancy Fred's undead ass. But hoping that he would, just maybe even a little, was worth making sure he walked out of this shit alive.

Well, as alive as he was, anyway.

Fred mulled that over as he listened to his clients continue to bicker.

"Beneath these paintings is everything we need," Jeff was insisting. "The ritual must be here. Salgumel's time is soon. Never fear, my brothers!"

"But what if it's more godstongue?" the squeaky one cried. "How are we going to translate it?"

"One problem at a time! Let's deal with the corpse first."

"Brother... why.... Why isn't he bleeding?"

"He's bleeding plenty, it's just...." There was a long pause. "Oh fuck."

Ghouls only bled black.

That was Fred's cue to move. He slapped his hands against the floor, growling fiercely, "*Ignis combustus!*"

Fire burst forth from his palms in a wild wave, instantly catching the floor and the legs of the men who were standing too close. They screamed, panicking as they fled the room.

Dragging himself up to his feet, Fred squinted his good eye to focus the flames right at the paintings. If he wasn't getting paid, they weren't getting their stupid paintings.

"No!" the squeaky one howled. "Stop him!"

The burn of bullets lit up Fred's back, more down around his hips, and shit—one had grazed the soul binding mark hidden deep inside of his stomach. The angle had nicked the edge of one of the arrows, a critical part of the design, and he immediately fell to one knee.

The fire spread within the room and over the furniture, licking its way up to the ceiling. The traitorous clients were gone with at least two of the paintings. The others were burned to a crisp, and Fred allowed himself a moment of satisfaction.

It was fleeting as the fire grew, and he could feel his body getting weak. The connection of his soul to his vessel had been damaged, and he had to move. He had to get help, or he was going to die.

Again.

He managed to make it outside to his truck, and the bar behind him was currently caught in an incredible inferno. He could hear distant sirens wailing and the honking of fire engines. He had to get the hell out of here.

Fred drove, squinting against the harsh glare of streetlights. Everything was too bright, and his vision was getting fuzzy. He tried fumbling around on his phone to call Lochlain. No, fuck that, call Sloane. Azaethoth could probably help him.

Someone.

Anyone.

His clumsy fingers accidentally reactivated the GPS route from earlier today, and he found himself mindlessly following the directions. The pain was overwhelming, and his consciousness was slipping away.

Logically, he knew it was his soul trying to leave his vessel. The binding mark holding it in place had been weakened, and his soul was moving on to the other side.

No, not yet.

Fred would not go yet. He was going to survive and make those bastards pay for this. He thought he heard a distant explosion behind him, but he kept driving. He had to keep moving.

Left, yes, the GPS wanted him to turn left.

He could do that.

The electronic voice was a beacon in the darkness of his shattered mind, and it took everything he had to focus on it. He could feel liquid pouring out of his mouth from the internal damage, but he refused to let go of this vessel.

The drive seemed like it took hours, and when he arrived at Ell's cottage, he drove right through the delicate white trellis. He was able to put the truck in park and then stumble out into the yard, the entire world spinning around him.

The next sensation was the cool grass against his face as he plummeted into the lawn. It seemed far away, but real enough that he realized there was grass poking into his damaged eye. It itched terribly.

"Freddie?" Ell's voice called out timidly. There was a pause, and he screamed, "Fred!"

Ell's hands frantically patted his shoulder, but Fred didn't move. "Ughhh… hey."

"Oh, by the gods!" Ell gasped. "What happened to you? You're hurt!" He tried to pull Fred up, grunting from the effort. "Come on. Crap, you're heavy. Ugh. We gotta get you in the house!"

Fred realized there was no way Ell could move him, and he willed himself to stand once more. Ell was trying to support him and stumbled alongside him as they walked inside.

"Here, sit down!" Ell steered Fred to the sofa. "What happened? You're bleeding everywhere!"

Collapsing the moment he could, Fred flopped against the cushions. "Shot… I was shot… my… my mark…." He gestured at his stomach. "Hit."

"Oh no. Okay, just hold still." Ell touched Fred's face, mumbling, "Your eye is majorly creeping me out. I'm so sorry. I gotta fix it."

A rush of warmth bubbled through Fred's skin, and he was certain now that Ell's touch was always going to feel like this. He savored the slide of Ell's fingers along his cheek and the smooth texture of his palm. The pain was fading, and within seconds he could see again.

Ell gradually came into focus, wearing only pajama pants and fluffy slippers. His young face was crinkled in concern, and in the dim light, Fred thought his eyes looked weirdly purple again.

"Here, let me see." Ell pulled at Fred's shirt, and he grimaced as he ripped the fabric to get it out of his way. "Sorry! I swear I'll get you another one."

"You save me, you can tear up as much of my shit as you want," Fred said with a weary smile. The pain in his head was completely gone now, and he watched Ell's quick hands glide over his stomach where the bullets had torn through him. "There… right there."

"I've got you," Ell said softly, his eyes glowing bright as he healed the damage.

The warmth of Ell's hands quickly became boiling hot, and Fred groaned loudly. It was a new level of agony, and he slammed his fist into the side of the couch with a terrible cry.

"I'm sorry, I'm sorry, I'm sorry!" Ell chanted. "Just hang on! I've almost got it! Just a little bit more!"

Fred squeezed his eyes shut as he braced himself, grinding his teeth fiercely. He thought it was never going to end, it was worse than dying, and suddenly… it stopped.

The pain was gone.

In its place was warmth, pressure, and the sweet sensation of touch. Fred was panting, his arms trembling from the intensity, and his eyes were hot. He blinked rapidly, and all he could see was the beautiful boy next to him.

Beautiful and exhausted.

Ell was fading right in front of him, pale and sweating, and even the color of his eyes had dulled into nothing. His hands, caked in black blood, dropped into his lap, and he swayed unsteadily.

"Ell?" Fred reached for his shoulder. "Was it too much? Are you okay?"

"It's okay." Ell's expression was glazed over as if he was drunk. "I've got you… just… please…. Please don't hurt me."

"Hurt you?" Fred scoffed. "I wouldn't… hey!"

Ell's eyes rolled back, and he tipped forward with a soft moan.

Fred caught him and was immediately shocked by how cold he was. It was like Ell had just come out of a bath of ice water. He patted his back. "Hey, hey. Wake up. You gotta wake up for me."

"Bed," Ell mumbled. "Blanket… I need blankets. I'm… I'm so cold."

"Come on," Fred said, scooping Ell up into his arms. "I've got you, little one. Let's get you warm, okay?" He hurried through the house to Ell's bedroom, finding the blankets askew and the pillows on the floor.

Probably from Ell hurrying out of bed to see what was happening in his front yard.

After carefully laying Ell in bed, Fred grabbed the pillows and tucked him back in. There was a quilt at the foot of the bed, and he grabbed that too. He could feel him shaking, shivering violently, and he was afraid. He didn't know what saving his life might have cost Ell, and a bubble of guilt crept up alongside the bile in his mouth.

The emotional rush was nauseating, and he pressed a hand against Ell's forehead. Even under the blankets and quilt, he was still freezing to the touch.

Shit.

"Please… help?" Ell whimpered, trying to curl up with the blankets as he trembled. "I'm so c-cold… please…."

"Okay." Fred couldn't think of anything else to do, but he was desperate to help Ell. He crawled into bed beside him, saying, "All right, look. I ain't tryin' nothin', okay? I just wanna get you warmed up."

"Please." Ell's voice was a breathy, pained whisper.

Fred hated how the bed creaked beneath his weight—by all the gods, he hoped this damn thing didn't break—and he wrapped thick arms around Ell, pulling him against his chest. He closed his eyes to concentrate as he murmured, "*Calidum.*"

He could feel the magic working through his hands, an invisible cloak of warmth enveloping them both. It was a spell for chilly mornings and brisk winds, one Fred had always found useless but was so grateful he knew now.

Fred kept it up, rubbing Ell's back as he cast the spell over and over again. He didn't stop until Ell's shivering finally eased, and he sighed in relief. He didn't let go yet, keeping Ell close as he asked, "Are you gonna be okay?"

"Yes," Ell replied, burrowing into Fred's chest and closing his eyes. "Need rest… please… please stay."

"I ain't going anywhere," Fred said immediately. "I've got you." It was so nice to hold someone, and he let himself enjoy it while he could. Ell was so small that it was almost like hugging a big teddy bear, except this teddy bear was real and alive and very, very beautiful. He listened as Ell's breathing slowed and peered down at his sleeping face.

This young man had saved his life, and Fred knew this was a debt that would not be easily repaid. Hell, he might as well skip the repairs and build Ell a new house from the ground up.

The odd thing was that Fred didn't mind. Hanging around with Ell didn't sound the least bit unpleasant, and he didn't even care what they would be doing. Fred knew he'd have to go handle the incident with his traitorous clients, but that didn't matter now. He had to make sure Ell was going to be okay first, and there was nowhere else he'd honestly rather be than right here.

Before Fred knew it, it was morning.

There was sunlight peeking in through the bedroom windows and birds chirping away. He blinked as he looked around, instantly confused. It wasn't uncommon for him to zone out for a few hours here and there, part of the fun of being a ghoul since he didn't sleep, but he had never lost time like this before.

Had he actually dozed off?

That wasn't possible.

Ell was still curled up against Fred's chest, his thin arms out of the blankets and hugging his waist as he slept. He looked peaceful, and he was definitely warmed up now. Ell's soft breath was tickling his collarbone, and it made Fred smile.

Fred delicately brushed some hair out of Ell's face and caught himself staring down at his lips. He had the weirdest urge to kiss him, and that was totally insane for a myriad of reasons.

Top of the list was that Ell was asleep, and this wasn't some silly Lucian fairy tale. Not to mention they barely knew each other, and there was no way Ell could be interested. One smiley face in a text message did not mean anything.

But Ell had obviously risked his life to save Fred's.

Maybe that meant a little something.

Fred's gaze traveled down to Ell's throat; he studied the scar there. It was thick, smooth, and from Fred's experience, it looked like the handiwork of a knife.

Fuck.

He wondered why Ell hadn't removed it with his healing powers, and he knew better than to ask….

But he was pretty sure it had something to do with Ell pleading with Fred not to hurt him.

Lingering on Ell's lips once more, Fred swore his heart thumped, and he had the overwhelming urge to protect this young man from anyone ever hurting him again. Fred had no idea what to do with that. It was impossible to focus with Ell cuddled so close, the very sensation of his warm body in Fred's arms making his mind overload. He needed to get some space between them so he could think clearly.

As Fred shifted back, he could see some of the dried blood fleck off his chest like the most vile confetti imaginable. He and Ell were both covered in it from last night's little adventure, and the bed linens would definitely need to be washed.

He couldn't go very far or else he'd fall off the bed, and Fred froze when Ell suddenly lifted up his head. His arm was still draped over Ell's side, and he wasn't sure whether he should move it or not. He stayed as he was for now, murmuring, "Good morning."

"Morning." Ell yawned and then smiled sleepily up at Fred. He dropped his head, hugging Fred's waist. "You really stayed."

"You okay?"

"I'll be okay. That happens, eh, if I try to heal too much."

"Yeah?" Fred frowned. "You felt like you were freezing to death."

"I'm okay now. Thank you. You kept me warm." Ell tensed, and the expression of distress on his face was almost comical.

"You sure you're all right?"

"Fine."

Hoping to ease whatever was bothering Ell, Fred teased, "You got to cuddle some of my squishy bits, and you didn't even have to buy me a meatloaf dinner."

"I really wasn't trying to get at your squishy bits! Not that I wouldn't want to, but, oh gods." Ell's cheeks turned bright red, and he rambled, "I'm sorry! It's just you're the first person to stay in my bed who isn't me. Like ever. I'm so sorry if I snored or stole the covers from you. Oh gods, I totally had all the covers, didn't I? I'm sorry, I've never done this—"

"Hey, kid." Fred grunted. "We just shared a bed. It's no big deal."

Blushing even brighter, Ell stuttered, "R-right. Just shared a bed. With no shirts on. No big deal."

"Thanks." Fred fidgeted as he struggled to properly articulate his gratitude. "You know. For not letting me die."

Smooth.

"Hey, no big deal," Ell repeated, finally pulling away from Fred and sitting up. He kept the blankets wrapped around himself as he scooted back against the headboard. "Are you really okay? I can try to heal you again if you need it."

"I'm good." Fred was better than good, glancing down at his torso. Other than the dried blood, he looked fine. Everywhere Ell had touched was not only free of bullet holes, but any old scars of rot in those areas were gone as well.

There were even some places up on his shoulders that seemed better, but he didn't think Ell had even touched him there.

"What happened to you?" Ell asked.

Fred grunted.

"Come on." Ell frowned. "I saved your life, right? We're both literally covered in your blood. Can't you at least tell me what happened?"

Fred grunted again, but then he finally replied, "Job went bad."

"Job?" Ell tilted his head. "What kinda job goes bad that gets you shot?" His eyes widened. "Fred, are you a *criminal*?"

"Don't think it's a good idea if I answer that," Fred grumbled.

"Well, you're a ghoul. Getting legit work is probably really hard." Ell scooted back toward him, his eyes big with excitement. "Have you… have you broken the law?"

"Maybe," Fred replied carefully.

"Will you tell me if I make you a meatloaf dinner?"

"Why?" A smile tugged at the corner of Fred's mouth. "You got a thing for crooks?"

"What? No!" Ell sputtered. "It's just, well, it's kinda cool. You know, it's really cool actually. Okay, that sounds lame, but I never even broke curfew. I had perfect attendance and everything."

"Honor roll?"

"Ugh, totally. Even when I was homeschooled. My parents were so super crazy protective and…." Ell stopped, shaking his head with a huff. "Anyway. Right."

"What's the matter?"

"I talk way too much," Ell replied sheepishly. "I always tell myself that I'm not gonna do it, and boom, my whole life story just tries to explode out of my mouth."

"I really don't mind." Fred couldn't remember the last time he'd tried to get to know anyone, and Ell's peppy energy was charming.

"That's sweet of you," Ell said, freeing himself from his blanket nest and crawling out of bed, "but it's safer if I don't."

Fred thought back to what Ell had said before he had passed out last night. "Someone hurt you?"

Ell's hand moved up to touch his scarred throat, and there was something broken in his usually bright expression. He dropped his hand quickly. "Look, if you're all healed up, maybe you should go. I, uh, I need to get cleaned up, and I really gotta wash the sheets—"

"I owe you." Fred stood. "You wrecked yourself saving my life, and you got a light that needs fixing, right? Maybe some other stuff around here that needs some work?"

Ell frowned.

"If you won't let me pay you, I gotta make this square some way." Fred crossed his arms. "I don't like having any kind of debt."

"Okay," Ell said, rocking on his heels for a moment. "I guess, yeah, you could fix the light and… well, you did sort of run over the stuff in my front yard."

"Sorry about that."

"Yeah, okay." Ell headed to his dresser, fumbling around for something. He offered a T-shirt out to Fred. "I can replace the other one, I promise. I'm sorry, but I don't think I have any pants that will fit."

"It's fine." Fred took the shirt. "Is it okay if I use your bathroom?"

"Use the… right!" Ell grinned. "To clean up. Because of the blood. Yup, sure. Yes. I'll go…. To the kitchen. Yup, because there's a sink there."

Fred nodded, wordlessly heading into the bathroom. He ran the sink and wiped himself down as best as he could. He really needed a shower, but that would have to wait for now. He pulled the new shirt over his head. It was a little tight but fit surprisingly well. It would have swallowed Ell up, and Fred hated himself for wondering who it belonged to.

He came out to find Ell waiting for him, and he saw that Ell had cleaned up too.

The blood was gone, and he was wearing a shirt with puffy cartoon rainbows and skinny jeans that hugged Ell's long legs like a coat of paint.

Fred tried not to stare as Ell stripped the bed. "Thanks for the shirt."

"Sure! It was my brother's."

Ah, mystery solved.

Ell smiled, and it seemed a little sad. "He's big like you, thought it might fit okay."

"It's good. Thank you." Fred eyed the dirty blankets and sheets. "You, uh, want me to grab that for you?"

"Oh! Thanks. Washer's in the kitchen."

Fred followed Ell to the kitchen where Ell opened a set of folding doors to reveal a washing machine and a dryer. Ell took the linens from Fred and loaded what he could in the washer.

While Ell added a very large amount of detergent, Fred looked out the kitchen window to the current disaster of the front yard. "I'll start out there and come back in to work on the light." He turned, surprised to catch Ell staring at him very intently.

More precisely, Ell had been staring at Fred's chest in his very tight shirt.

"Okay, good!" Ell squeaked.

"You okay?" Fred raised his brows.

"I'm great. So great. I'll… I'll be here. I will be here doing… stuff."
Ell nearly tripped over himself as he headed to the sink. He grabbed a pot
from the dish strainer next to it. "So busy, uh, with all this stuff. Washing
things. Yup. That's what I'm doing."

"You sure you're all right?" Fred frowned. "You're all healed up
from last night, yeah?"

"Oh! Yes!" Ell accidentally dropped a pot into the sink as he was
trying to fill it, making himself jump from the loud clanging. "I'm fine,
thanks. Thank you."

Without another word, Fred headed outside to move his truck. He
wondered why Ell had been gawking at him like that, and he dared to
wonder if Ell had been checking him out. He smiled, though it quickly
turned into a grimace when he heard the remains of the trellis crunch
beneath his tires.

Yeah, definitely gonna have to replace that.

After picking up the shattered wood and hauling it to the bed of his
truck, Fred tried to clear his head. The weirdness with Ell aside—Fred
refused to call it a crush because that seemed far too juvenile and didn't
exactly capture the depth of whatever the hell it was—he had a damn hell
of a problem to deal with.

The job had gone terribly. His clients tried to kill him. When the
time was right, he would reach back out to his contacts and find out
what was going on. Honestly, lying low here in the country with Ell was
probably the best thing to do right now.

He caught Ell peeking out the front door at him, and he waved.

Ell waved back, smiling wide before ducking inside the house.

Damn that kid.

Fred couldn't explain the effect Ell was having on him. The
powerful healing was insane enough, but the laughing and flirting and
the rest was something so big that he didn't even know the right words
to describe it.

Being with Ell…. Fred felt human again.

It was all happening way too fast, and Fred suspected that Ell was
hiding something about his abilities. How much it drained him was a
concern, as was the odd scar around his neck. Not that Fred had any
problem with scars, but Ell's must have quite the story.

"You don't question his age, his scar, or anything else about him."

Fred remembered Doc's warning, and he tried to convince himself that he had enough problems to worry about.

Some doe-eyed healer should be the least of them.

After he'd cleared the broken trellis, he tried to mend the surrounding fence that had suffered. He was fighting a losing battle against one of the cross beams when his phone rang.

A break wasn't such a bad idea, he decided. Not that he was tired being a ghoul, but he was about to snap the broken cross beam out of frustration.

When he saw it was Lochlain calling, he was instantly relieved. His best friend calling in his time of need felt like fate, and he was even smiling when he answered. "Hey."

"Hey! Are you okay?" Lochlain sounded worried.

"Been better." Fred grunted. "Job went bad."

"That's why I'm calling," Lochlain said urgently. "I'm guessing you haven't seen the news. There was a little bit of a fire downtown?"

"Hmm."

"And there was a break-in the night before and some paintings got jacked. Paintings that they're saying were in that fire. Was that you?"

"Told you. It went bad."

"Okay, right, so that little bit of a fire took out half a city block. Two bars, a restaurant, a soup kitchen, and a day center for deaf and blind children."

Fred cringed.

"Oh! And then the fire spread to a dog park."

"A dog park?"

"Uh-huh."

"Huh." Fred considered this new information very carefully.

"Well?"

"Okay," Fred said at last, "so, it went *really* fuckin' bad."

CHAPTER 4.

"WHAT HAPPENED?"

"Clients shot me." Fred leaned against the side of his truck with a scowl. "No pay, but I toasted most of the product before I got outta there. Fuckers."

"Are you hurt? Are you with Doctor York?"

"Nah, I got a new doctor."

"Name?" Lochlain pressed.

"Can't tell you that, but he's real good."

"Yeah? Wow, must be."

"Huh?"

"You're smiling." Lochlain laughed. "I can hear it in your voice."

Fred growled.

"Ahem. Got it. No comments about your sudden ability to smile." Lochlain chuckled. "Now, these new clients. Who were they?"

"Found them through Roger Lorre," Fred replied. "Thought it was legit. They were just supposed to be some kooky collectors. Wanted me to jack some old paintings. Tried to smoke me as soon as I walked in to make the drop."

"Why didn't you tell me?" Lochlain demanded. "I could have gone with you!"

"You were busy." Fred grunted, recalling the text message about hanging out with him and Robert with a grimace.

"Never too busy for a heist," Lochlain countered.

"Right."

"Come on. I would have come."

It would have been easy to accuse Lochlain of being stuck so far up Robert's ass that he couldn't see daylight, but Fred resisted the urge. He didn't want to lose his temper with his best friend and instead replied, "What's done is done."

"Yeah," Lochlain said, something rustling on his side of the line. "I'll go pay Roger a little visit. Find out what he knows about these passionate art collectors. You probably shouldn't stay at your place. You need to stay out of the city for—"

"Thanks, Mom."

"Hey!" Lochlain snapped unexpectedly. "I already lost you once, Fred! I'm not losing you again because you're too stubborn to ask for help!"

"Oh yeah?" Fred's temper surged. "And how long exactly would it take you to notice something had happened to me? Is this before or after you come up for air from sucking Robert's dick?"

"Fred!" Lochlain was clearly stunned, taking several seconds to stammer back, "Hey! Hey, you *asshole*! That's not fair!"

"Fair?" Fred snarled. "You wanna talk about fuckin' fair? To me?"

"Fred—!"

"When you died and came back, you got a brand-new body and the man of your fuckin' dreams! The fuck did I get? *Pain*! All I have is fucking *pain*! You get kisses and fuckin' hugs, and I got parts of me fuckin' rotting off!"

"I've told you I was sorry!" Lochlain protested. "I've told you I was sorry a thousand times! I'm fucking sorry about the Willam job—"

"Sorry don't fuckin' fix me!" Fred roared back. "It don't fix my life! Where was your precious fuckin' god then, huh? Where was he when you fucked up and left me to burn?"

Silence.

"That's what I fuckin' thought." Fred hung up and threw his phone as hard as he could out into the grass.

Anger was so natural, the primal emotion always taking right over and overwhelming his senses. It made him feel strong, alive, and it was impossible to escape. It filled every pore until he was bursting with sensation, his vision going red and waves of pressure snapping off inside of his head.

He didn't even realize what he was doing until he heard the front door open, freezing in place to stare down at his busted hands and the dents in the side of his truck.

"Freddie?" Ell called out, poking his head outside and peering at Fred. "Everything okay?"

"Fine," he snapped, instantly regretting it when Ell cringed from his harsh tone. He struggled to get his rage in check as he bit out, "I'm fine."

"You're hurt!" Ell scampered out from the house and hurried up to Fred. His brow was pulled up with concern. "Your hands."

"It's nothin'." Fred tried to turn away, but Ell was too fast and grabbed him. He couldn't deny the soothing warmth of Ell's touch that he was becoming quite fond of, and he was embarrassed for how carried away he'd gotten.

"Oh, Freddie," Ell murmured as he gave Fred's hands a very gentle squeeze. "I heard you shouting. What happened?"

"Don't worry about it," Fred said gruffly, keeping his eyes on the ground. After blowing up with Lochlain, the last thing he needed was someone else being upset with him—or worse, their pity.

"Okay." Ell's fingers began to move, gliding over Fred's busted knuckles. "Just hold still for a second."

"Hey," Fred protested, "you sure you got enough gas in the tank to be healin' me again so soon?"

"Well, if I don't, you're not gonna be able to do any of the repairs you promised me," Ell said with a snort. "Can't be very handy if you can't use your hands, now can you?"

Fred had to look at Ell then, but he only found a pinch of concern and a very determined pout. He sighed. "Fine."

Ell preened at his victory, summoning his magic to heal the tears in Fred's hands. The wounds were small and closed quickly, though Ell still wobbled when it was done.

The healing seemed to have unlocked a new level of sensitivity because now Fred could feel little calluses on Ell's hands he hadn't noticed before. He didn't think Ell's hands would be so rough, but he enjoyed how they felt nonetheless. He didn't even realize how captivated he was by them until Ell spoke again.

"It's the healing." Ell smiled as he watched Fred exploring his hands. "It's okay. You'll start feeling a lot more as you get better."

Fred jerked away. "Sorry."

"It's okay." Ell tucked his arms behind his back with a shy grin. "I don't mind. If you wanna hold my hand, you could just ask me, you know."

"How do you do it?" Fred blurted out. "Are you a witch of starlight?"

"Oh gods no!" Ell laughed. "I wish I had starlight. I could just clap my hands and fix everything. I was officially registered as a void. My parents were Lucian, you know. They did their best."

A void was the official label for someone with no magical ability in the government's system of classification. It was heavily influenced by

Lucian teachings. Sages called people who had no magic Silenced, but there was no way Ell was one with what he could do.

"Bullshit. How do you do it?"

"What were you fighting about on the phone? Sounded bad. Wanna talk about it?"

"No."

Ell smiled sweetly.

"Right. No questions." Fred scowled and flexed his hands.

Looking around, Ell noted casually, "Well, it looks like you got the worst of it out here. Think you're up to tackling the sink?"

All that remained in the yard were a few splintered pieces of the trellis. The fence was still leaning, but Fred was tired of being outside. His sour mood was lingering, and a few of his old aches were returning. Ell's invitation was a welcome distraction, and he decided to worry about finding his phone later.

He didn't want to talk to anyone else anyway.

"Sure."

Fred grabbed his tools and then lumbered his way through the house into Ell's bathroom, focusing on taking the faucet apart to find the source of the problem. He tried to forget about his fight with Lochlain, and he was pleased to find the source of the leak was a worn-out O-ring.

It was an easy fix. He had a variety of random hardware in the bottom of his toolbox and rooted around to see if he had something that could replace it. He tried a few, but none of them fit. He happened to turn in the direction of the tub as he examined a few more washers, and something bright caught his eye.

Curious, he peeked around the shower curtain into the tub.

There was a fancy tray that fit across the tub, and there were three colorful dildos of varying sizes and shapes lined up across it. One was neon green and shaped like a tentacle.

So, that was why Ell didn't want him looking in the tub.

Fred's mind was immediately flooded with images of Ell using those toys, and he was surprised at the sudden rush of heat coming over him. He hadn't experienced an inkling of desire since his death, and he wasn't sure if it was because of Ell's magical healing, Ell himself, or a mix of both.

He ignored it.

Fred couldn't manifest passion in any physical sense, and it had never been an issue before. Faced with an erotic fantasy of Ell sliding down into that tub with that damn tentacle toy going between his legs definitely made it *something*, and he decided it was best left alone.

He sighed, closed the curtain, and got back to work.

Unable to find a piece of hardware that would fit the sink, he put his tools away. He couldn't do anything without the right part. As he tidied up, his ear was drawn by familiar music, and he peeked out of the bathroom to see what it was.

Ell had come into the bedroom, made the bed with fresh linens, and was watching some show on the little television while he put away some more laundry. He was humming along with the theme song, and Fred was surprised when he recognized it.

"You're watching *Legends of Darkness*?" Fred asked.

"Oh! Sorry!" Ell dropped the shirt he'd been folding. He hurried over to the television, his hand out to adjust the knob. "I can turn it down."

"No, it's okay," Fred said, stepping out of the bathroom to glance at the screen. He knew the grainy introduction to his favorite television series by heart.

"Do you… do you like this show?" Ell sounded hopeful.

"Yeah, a bit," Fred replied as casually as possible.

He didn't want Ell to know he was obsessed with this particular show, and the memories of watching it for hours on end with Lochlain were some of the best from his childhood. Thinking about Lochlain again so soon spoiled the recollection since he was still angry with him, but Fred decided to focus on his surprise that Ell was watching such an old show.

"Were you even alive when this was on?" Fred smirked.

"Hey!" Ell huffed. "Don't tease. It's my friggin' favorite show. I know everything about this show."

"Oh yeah?" Fred crossed his arm as he challenged, "Then who was Princess Daisy supposed to marry?"

"Trick question." Ell planted his hands on his hips. "Everyone always says Baron Tiberius Grappenhall because he's the big bad, but she was actually engaged to his brother first, Franz Grappenhall. Halfway through season one, they wrote Franz out of the show, and Daisy is then engaged to the Baron with zero explanation."

"Hmmm. And Princess Daisy—"

"Was played by Tia Sarah. She was only fifteen when she auditioned, and she lied about her age to get on the show. She's the one who convinced the writers to kill the whole marriage plot line so Daisy could have a bigger part and not just be a damsel in distress all the time."

Fred refused to show how impressed he was. "Yeah, well, and Sappy Gump—"

"Was played by award-winning actor David Beniwasp, but the producers dubbed over his voice because they were worried viewers wouldn't like his heavy German accent." Ell took a bold step forward, staring up at Fred. "The actor who played the goblin king, Alex Playten, provided the dub."

"Fuck," Fred said without meaning to. "All right. You know your shit."

Ell kept his head held high. "So, who's your favorite character, huh? Trip, the idiot hero? Maybe you liked Sappy?"

"The goblin king." Fred scoffed. "Obviously. Blix was the most fuckin' badass swordsman, he had the best character development, even though he never got his happy ending—"

"His happy ending," Ell said, their voices overlapping. His defiant posture relaxed, and he grinned sheepishly. "You really like the show too, huh?"

"Yeah, I do." Fred smiled. "I like it a lot."

"I watch it all the time," Ell confessed happily. "Me and my brother used to binge it together, and I swore we were the biggest fans ever. He kinda grew out of it, but I never did. I still wanted adventures and romance and… well, yeah. I could never forget the goblin king."

"Sticks with you," Fred agreed.

"Wanting a happy ending?" Ell asked, something sad in his eyes.

Those words hit Fred right in his gut. "Yeah. That too."

Ell stared at Fred expectantly, as if he was waiting for him to say something else. He was leaning in closer and looking up at him with the weirdest expression on his face. He kept glancing at Fred's mouth, and his lashes fluttered in a way that made Fred remember what he'd seen in Ell's tub.

Dammit.

Not knowing what to do with any of that, Fred grunted. "You, uh, need a new O-ring for the faucet. I ain't got one that fits. Got the water turned off now so it won't leak, but uh…."

"Oh, right." Ell took a step back, wringing his hands. "The sink."

"I can go out later and get the part that I need," Fred went on. "I'm gonna go work on that light, okay?"

"Thank you." Ell brightened back up a little. "Maybe after that, would you, well, would you like to watch some *Legends*?"

"You wanna watch the show?"

"I wanna watch it with you," Ell clarified as he returned to folding clothes. He kept his eyes on the laundry, trying and failing to mask his excitement as he said, "I have the special edition DVDs with deleted scenes, commentary from the directors, and, well… I thought it would be fun to watch with another fan. Uh, if you'd be interested?"

Fred ducked into the bathroom to retrieve his toolbox, trying to drag the decision. The immediate reply bubbling up in his mind was positive, but he found himself hesitating.

He needed to square things up with Lochlain and find out what was going on. He couldn't shake the sense of dread tapping away on his shoulder that those art collectors were more than avid fans of antique Sagittarian art.

Why try to kill him? Why risk that kind of heat? What was so important about some old paintings that would be worth murder?

Ell was a lovely distraction, but maybe Fred needed to keep things professional between them. After all, Doc had warned him about Ell not wanting to get too personal. Even Ell himself had dodged questions and specifically avoided explaining his unique powers.

When Fred came back out and saw Ell folding a pair of fuzzy llama pajama pants with such an earnest smile, however, there was no other answer he could give.

"Sure."

"Really?" Ell hopped in place. "Yes!" He quickly tried to rein it in, clutching the pajamas to his chest and keeping his feet on the floor. "Yeah, uh, I mean, that, that would be cool."

"Okay." Fred didn't know what else to say, so he left the bedroom. He found the light switch in the living room that didn't work with a few clicks, and he recalled he'd brought his drill. He headed back outside to his truck. He could hear his phone ringing somewhere off in the grass, and he scowled.

Later.

He grabbed the drill and went back in. After removing the plate over the switch, he checked the wiring. A bad short seemed to be the problem, and he grunted when he got a small zap for his trouble.

Good thing he was already dead or he might have been electrocuted.

"How fucking old is this house?" he grumbled under his breath. He grabbed wire snips to work around the corroded copper so he could make a fresh connection. When he was done, he flicked the switch.

Fred was pleased to see the light turn on, allowing himself a moment of pride that he'd actually been able to fix something. The fence and trellis were going to need more work, and the sink still needed a new part, so he was going to take this as a win.

"Hey, you did it!" Ell exclaimed as he walked into the living room, admiring the new light. "Wow."

"Don't sound so surprised."

"I'm not! I'm just excited."

"Didn't think I could do it, huh?"

"No. I had faith in you the entire time." Ell grinned. "Promise."

Fred pretended to be skeptical. "Sure you did."

Ell laughed. "I really did! Pinkie promise."

"Hmm. I guess." Fred smiled. "So. Got anything else that needs fixin' around here?"

Ell arched his brow. "Do you want the short list or the long list?"

Fred thought he heard his phone ringing again out in the yard, and the immediate and visceral reaction was to ignore it. He decided Lochlain and the rest of his headaches could wait a little longer.

"Hit me with the long list," Fred said. "I got some time."

Fred reasoned he could handle at least a few more repairs before he had to leave, but he was not prepared for everything Ell needed help with. There was another light in the hall closet that didn't work, the sink was clogged in the guest bathroom, something had eaten a hole in the wall of the spare bedroom, part of the ceiling in the kitchen leaked whenever it rained, and on it went.

As Ell showed him through the house, Fred tried to keep up with the growing list of supplies he was going to need to make the repairs. It was going to make for one hell of a shopping trip.

When Ell finished the grand tour of damages, Fred asked him, "You ever think about setting this place on fire and just startin' over?"

"What? No!" Ell wrinkled his nose. "Okay, I know it's kinda busted, but you know, it's home."

"I'll do what I can today, but I'm definitely gonna have to get more stuff."

"That's fine. I gotta finish my laundry and stuff." Ell gestured behind him. "I'll get the DVD ready. You know. For whenever."

Fred got back to work, finding another corroded wire in the hall closet and what was possibly the biggest wad of hair in the universe down in the guest bathroom sink. He tended to some loose door hinges, adjusted the legs of the wobbly kitchen table, and decided he had accomplished just about everything he could with what he had.

The sun was setting now, and he headed to the bedroom to find Ell. "Hey."

"Hey!" Ell was sitting in his bed with a book, and he smiled. "All done?"

"As much as I can be. You, uh, still wanna watch the show?"

"Totally!" Ell closed his book and scooted over. "Here. You can sit here with me if you want?"

"That's okay. I can stand."

"Well, I can try to heal you while we watch if you want," Ell offered.

"Won't that tire you out?" Fred frowned.

"Trust me." Ell patted the mattress invitingly, urging, "Come on. I'm not going to try and do anything too crazy, but I can help you."

Fred lumbered over to sit down on the very edge of the mattress.

"Closer," Ell said with a soft snort. "It's not like I'm gonna bite you and infect you with the dark plague."

Fred smiled at the reference to the show, finally swinging his legs up. He braced himself against the headboard next to Ell, flinching when Ell laid his hand on his arm. "What are you doing?"

"Is this okay?" Ell asked. "I still have to touch you to heal you."

"Sure." Fred kept his hands firmly in his lap, silently enjoying the warmth of Ell's palm. He could feel something happening, something faint but warm, and it was radiating all over his body.

Weird.

Ell grabbed the remote and pressed play, grinning as he declared, "Here we go!"

Fred's lips twitched up in a smile as the opening credits played, and Ell hummed along. Perhaps a bit more quietly, Fred hummed along with him.

The first episode opened with the young hero Trip being transported to the fantasy world of Palmyria after reading a magical book as a little boy. He got lost in the forest and met Princess Daisy, and they formed a fast friendship. Trip returned to his world with Daisy's help, and he grew up wondering if it was all a dream.

There was a dramatic cut to a montage that showed them growing up in their own worlds, thinking of each other often, but not yet reuniting. That didn't happen until later when Trip, all grown up, finds the magical book and reads it again.

"Oh, oh, oh! Here, they included the deleted scene of Daisy singing to call to the birds!" Ell exclaimed. "They recorded both actresses, both young and old Daisy, and like, they mixed them together for the chorus! It's so cool!"

"They cut it because some songwriter threatened to sue over the lyrics," Fred recalled. "Which makes it so fuckin' stupid later when Princess Daisy calls the birds to send her cry for help to the neighboring kingdom when the baron takes her."

"Right?" Ell laughed. "It's so dumb! It's like, when did she learn to talk to birds? When did that happen? And she always knew how!"

"But they never showed it and everyone thought it was bad writing!"

"Friggin' exactly!"

Fred's entire body was buzzing, and he was smiling so wide that his cheeks were actually sore. He couldn't remember ever being so happy. He and Ell traded stories and trivia as the episodes continued on late into the night, and Ell soon had his head resting on Fred's shoulder in clear danger of falling asleep.

When the next episode ended, Ell got up to go grab snacks and wake up, saying he was determined to finish the first season.

Glancing at his arms after Ell had left the room, Fred saw that his scarring looked... different.

The bumps and edges were still there, but they were smoother. He quickly lifted his shirt to investigate his torso, finding that his skin there was also changed. The scars were softer, and areas that were rotting were pinker than before.

"How do you do this?" Fred asked when Ell returned.

"Do wah?" Ell mumbled through a cheek full of food, clutching a bag of strawberry poofies to his chest.

Fred held up his arm. "We've just been sitting here, and you've fuckin' healed me more than going for weeks of treatment with Doc York."

"I can't, I can't talk about that." Ell hovered anxiously by the door. Fred fell silent.

"Can we… can't we just go back to watching the show?" Ell asked hopefully. "The goblin king's about to be crowned, you know."

"Yeah, sure." Fred forced a smile as he got up from the bed. "Sorry about pryin'."

"Oh! Wait! Where are you going?" Ell asked in alarm.

"Just taking my tools out to the truck," Fred replied. "Don't start the coronation without me."

"Okay," Ell promised. "I won't." He bounced back into bed with his snacks, beaming sweetly. "Hurry back!"

Fred lumbered outside with his tools and secured them in his truck with a haggard sigh. Whatever Ell was doing to him had some very unexpected consequences.

It wasn't just the healing, of course.

It was how much Fred wanted to be near Ell, to hear his voice and his laughter, and the alien urgency of wanting to know everything about him. The time they'd spent together was minuscule compared to the years he had invested with a childhood friend like Lochlain, and yet Fred hadn't been this happy since his death.

Shit.

Lochlain.

He searched through the yard for his phone, squinting in the darkness. He hadn't realized how late it was, and it was too dark to see where he had thrown it. There was a slim chance Ell had a flashlight, or he could ask him to call it.

Fred walked back into the house and headed to the bedroom. "Hey, could you…."

Ell was curled up with the poofies in one hand, remote in the other, sound asleep.

Smiling, Fred turned off the lights. Their marathon could continue another time. He left the television on so he could see to straighten up Ell's tangle of blankets and tuck him in. He then began to very carefully pry the remote out of his hand.

Ell stirred, sleepily gazing up at Fred. "Mmm, don't go. We didn't get to the coronation yet."

"You're asleep."

"No, I'm not," Ell argued even as his eyes closed. He patted the pillows beside him. "Come on, we almost finished the first season. We're so close."

Fred knew he needed to go find his phone and see if Lochlain had any news for him. He should probably head home, check the news, do anything but stay here again.

He couldn't possibly resist Ell's sleepy smile, and he grunted impatiently. "Fine. We'll finish the first season, and then I'm leaving."

"Deal."

CHAPTER 5.

ELL WAS back asleep before the next episode ended, and Fred kept watching. He didn't have to worry about needing to rest, and he was determined to finish the season. Watching his favorite show without the fuzz of the old VHS tapes he was used to was pretty awesome. One minute he was enjoying the big climactic battle in the magical forest, and the next he was staring up at the ceiling and it was morning.

The hell.

He was lying on his back in bed with Ell glued to his side like a koala bear. He glanced down and saw he was still sleeping. He tried to plan his next move.

If Fred got out of bed, he would definitely wake up Ell.

If he stayed here, well, nothing necessarily bad would happen, but he had shit that needed to be handled and had been waiting for far too long already.

Ell made a soft sound, his hand sliding over Fred's chest as he cuddled closer.

Maybe a few more minutes wouldn't hurt.

Whenever Ell got up, Fred decided he would too. It was important for Ell to be well rested so his healing powers would recover. That was totally why Fred was staying.

It had absolutely nothing to do with the warm body currently snuggling him.

He'd experienced a lot of strange things since meeting Ell, but nothing could have prepared him for the lurch of pressure beneath his ribs. It was uncomfortable, an eerie dip like the bed was being pulled out from under him, and he couldn't stop staring at Ell's sleeping face.

There, for a moment, he thought his heart beat again.

"Mmm…." Ell's eyes peeked open, and he smiled. "Hey, you're still here. Did we make it to the coronation?"

"Nope." Fred rested his hand on top of Ell's, and he teased, "You didn't even make it to the part where Blix goes down to the wine cellar to talk to the drunk wizard."

"Damn." Ell laughed, breaking off into a big yawn. "Mmmph. Sorry I'm so lame. I never stay up that late."

"I never sleep," Fred said out of habit. He paused to reflect on recent events and then amended, "Until I met you."

"Really?" Ell's eyes widened.

It was hard for Fred to read Ell's expression—shock, pride, interest? Maybe all of the above. It was difficult interpreting emotions he wasn't used to experiencing himself.

"Is that…." Fred paused, debating his options of what to ask. "Is that because of you?"

"Yes!" Ell exclaimed, sitting up and excitedly grabbing Fred's arm. "That means it's working. And wow, this is a lot faster than usual. This is great, Freddie!"

"You've done this before?"

"Of course. I've healed a lot of ghouls!" Ell flushed. "Wait, do you, do you mean the bed? No! Oh gods, no! This, I don't do this—"

"It's fine," Fred soothed, hoping he didn't sound too gruff. Ell continued to look mortified, so he tried, "The other ghouls? I guess they weren't into *Legends of Darkness*, huh?"

Ell smiled at that. "Nope. Just you." He wiggled out of bed, trying to smooth down his rumpled hair. "It's, uh, been a lot of fun! I'm totally game to keep going with the marathon if you're okay with maybe backing up a few episodes."

"Yeah." Fred got up and resisted the urge to reach out and pet Ell's hair. "I'm gonna go into town, check some things out, and get the stuff I need to do more repairs."

"And then you'll come back?" Ell asked hopefully. "I mean, you know, you still need more healing. Those spots on your hips definitely need some attention before they start to turn."

"You feeling okay after what you did last night?" Fred gestured to his arms.

"Yeah! I'm fine! Healing that way is… it's, it's just different." Ell scurried off into the kitchen.

Fred followed him, watching Ell fumble around with a kettle and rub the sleep out of his eyes. He looked very adorable when he first woke up.

After clearing his throat, Fred asked, "Anything else you need while I'm out?"

"No, I'm fine," Ell replied. "I'm still set from the last trip."

"It don't feel right." Fred frowned. "There's gotta be something else I can do for you to make this square."

"Well," Ell said thoughtfully, "you can watch the rest of *Legends of Darkness* with me—"

"Yeah, okay—"

"—with the director's commentary on!"

Fred laughed. "Sure, yeah. Why not. We'll finish it up and watch it again with the commentary track on. Yeah?"

"Sounds good." Ell put the kettle on the stove. "So, see you in a bit? You can text me whenever you're headed back this way. Or not. You don't have to text me. You can just show up. I'll be here."

"I'll text." Fred smiled. "Later."

"Bye, Freddie!"

"Bye." Fred was still smiling as he headed outside. Trading hours of watching his favorite show for top-notch healing was a very sweet deal.

It helped that the healer was a pretty awesome cuddler.

Fred didn't think it was a fair trade, if he was being honest. There had to be something else he could do other than fixing up the house and binging television to repay Ell. He thought it over as he searched through the grass, hoping he could think up something good.

He found his phone and then sat behind the wheel of his truck before glancing over the screen.

There were dozens of missed calls and unread texts.

They were all from Lochlain, and Fred's undead guts twisted as he rang him back. The texts were frantic and strange, and he was left waiting for the line to pick up before he growled, "What the fuck is this 'you're in danger' shit?"

"Talked to Lorre," Lochlain replied quickly. "The art collectors are looking for you. They're pissed about the fire—"

"Good."

"Fred!" Lochlain pleaded. "Tell me where you are. I can come help protect you! Robert too! Azaethoth is still gone with Sloane, but I'm sure if I prayed—"

"Fuck your prayers." Fred's anger was rapidly boiling up again, and he struggled not to be too heavy on the gas as he left Ell's so he wouldn't kick earth everywhere.

"Fred, please. Listen to me. These guys aren't just art collectors. According to Lorre, they're seriously intense Salgumel worshippers. At least one of them worked at the same museum as a certain Bad Robert."

Fred flinched at that.

"Ring any bells?"

"Tollmathan," Fred recalled, naming the god who had possessed a museum curator, also known as Bad Robert, and tried to bring about the end of the world by waking the old god Salgumel out of his sleep.

He'd also been the one who murdered Lochlain.

"Everything in my gut is telling me these guys are really bad news," Lochlain said urgently. "If you don't want my help, fine. Please just tell me you're going to be safe? That you have somewhere to lay low for a bit longer?"

"Yeah." Fred thought of his promise to marathon *Legends of Darkness* with Ell a few times over. "I got somewhere."

"Stay there and keep your head down," Lochlain advised. "When Sloane and Azaethoth return, I'll let them know what's going on. You don't have to do this alone, Fred."

"Yeah."

"Did you tell him?" Robert's voice came through the line, close enough to the phone that Fred could hear him.

"Not now," Lochlain said gently, his voice muffled as if he was trying to put his hand over the speaker. "It's not a good time—"

"But it's our wedding!" Robert protested.

"You guys are getting hitched?" Fred knew Lochlain had been thinking about asking Robert, but this seemed awfully sudden.

"Well, yes," Lochlain said, more clearly now. "I didn't want to tell you yet. Not until all of this shit had settled down."

Fred scowled.

"I can hear you making a face," Lochlain drawled. "I know you're in a very bad situation right now, and the last thing I wanted to do was make it seem like I was rubbing my happiness in your face."

Fred knew Lochlain meant well, but it still hurt. Considering their last conversation, it hurt a lot. "Yeah, don't worry about it."

"Really?" Lochlain perked up.

"You do plenty of that rubbin' shit in my face anyway."

"Fred!"

"Good luck with the wedding. Call me if you have somethin' useful." Fred hung up, letting his phone fall down to the floorboard as he fumed.

The drive back to the city was long enough for him to cool down and sort out the unexpected guilt that was eating at his stomach. He knew he was being hard on Lochlain, especially for a guy who had also died, but he couldn't stop himself from being so bitter.

He got in and out of the local hardware store with what he needed for the repairs and thought over his next move. The cultist art dealers or whoever they were wouldn't take long to figure out where he lived.

If they didn't know already.

The best thing he could do was return to Ell's house and hunker down there.

Thinking again of Lochlain, Fred considered driving over to his place to apologize. He hated how his temper always surged to the front of his emotions and was turning every conversation into a battle.

Fred was trying to be a good friend, but he was a ghoul. His emotions were limited, and he was frustrated by how quickly his anger took over. His best friend had been blessed with a miraculous second chance. He needed to be happy for Lochlain, not bitter.

Besides, Fred had whatever it was going on with Ell now, and his emotions were not limited when they were together. It was too early to say what it was exactly, but it was something. Fred *hoped* it was something anyway. He was struck by another wave of unexpected guilt because he didn't want to take advantage of Ell's sweet nature, and he wished he knew of some way to show Ell how much the last few days had meant to him.

There had to be something he could do to bridge the uncomfortable void left behind by his fight with Lochlain and try to show Ell how truly grateful he was. Fred thought and thought, and he came up with absolutely nothing. Trying to make people happy was hard. He was reminded of the goblin king in the show trying to mend the tensions between all of the warring kingdoms and build new alliances.

King Blix brought a rare gift to appease Princess Daisy, something special and….

Oh, of course!

Fred started driving back to his apartment, smiling proudly. He knew how to solve both of his problems. All it would cost him was a quick visit home. He needed a shower and a new pair of pants anyway. What appeared to be oil or paint would be recognizable as dried ghoul blood to some. It was risky, he knew, but he would make sure to stay on guard.

Spying an unfamiliar sedan with white racing stripes made him uneasy, though he didn't see anyone hanging around. There was no immediate sign of his neighbors or any screaming kids about either. It was lunchtime, and he assumed everyone was at work or school, which made the sedan even more out of place as the parking lot was nearly vacant.

Fred watched his back as he headed to his apartment. Even after he'd locked the door, he checked the peephole to see if anyone was coming up the hallway. He saw no one, but that didn't mean someone wouldn't be waiting for him later. He took a quick shower, changed into fresh clothes, and then debated what to do with the shirt Ell had lent him. He'd prefer to wash it and return it clean, but he couldn't stay home that long.

Knowing it had belonged to Ell's brother gave him pause, and he decided bringing it back dirty was better than not bringing it back at all.

Fred grabbed the box of VHS tapes from the living room, a battered book from his bedside table drawer, and he was ready to go. He looked through the peephole and saw nothing but an empty hallway. He stepped outside, looked around again, and then locked his door. He turned to head down the hallway, but he smacked right into a thin man he would have sworn wasn't there a second ago.

So great was Fred's girth that he nearly knocked the man down just from bumping into him. He growled low, "Pardon me."

"Sorry, didn't see you…." The man trailed off as he looked up at Fred, and still more up to finally meet his eyes. "Wow. Yeah. My bad."

Fred bared his teeth and lumbered toward the stairs without another word. He'd never seen that man before, and he wondered if it was one of the cultists following him. He hadn't seen many of their faces, but he'd heard a few of them talking. He didn't recognize the man's voice as being one of them, but that didn't mean anything.

Having been shot in the head at the time, Fred didn't think his memories from that evening were the most reliable.

He stopped at Lochlain's, knocked, and left the box of VHS tapes on his doorstep after he'd written a quick message on the lid:

The Goblin King sends his regards

Fred couldn't think of a better apology, and he hoped Lochlain would understand the message.

The old book was safely tucked in his glove compartment, and it was just as precious to him as those dusty tapes. It was a first edition of the novelization of the first season of *Legends of Darkness* Fred had bought with allowance from his parents years ago.

It was long out of print and hard to find. Just for fun, Fred had once looked up how much a copy was going for, and even later editions sold for hundreds of dollars. Dogeared and tattered, his copy wouldn't be worth squat, but to a fellow fan like Ell?

Maybe it would be worth a bit more.

Fred got back in his car, scanning around for the mysterious sedan he'd seen over at his place. He saw no sign of it, but he decided to take the extra-long way out to Ell's just to be safe. The last thing he wanted was anyone following him and putting Ell in danger.

He checked his mirrors often for the mysterious sedan or anyone else who might be tailing him as he drove around the city in sporadic circles, but he had the road to himself by the time he finally turned onto the country highway that led to Ell's house.

Maybe he was just being paranoid.

When Fred pulled up into Ell's yard, Ell was out watering the flowers around the windows.

Ell waved excitedly, nearly dropping his watering can.

Fred parked, grabbed the book and the borrowed shirt, and lumbered out of his truck. "Hey."

"Hey!" Ell grinned, adorably crooked as always.

"Here. Thanks for letting me wear this. Sorry I didn't wash it." Fred thrust the shirt out first. "I couldn't hang around long."

"That's okay." Ell took the shirt and hugged it to his chest. "My washer works just fine." He eyed the book. "What's that? I'm not a plumber, but that doesn't look like a part to fix my sink."

"Come on." Fred nodded at the house. "I'll show you."

"Oh, okay, Mr. Mysterious." Ell finished watering the last row of flowers and then headed inside, stopping in the kitchen to drop the watering can in the sink and the shirt in the laundry nook. "Well, what is it?"

Fred offered out the book.

Frowning, Ell took it and finally looked at the cover. His eyes widened with a soft squeak, and he reverently turned to the first page. "This… this is… where, where did you get this?"

"Bought it when I was a kid," Fred explained, pleased that Ell seemed so thrilled. "Sorry it's kinda beat up."

"No, it's great! This, this is amazing!" Ell clutched the book to his chest. "You're, you're really giving this to me?"

"Yeah, thought I might," Fred said with a shrug. "Figured you could appreciate it, you know? I wanted to say—"

"Thank you!" Ell leapt up into Fred's arms, hugging his neck fiercely. "I love it, I love it, I friggin' love it!"

"Whoa!" Fred laughed, wrapping his arms around Ell to hold him up. Ell's warmth enveloped him like a blanket, and the brush of his fingers at the nape of his neck made Fred shiver. As he hugged Ell back, he could feel the worn fabric of his shirt and the lean muscles of his shoulders, and nothing had ever felt so right.

"Thank you, thank you!" Ell turned his head, planting a sweet kiss on Fred's cheek.

Fred's body then did something he never thought would be possible; he blushed. Ell's lips were damp, hot, and the simple affection made Fred's chest tighten up. He returned Ell's feet to the ground, but he hesitated to let go of him. He wanted to keep holding Ell like this forever, watch *Legends of Darkness* and make tea and fall asleep together….

Even when he'd been alive, Fred didn't think he'd ever been so drawn to someone before.

"This is seriously the most thoughtful thing ever," Ell gushed, beaming up at him. One of his hands lingered on Fred's broad chest. "Thank you, Freddie."

"Yeah," Fred mumbled. "It's uh… it's no big deal. Look, I wanted to say thank you. For the healing, and…." He struggled to find the right words. "The other stuff."

Perfect.

"What other stuff? I mean, you need to be more Pacific, and not so Atlantic." Ell grinned expectantly.

Fred groaned at the reference from the show, one of Trip's many corny jokes. "Look, that was awful when Trip said it to the king of the fairies, and it's fuckin' awful now."

"Hey! The only reason it was awful is because the fairies didn't get it 'cause they live in Palmyria and don't have the same oceans we do. So, of course, they wouldn't find it funny."

"We have those oceans, and it's still not funny."

"It's totally funny."

Fred laughed despite his best efforts not to, and he smiled down at Ell. "You're ridiculous, little one."

"Is that part of the other stuff you, uh, wanted to thank me for?"

"Not exactly, uh…." Fred became hyper aware of Ell's hand still on his chest and how closely their bodies were now pressing together, unconsciously having closed the distance between them while they were talking. He gazed down at Ell, searching his bright blue eyes as if he could find what to say there and then getting distracted by his lips.

Fred's hands were at the small of Ell's back, and he was already imagining sliding one of them into Ell's hair to tilt his head up for a kiss.

Ell hadn't moved, though his fingers tightened ever so slightly in the fabric of Fred's shirt as he looked up at Fred with a shy little smile. "Well?"

"I just…." Fred bowed his head, sliding his hand higher up Ell's back. Maybe it was his imagination, but Ell seemed to be leaning in closer, and Fred couldn't help but wonder if his lips would be as soft as they looked.

"Oh!" Ell blinked, startled by something outside and pulling away from Fred. "What's that?"

Fred silently cursed and turned to see what had caught Ell's attention through the window. It was an old sedan with white racing stripes pulling into the yard next to his truck.

Fuck.

"Expecting anyone?" Fred asked warily.

"No." Ell frowned. "I don't have any other patients right now except you. No one ever comes out this way unless they're friggin' lost."

It was definitely the same sedan Fred had seen at his apartment complex.

"Stay here," Fred growled, leaving Ell stuttering as he stormed outside. He didn't want Ell to see what he was about to do, but he had to make sure he was safe.

There were two men getting out of the car, and one was the same asshole Fred had bumped into outside his apartment.

They had to have tagged him with a watchman spell, Fred realized. That was why he hadn't seen anyone following him because they didn't have to. All they had to do was hang back, track him with the spell, and then they could close in whenever he stopped.

Right here at Ell's.

"Hello there, Mr. Wilder," the asshole said cheerfully. "You're a hard man to find. We got some unfinished business with you, you know."

"You mean like all that money you owe me?" Fred huffed sarcastically.

"I mean like I tried to kill you, and you didn't stay dead," the other man spat.

Fred recognized his voice as the one who had shot him the other night.

Jeff.

"You're a damn ghoul, aren't you?" Jeff sneered. "Guess we got to make sure you're double dead."

Summoning fire into his hands with a few whispered words, Fred reared back to attack. He was going to reduce them both to ashes and….

Wait.

Nothing was happening.

"Nice try." The asshole laughed, holding up a large wooden block carved with twisting symbols. "This is a silencing totem. It will keep you from casting any magic—"

Fred ran right at them. He lunged at the asshole with the totem first. He punched him as hard as he could, summoning all of his ghoulish strength. He heard a loud crunch, and he leered as the asshole dropped to the ground and didn't move. "Silence that."

"Hey, you rotten fuck!" Jeff had a gun, and it was pointed right at Fred.

Ducking beside the car, Fred flinched as the glass of the passenger-side window burst over his head. Bullets pinged off the truck behind him and off the hood of the sedan.

The asshole with the totem was stirring, groaning in pain. He jerked up when he heard the shots.

Fred punched him again.

Counting down the bullets whizzing around him, Fred figured he had a good chance to make it around the car before Jeff reloaded. He couldn't see where the totem was, so he'd have to use his hands.

And anything else he could grab.

Leaping up, he reached for the toolbox in the back of his truck. He hurled it as hard as could, and it struck Jeff right in the chest.

Jeff teetered over, gasping as the air was knocked right out of him. The gun flew from his hands, and Fred leapt on top of him.

Fred wrapped his hands around Jeff's throat, snarling, "In ten seconds, I am going to let you go, and then you're going to tell me how you fuckin' found me and what the fuck you want from me. Then, if I'm feeling really nice, I ain't gonna grab you again—"

The world spun as something struck Fred in the side of his head. His vision blurred, and it hit him again. He had to let go and was sent reeling backward. The pain was strange, closer to the forefront of his mind and impossible to ignore.

He managed to focus on the object Jeff was hitting him with before it crashed into his face.

Ah, a hammer from his toolbox.

Just as Jeff was about to swing down on his head again, Fred heard the front door opening and Ell screaming.

"Leave him alone!" Ell was absolutely enraged, thrusting his hand against Jeff's face.

The instant he touched him, Jeff screamed in agony and dropped the hammer.

Fred could hear skin sizzling and popping, and he smelled something absolutely foul. "Ell! Go! Hey, get out of here!"

"I'm not leaving you!" Ell shouted stubbornly.

"Ell! For fuck's sake!" Fred roared, trying to get up and falling right back down. All of his energy was focused on trying to protect Ell. "Get the fuck out of here! Right now!"

Ell either didn't hear him or chose to ignore him, keeping his hand plastered against Jeff's cheek and driving him away from Fred.

"The fuck! The fucking fuck!" Jeff screamed, flailing in pain as he twisted away from Ell's touch. He now had a nearly perfect handprint on the side of his face, so black and rotten that Fred could see his teeth shining through what used to be his cheek.

Ell wasn't moving, standing firm with a curiously blank expression as he watched Jeff scrambling to get inside to the driver's seat of his car while clutching his face.

The asshole with the totem managed to climb into the car next to him, and he screamed hysterically at Jeff to leave. They sped away, tires squealing and kicking up grass.

Whatever strange trance Ell was in broke when he turned back to Fred. "Oh! Freddie! Your poor head!"

"I'm fine." Fred grunted as Ell kneeled beside him and pawed at his injuries. He was able to sit up, and he patted Ell's side. "I'm okay, really."

"No, you're not! You're really hurt! By all the gods, I was so friggin' scared! I heard the shooting and all the yelling and I, I didn't know if you…. Oh gods." Ell suddenly hugged Fred's neck and kissed him right on the lips.

Ell's kiss was hot, his mouth holding Fred's so deeply that he felt it down in the mark binding his soul to this vessel. It woke up a new wave of sensations Fred didn't think he was capable of anymore—passion being right at the very top of that list—and it ended all too soon.

"Sorry." Ell pulled away awkwardly, and he ducked his head against Fred's shoulder. "I was, uh, I'm just really happy you're okay."

"Thank you." In spite of the pain, Fred smiled. He hugged Ell's waist, savoring the warm body in his arms as he stroked his back. He wanted to kiss him some more, hold him for hours, and never let go again.

But first, his brain spoke up, he probably should find out how Ell decomposed someone's face off in the presence of a silencing totem.

"Oh, hey, glad to save the day anytime. I'm just like Trip, a knight in shining—" Ell glanced down at his shirt. "—uh, a shining rainbow llama shirt." He had a smear of black blood on his face from where they'd kissed, his face quite flushed as he petted Fred's aching skull. "Hold still. I've got you."

The pain in Fred's head began to fade, and his vision returned to normal. He hugged Ell closer. "Are *you* okay?"

"I'm okay." Ell offered a weary smile as he petted Fred's cheek, fussing over the blood. "I'm sorry I didn't come out sooner."

"I was doing all right," Fred insisted. "You should have stayed in the house—"

"And watch you get murdered to death with a friggin' hammer?" Ell's eyes were suddenly full of tears, and he grabbed Fred's shirt. "No! I couldn't, I couldn't just let you die!"

"Hey, hey." Fred gently touched Ell's wrist. "Already dead, remember?"

"Not to me!" Ell cried. "You're not some dead thing! You're alive! You're Fred! You're my friend, and I would do anything to keep you safe!"

"Anything, huh? Like rotting somebody's face off?" Fred raised his brow. "I know I owe you some answers about bringing danger to your front door, but *wow*. What the fuck was that?"

"Right. That." Ell fidgeted. "Uh, maybe we should… we should talk about that whole rotting faces off thing because I… might not be human?"

"No fuckin' shit."

CHAPTER 6.

"So, I was adopted." Ell started speaking once they were back inside, sitting on the sofa and wringing his hands. "See, my parents literally found me on their doorstep. Totally abandoned. They said there wasn't even a blanket with me. I didn't even have a diaper on."

"Okay," Fred said, hesitantly sitting beside him.

"They were so happy," Ell said with a wistful smile. "They already had my brother, but they'd always wanted more kids. Mama… she…. My mother couldn't have any others, so I was their special little blessing from the Lord of Light. They spent a fortune making sure they could keep me. I didn't actually know I was adopted for a long time. Not until…."

"Until?" Fred gently prompted.

"Not until I almost killed my brother."

Fred flinched, scanning Ell's worried face. Ell looked like he was on the verge of tears, and Fred reached over to take his hand.

Ell squeezed hard, continuing urgently, "It was an accident. Totally an accident. I didn't know what I was doing. We were just goofing around, and he was trying to pile all of these stuffed animals on top of me. But… but then I couldn't breathe.

"I tried to tell him to stop, but he just kept going. They were on my face and in my mouth and… and… I was finally able to get a hand out, and I pushed him as hard as I could. When I touched him, something happened. He, he just sort of fell over and…."

Ell was about to cry.

"Hey." Fred leaned closer, resting his other hand on top of his joined with Ell's. "It's okay."

Ell nodded and sniffed back his tears. He took a deep breath before he continued, "So, my parents totally friggin' freaked. Called paramedics, my brother had to go to the hospital and stayed there for months in a coma. They were all saying it looked like someone had sucked the life right out of Ted. They said they'd never seen anything like it.

"No known magic, no such spell, not even one recorded in the forbidden arts, could do what I did. One second he was a perfectly healthy boy, and then it was all gone. Like someone had just strolled on over and slurped it away with a straw.

"After that, I couldn't touch anyone. My brother got better, and he didn't remember anything. My parents lied about what happened, said he had some sort of seizure, but I knew the truth. It was me. Something happened to me. This power... it woke up that day, and I could never put it back."

"It got triggered by your brother trying to smother you?" Fred asked carefully.

"Maybe because I was so scared. Maybe it was from some sort of crazy adrenaline spike... I don't know." Ell hung his head. "I know now he wasn't really trying to hurt me, but I guess six-year-old me didn't."

"Is this why your parents kept you under fuckin' lockdown and all that curfew shit?"

"Yes," Ell confirmed. "They took me out of school, and they started making me wear long sleeves and gloves. I couldn't have any friends, I couldn't see my brother, and I could never leave my room. No hugs, no high-fives, nothing. They told everyone I was really sick, anything to keep other people away."

"And they did this shit when you were six?" Fred cut in sharply, his anger quick to rise. "You were just a fuckin' kid!"

"They were worried I would slip up, have an accident, hurt someone again." Ell wiped away a tear. "Me and my big brother grew really far apart, and my parents... I think they were scared of me. They probably still are, but we haven't spoken in years, so who knows. They always claimed they were trying to protect me." He wiped another tear from his cheek. "I knew that was a lie. They weren't really trying to protect me. They wanted to protect other people *from* me. I wasn't their miracle anymore. I'd become a monster, and they didn't know what to do with me. So. Uh. When I turned sixteen, I ran away."

Fred wanted to tell Ell that he was sorry, but a simple apology didn't sound like enough for what he had been through. He raised Ell's hand to kiss it.

Ell smiled, and he turned his head to rub a few more tears off on his arm. "Yeah. So. That's, uh, that's season one of my epically tragic backstory. Next, we get to talk about how I started healing ghouls and got this super awesome scar. Heh."

"We ain't gotta go into season two just yet if you don't wanna," Fred soothed. "We can take a break. You want some tea or somethin'?"

"No. It's okay." Ell laced his fingers with Fred's, anxiously rubbing their thumbs together. "Uh, so, season two kicks off with me figuring out that I could heal ghouls."

"Yeah?" Fred cleared his throat. "How did that happen exactly?"

"An accident actually. I met a very nice ghoul named Doyle at a homeless shelter I was staying at. He'd run away from his family when he started to rot."

"Sounds like you had a lot in common, both bein' runaways."

"Yeah. He didn't like *Legends of Darkness*, but he knew the best jokes and always gave me his food when the soup kitchen was open." Ell managed a brighter smile. "That's where we were when it happened. There were these big stairs at the front of the building where they served the food, and one day I tripped walking up them. Caught my sleeve on the railing by the door and tore it open. When Doyle helped me back up, he accidentally touched my arm."

"But nothing happened?"

"Nothing. He didn't get sick. He wasn't hurt. It was incredible. I maybe went a tiny bit crazy and found every excuse to touch him that I could. It had been so long since I could actually touch anyone, and I was so desperate for hugs, handshakes, whatever. He humored me, and well, then he started to get better."

"Did you tell anyone?"

"Oh gods, no!" Ell grimaced. "Even at that age, I knew what I had was special and dangerous. I was already registered as a void, and people would have so many questions. So, I learned how to focus my power, heal specific parts, met Doctor York through another ghoul that Doyle knew. I got her patients that needed the most help, and well, I've just been doing that ever since."

Fred paused, turning the new information over in his mind. He'd never heard of any creature being able to wield this kind of magic except maybe a god. Eyeing the scar on Ell's neck, he asked, "And that?"

"Uhm." Ell fidgeted awkwardly. "So, Doyle.... Doyle was my best friend, but he.... You see, he was...."

"*Was?*"

"He's dead." Ell gave Fred's hand another squeeze. "After I started healing him, he was able to go back to his family. They gave me the money for this house as a thank-you for healing him. His family were all so happy to have him back, but his mother… she wanted me to do the same for her."

"To heal her?"

"Yes." Ell closed his eyes. "She had some kind of cancer that wasn't responding to any medicine or magic. I tried explaining to her and Doyle that my powers didn't work like that. If I touched her, she would get hurt. She might die."

"Lemme guess." Fred sighed. "They didn't listen?"

"Doyle waited until the next time I healed him to try it," Ell said quietly. "I was weak, tired… I couldn't stop him from letting his mother into the house. No matter how much I screamed for her to stop, she grabbed my hand, she wouldn't let go, and she… she just started rotting.

"Doyle called me all these nasty names, grabbed a knife from the kitchen… and well…." Ell trailed off, gesturing to the long scar across his neck. "He and his mother left me there to die, but, heh, I didn't. I woke up with a brand-new scar, and I never saw either of them again."

"No cops?" Fred asked flatly, trying to hide his shock at Ell surviving having his throat slit. The scar was ghastly. No mortal could have taken that and lived to talk about it.

"I sure as hell wasn't going to call them." Ell made a face. "There was nothing Doyle could do either. If he tried to have me arrested for magical assault, I could out him as a ghoul and his family for harboring one. Not that I really would do that because that's mean, but well… just in case."

"He still around? You keep sayin' he *was* your best friend."

"They're both dead. Doyle's mother died from her cancer or maybe whatever I did, and Doyle didn't come back to me for treatment again. I would have helped him, even after everything he'd done… but I saw an obituary for him that winter. There wasn't anything about him being a ghoul, but I think… I think he let himself rot."

"Good." Fred was struck by another surge of rage. "He didn't have any right to take advantage of you like that."

"He loved his mother," Ell insisted. "He did what he thought was best to help her—"

"But not you. He tried to fuckin' kill you."

"People do crazy things for the ones they love," Ell said, smiling mournfully. He appeared so much older in that moment, exhausted and worn down. "Well. There you have it. That's my story."

"What are you?" Fred didn't mean to sound so blunt, but he couldn't stop himself. "Are you a god? 'Cause it kinda seems like you could be."

"A god? Ha, no!" Ell laughed. "I really don't know what I am. I don't think I'm human, not entirely. After a lot of research, I think I might be part Eldress with maybe a tiny bit of Asra."

"The undead unicorn things and the cat people?" Fred blinked.

The Eldress were a race of equine creatures with horns who appeared to be actively decomposing and yet alive. They were the third of Great Azaethoth's children. The Asra were the first, giant cat monsters who had been created to serve the gods before they rebelled. After winning the war, the Asra were gifted rule over the magical world of Xenon, the bridge between the human world of Aeon and Zebulon, the home of the gods.

Like the other monstrous everlasting races, none had been seen on Aeon since the gods went into the dreaming.

"Yup." Ell said, brightening back up a bit. "I know everyone thinks the everlasting people are dead or they fled to Xenon, but I don't think all of them did. I think some of them stayed here."

"Probably be hard not to notice a zombie unicorn running around."

"They could have learned how to change their appearance!" Ell protested. "Bones of the Asra are supposed to help with magical stuff—"

"Like astral projection."

"And shape-shifting!" Ell was excited again, his eyes wide as he continued, "We know there aren't any Asran graves left here on Earth, so what happened to the bones? I think some of the other races, Eldress, Vulgora, even some Asra, stayed behind, used the bones, and lived with humans and totally had kids!"

Fred stared, scrambling for something to say. This all probably would have sounded insane to anyone else, but not just anyone had a best friend who had been recently resurrected by a god after their body was possessed by another god to solve their murder.

But Fred very well couldn't say *that*, so he was left fumbling.

"It could have happened!" Ell clearly took Fred's silence as doubt. "What about Fish Boy?"

"That really badly photoshopped thing that pops up in the tabloids at the grocery store?"

"What if he's real?" Ell pressed. "He might be part Vulgoran! I could be part Eldress! They existed between the edge of life and death, right? Always rotting but still totally alive? And the Asra can't ever be silenced! It would explain my powers!"

Fred pressed his lips together in a tight line as he tried to plan what he was going to say next very carefully. He cared about Ell very much, but there were some secrets he didn't think were his place to share.

"My mother was Tauri," he said at last. "In the Tauri religion, the everlasting races are seen as helpful spirits that answer prayers when the gods ain't up to it. Some of 'em got turned into gods for doin' such a good job, like Ekiya the Kind, who was like half-horse with these ram horns, or Prisha the Brilliant, a lady with a cat head and a big long tail."

"See!" Ell beamed. "I bet that's who they were! They were descendants of the everlasting people like me."

"Yeah, but it ain't like you got a big cat tail or some horns pokin' out from anywhere." Fred was surprised when Ell looked particularly sheepish, and that prompted him to ask, "What?"

"About that." Ell reached behind his neck as if he was taking off a necklace, though there was nothing there. There was a click, and a silver chain suddenly appeared, and he set it in his lap.

A glamour charm.

It was a spell to alter someone's appearance for long periods of time, even beyond the duration of shape-shifting, but it was only active as long as the wearer kept the enchanted item on.

Fred looked over Ell, and at first, he didn't notice anything different.

Until he looked at his hair.

Poking out through Ell's blond hair were two small caprine horns. They were lightly colored, almost blending in with his hair, and Fred was left positively speechless.

Ell's cheeks flushed, and he went to put the necklace back on. "It's, uh, it's a really powerful glamour charm. When I have it on, you can't feel them, much less see them—"

"Hey, no," Fred cut in, staying Ell's hand. "You ain't gotta do that. I was just… surprised. I like 'em."

"You don't… you don't think they're weird?" Ell asked pitifully.

"Of course they're fuckin' weird. That's why I like 'em. Weird is good." Fred grinned, pleased when Ell smiled back.

"Really?"

"Really." Fred glanced up again at the little horns. "Can I touch 'em?"

"Uh, sure?" Ell fidgeted. "No one's ever… no one else has touched them. I guess, uh, just be gentle? They're kinda sensitive."

Fred moved slowly, reaching up to carefully touch the tip of one horn.

Ell inhaled sharply, and his eyes closed.

"This okay?" Fred asked, aware how the energy in the room was now charged.

"It's… it's okay." Ell eagerly leaned into Fred's touch. "They popped up after that stuff happened with Doyle and his mom… and it… *wow*, that… that feels really nice. Please don't stop."

Fred stroked Ell's horn, finding it smooth and warm, tracing it down to its base. Ell gasped again, and he shifted his hand so his palm could cradle the side of Ell's head while he continued to explore.

He'd felt the true touch of a living god, but it didn't compare to this. Not when Ell was pressing against his hand like a desperate kitten and Ell's hand was now squeezing Fred's thigh. Fred had no idea what Ell really was, but fuck if he wasn't the most beautiful thing Fred had ever touched.

"Freddie," Ell murmured, his eyes slowly opening again to find Fred's. "I've never…."

"What?" Fred caught himself looking down at Ell's lips. He aimed for teasing, joking, "Never gotten your horns jerked off by a ghoul?"

Ell laughed, bright and happy, and his blush deepened. "That, and well, everything else."

"Everything," Fred repeated dumbly before his mind caught up.

Of fuckin' course, he realized. Ell couldn't touch anyone.

And if Ell couldn't touch anyone, that meant no one could touch him, and well….

Shit.

Fred didn't know at first what to do with that. He couldn't explain the rush of heat inside of his body that continued to grow as he toyed with Ell's horn and listened to all the soft little sounds he was making. It was an ache he hadn't known properly in years, a longing that was completely overwhelming his senses.

Lust.

He didn't want to take advantage of Ell's obvious inexperience, but he wanted to keep going. He hadn't done anything like this since before his death, and the deep lonely chasm in his undead heart was flooding with an irresistible yearning.

"You were my first kiss," Ell confessed even as his fingers gripped Fred's leg. "Maybe… you could be my second? And, and maybe my third—"

Fred surged forward, kissing Ell hard.

"Mmmph!" Ell squeaked, his hands shooting up to brace himself against Fred's chest and freezing in place.

Shit, too much.

Fred dialed it back, kissing Ell more softly and moving his hand down to his shoulder. It was a warm press of lips, and then another, and one more until Ell relaxed again.

Ell's hands shakily slid up Fred's chest, and he began to kiss back more confidently.

When Ell moaned, Fred growled in reply and felt him shudder. He wanted to take more and more, but stopped himself from moving too fast. Ell had saved him—his body from rot, his life from some asshole with a hammer, and his heart from dying. The least Fred could do was be patient.

This needed to be perfect.

Whatever Ell was, he was sweet and generous and kind, and Fred wanted to protect him and make him smile and be with him always. This feeling couldn't just be from the magical healing. Fred was certain the magic was Ell himself, and Fred couldn't get enough of this special young man.

The kiss was growing steadily more passionate, and Ell's reservations were dwindling. He was all but crawling in Fred's lap, and he scratched his nails over the back of Fred's neck.

There was too much spit, and Ell was digging in way too hard, but Fred wouldn't correct him for all the money in the world. Fred kissed Ell back with a passion he didn't know he was capable of even when he had a pulse, and Ell's needy whimpers were making Fred dizzy. He kept his hand on Ell's shoulder, rubbing him soothingly, but not advancing. It all felt good, so very good, and then….

No.

It wasn't possible.

Fred's cock was getting hard.

"Freddie," Ell sighed, pulling away to catch his breath. His lips were deliciously red and wet from kissing, and he was gawking up at Fred in utter amazement. His eyes had turned that rich violet color again, and Fred didn't think he'd ever looked so pretty, horns and all.

"You okay?" Fred asked, giving Ell's shoulder a reassuring squeeze while trying to ignore the stirring between his legs. He was not about to bring that up, nope, not right now.

"Is it… is it okay if we stop?" Ell shivered. "Not that I really want to stop because I don't. Like, wow. I really, *really* like doing that, but my skin feels all buzzy and weird and—"

"Hey," Fred soothed. He kissed Ell's forehead. "It's fine."

"It's just really new, and crap, when did it get so hot in here?" Ell ran his hands through his hair, digging around his horns. "Whew. Wow."

"It's new for me too." Fred cleared his throat, still trying to will his cock to stand down. "New for me, you know, like this."

"I really, really wanna maybe keep going, but uh, can we talk about why someone was trying to kill you with a hammer?" Ell took a deep breath and reached for Fred's hands. His eyes were blue again. "Please."

"Right. So, you know how you thought it would be really cool if I was a criminal?" Fred grimaced. "Surprise."

"Really?" Ell's eyes widened. "Ha! I knew it! Oh, oh, what kind of criminal are you? Are you an evil bandit like the goblin king was before he finally took the throne?"

"Eh, something like that. I steal stuff, usually very high dollar, and sell it off. The last job I was on didn't go so fuckin' well. The clients tried to kill me."

"That's how you got hurt?" Ell frowned.

"Yeah. Tried to bring them the loot, and they shot me."

"But why kill you if you did what they wanted?"

"Cheaper than paying me." Fred shrugged. "They're up to somethin' bad, but I dunno what."

"Have you always been a thief?" Ell asked hesitantly. "I mean… is this a ghoul thing, or did you always do this?"

"Always," Fred replied. "Me and my best friend were swiping lunch money from the cafeteria till in grade school. We were always lookin' to take a little somethin', and well… we got older, learned there's a whole lot more money out there than just some rolls of quarters if you're smart."

"Is that… is that how you died?" Ell gently touched Fred's arm.

Fred bristled initially at the idea of discussing his death, but he decided it was only fair to tell Ell his story too. "Yeah. Went on a job, everything went to shit. Got left behind."

"You weren't alone?"

"No," Fred said, shaking his head. "There were two of us. We got into the place, some big cushy penthouse downtown, no problem. It was gonna be a cinch. My partner was always real good at planning, you see, so I wasn't worried. But there was a fire trap on the fuckin' safe that he missed."

"What's that?"

"You open the safe without the password, boom. Fire."

"Right. Sorry."

"It's okay." Fred moved his arm to take Ell's hand, smiling wearily. "I really didn't know what one was either until it exploded right in my face. The whole place caught on fire in seconds, the alarms started blaring, all that shit. And the guy I was with… he left me."

"He left you?" Ell gasped in horror.

"Yeah." Fred looked down at the floor. "Guess he thought I was too fucked up. Maybe he got scared. Place was going up in flames, and he fuckin' bailed."

"I'm so sorry."

"It's fine." Fred grunted, trying to hide the pain that the old memories stirred up. "Cops and fire department showed up, got the fire out, and dragged my crispy ass to the nearest hospital. I was burned bad, real bad, and I wasn't gonna make it.

"And my partner's sister shows up. I mean, I don't remember none of this 'cause I was busy dying and all. But they told me after. She came over and worked some fuckin' magic with a wooden spoon and walked out of that hospital with my soul."

"A spoon?"

"Yup. She bound my soul to a spoon to take me out of the hospital." Fred smiled. "Damn spoon is probably still in her kitchen. She made my body, brought me back." He shrugged. "Wasn't much else for me to do after that, being dead, so I went right back to stealing. So, yeah, that's it."

"Thank you for telling me." Ell kissed Fred's cheek sweetly. "I'm so sorry that happened to you. I hope that awful jerk who left you behind got exactly what was friggin' coming to him. I mean, wow, what a selfish bastard!"

"Ha!" Fred chuckled. "You can tell him all that shit when you meet him."

"Wait, huh?" Ell tilted his head in confusion. "What do you mean? Meet him?"

"We need to leave," Fred explained. "They'll be back lookin' for me and you too."

"Me?" Ell squeaked.

"Yeah, since you decomposed that guy's face. They're probably not happy about that."

"Hey!" Ell pouted. "I only did that because he was hitting you with a friggin' hammer!"

"Which I very much appreciate, but we gotta go."

"Where? Uh… are we going to your place?"

"They already know where I live. Probably made my partner's digs, too, 'cause I stopped there on my way to your place. I gotta call him, see if he knows anywhere else we can lay low."

"Wait, the one who left you to burn to death?" Ell scoffed. "That's who you're calling for help?"

"He did apologize for it."

"He apologized?" Ell was clearly not convinced.

"He did. Like… a lot."

CHAPTER 7.

WAITING FOR Ell to pack was its own challenge, and Fred did his best to remain patient. He stayed at the bedroom doorway, watching him flit around and toss things into a tattered duffel bag.

Clothes and toiletries were expected, but Ell kept grabbing books. And then more books. And yet even *more* books. And then all the DVD boxed sets of *Legends of Darkness*.

"Ell," Fred warned as the bag bulged, "we ain't going to Europe. We've just gotta lay low for a few days."

"Are you sure?" Ell scowled. "Baron Grappenhall never gave up on hunting down Princess Daisy, just saying!"

"It ain't the first time I've taken some heat for a job." Fred wasn't sure who he was trying to convince more, himself or Ell, but he hated to see Ell so upset.

"Says the guy who died in a fire!" Ell countered as he stalked back into the bathroom.

"Technically, I died at the hospital."

"Whatever!"

Fred groaned, reaching up to rub his temples. He was getting a headache, and its sudden presence made him realize how little pain he'd actually been experiencing since meeting Ell. He could still feel the familiar aches in his body, but the scream of his daily agony had quieted down to nearly a whisper.

Except for the currently pounding migraine.

"What did you steal that made these guys so crazy?" Ell asked as he came back out with a bunched-up towel.

"Some old fucking paintings." Fred got his phone out and started flipping through his contact list. "Try to finish packing soon, okay? I gotta call Lochlain."

"That's your partner?"

"Yeah."

"Left you in the fire, that partner?"

"Yeah, that's the one." Fred offered a small but comforting smile. "Safest place I can think of."

Ell made a sour face, but didn't say anything else.

Fred stepped out into the living room, listening to the phone ring while he kept an eye outside. No telling if those guys would be back, but he was certain if they did that there would be more.

"Hey," Lochlain exclaimed cheerfully through the line. "I got the tapes. All is forgiven, and I'm so sorry. Can't believe you still had these damn things—"

"I need a place to stay," Fred said briskly, getting right to the point. "Me and Ell."

"Who the hell is that?"

"My ghoul doc," Fred replied. "The art collectors tracked me to his place. Tried to finish the job. They might be watchin' yours too. Ain't safe."

"By Great Azaethoth's fuckin' horns. Okay, okay, just get over here." Lochlain sounded upset but determined. "I'm at Robert's shop, and it's warded up to the seams. Come here right now."

"On our way." Fred hung up and returned to see how Ell's packing was going. He was relieved to see he had finished. He walked over to grab the bag, certain it would be far too heavy for Ell to haul out to the truck. "Ready?"

"Yes, except…. Uhm…. Is it… is it okay if I kiss you again?" Ell stuttered as Fred approached, trying to glance casually up at his lips and failing.

"You ain't gotta ask me." Fred smiled warmly and set the bag down. He took a long moment to enjoy wrapping his arms around Ell's waist and lifting him up to claim a sweet kiss.

"Mm…. Freddie." Ell hugged Fred's shoulders as his feet dangled off the floor, and he kissed him back with a burst of passion.

The kiss went much easier this time, deep and hot, and when Fred slipped his tongue forward, he was delighted to feel Ell's slide against his in reply.

"To be continued," Fred grumbled before they got too carried away. He gave Ell one last departing kiss and ran his fingers through his hair where the horns would be.

Blushing, Ell offered, "Maybe later… I could take the charm off again?"

"Definitely," Fred agreed, picking up the duffel bag and urging Ell to follow him. "Come on. Let's get going."

Ell locked the door and then met Fred out by the truck, bundled up in a scarf, coat, and a big floppy toboggan. He joined Fred in the truck and fumbled with his seat belt. "So, uh, um… does this mean…?"

"This isn't forever," Fred promised as he pulled out of the driveway. "Once we get these jerks taken care of, you'll be able to come back home. I promise."

"Oh!" Ell fidgeted. "That's really nice, but that's not what I was going to ask."

"What?"

"Does this mean… we're boyfriends now?" Ell had turned a very bright shade of red and couldn't even look at Fred.

"If you wanna be." Fred reached over to take one of Ell's fumbling hands, squeezing it reassuringly. He didn't know what to say, and he'd never been very good at communicating—especially romantically.

Ell made him feel things he never thought were possible, even before their sweet kiss. He made Fred laugh, made him smile, and for the love of all the gods, it was like being alive again.

"I definitely wanna be." Ell scooted as close as the seat belt would allow. "I don't really know how any of this is gonna work, but we don't need to have sex right away—"

Fred nearly drove off the road.

"Hey, what's wrong?" Ell cringed instantly. "Was that the wrong thing to say?"

"Just wasn't expecting that," Fred mumbled. "I mean, you're… you're a virgin."

"That doesn't mean I don't want to have sex!" Ell protested. "I think about it a lot! I do, you know, stuff by myself, so I understand how it works!"

Thinking of Ell's toys almost veered Fred into a ditch.

"I'm only freakin' nineteen!" Ell went on. "I have, you know, *ideas*, about things! I mean, not like, eh, not all the time! But a perfectly normal and healthy amount!"

Fred clenched his hand on the steering wheel. "You and the other ghouls… uh." He cleared his throat. "You never…? Nothing?"

"No, I never messed around with any other ghouls." Ell wrinkled his nose. "I guess I could have, but I never felt anything like that for any of them. I didn't want to do it just to *do it*, but I really wanna do it now. With you. Whatever that means for us, it'll be enough because it'll be with you."

A thousand more fantastic images popped up in Fred's mind, awash with fingers and toys and doing anything he could to please Ell since his own equipment was literally dead.

Some ghouls could still have sex, but he'd heard it was messy business as the rot went on. A ghoul with a penis couldn't get an erection, and orgasm for any ghoul was completely unheard of.

Whatever happened earlier on Ell's couch had to have just been Fred's imagination.

"Let's work on kissin' and go from there," Fred suggested. "I get that you're super up for it. You want what you ain't had because you couldn't have it. But…."

Shit, why wasn't he better at this?

What would Lochlain say?

Ugh, something mushy.

Robert's advice would be pretty sappy too. Lynnette would offer something really blunt. Sloane would probably blabber something about the gods and how much he loved Azaethoth.

Okay, what would Azaethoth the Lesser say in this situation?

Go in tentacles first and make sure to use lots of lube?

Shit.

"Ain't no sense in rushing into fucking," Fred said firmly, feeling bold and trying to speak from the heart. "It can be fun, really fuckin' fun, but it can also be… special. What you are, Ell? What I feel when I'm with you?"

"Yeah?"

"It feels like a lot more than just fuckin'."

"Oh, Freddie," Ell gushed, leaning over and snuggling his head into Fred's shoulder. "You're so sweet."

Fred smiled, happy in spite of the looming fear of what lay ahead of them. He was sure he had dealt with worse, and things were much different now. After all, if he really needed to, there was an old god just a phone call away.

If he and his mate ever came back from their damn porn temple trip, anyway.

The drive back into the city was punctuated with light conversation, and Fred found himself again thinking of Azaethoth. If anyone would know what Ell was, certainly he would. However, that would mean both revealing Azaethoth's godly origins and Ell's strange abilities.

"You know," Fred began, "I got a friend named Loch that's sort of like you."

"Loch? Like the partner who left you in the fire?"

"No, just Loch. Eh." Fred paused. "They're twins. Loch and Lochlain."

"I thought me and my brother's names were weird." Ell snorted. "What do you mean Loch is like me?"

"He's special," Fred said carefully. "Like, he has really special powers. He's old, uh, he's the older twin. And he's real smart… sort of, you know, godly almost."

"Okay?"

"I was thinking maybe you could talk to him," Fred went on. "Maybe you could find out what you are."

Ell laughed. "I don't even think the gods know what I am, Freddie. Besides, I already told you I'm pretty sure I've figured it out, and I'm part Eldress and Asra. I'm totally fine with that."

"Are you sure?" Fred pressed. "Because this friend of mine is *reeeally* special."

"Does he have horns and hurt living people with his touch?" Ell retorted dryly.

No, but he has a bunch of tentacles and an apparently insatiable libido.

Shit, couldn't say that.

"Not exactly. But if you wanted to talk to him, it could be good. Like a real good thing." Fred wanted to tell Ell the truth so badly, but it had been agreed upon between those who knew to keep it a secret.

"Maybe later," Ell said, a nervous edge sharpening his smile. "I'll meet him if you want, but I don't know if I'm ready for that. What I am, what I do… I've gone to a lot of trouble not to get caught, okay?"

"Caught?"

"For what I'm doing," Ell explained. "I don't just heal ghouls, okay. What I do is different. Fred, come on. Bringing life to those that are dead?" He sighed. "It's a form of necromancy. It's… it's illegal."

The realization struck Fred right in the gut.

Ell's abilities were beyond any other healer's because he wasn't just healing. He was literally resurrecting the dead flesh of ghouls' bodies into something more, into something alive. It made his magic even more powerful than Fred first thought, and a hundred times more dangerous.

Crimes of necromancy were considered very severe by modern law, and convictions carried a life sentence. Fred had always heard offenders went to some crazy government prison because the rulers of the world were desperate to learn the forbidden arts for their own gain.

Of course, he'd read that in the same tabloid magazine that published photos of Fish Boy, so probably not the most reliable source.

"I won't say nothin' if you don't want me to," Fred said, "but maybe when you meet him? Maybe you'll think about talking to him?"

"Sure. I'll think about it." Ell offered a shy smile. "You won't say anything, though? Unless I want you to?"

"Of course." Fred pressed a kiss to Ell's hand before guiding it into his lap. "I wouldn't never give up your secret."

"Like King Blix keeping the truth about who Daisy's parents really were to protect her from finding out about the ancient family curse?"

"Yeah, exactly like that."

Fred hit the gas a little harder once they got back in the city limits. He hoped Robert and Lochlain had some answers for them, but his first priority was making sure Ell was safe. He checked his mirrors often, keeping an eye out for the sedan or any other suspicious cars tailing too close, and he drove down several twisting backstreets just to make sure no one was following them.

He knew his efforts wouldn't matter if the cultists were still using a watchman's spell, but he had to try.

Fred pulled his truck down the alley behind Robert's jewelry shop, parking it there away from the view of the street. He got out and grabbed Ell's bulging duffel bag, nodding for him to follow to the back door.

Ell stayed close, his hands fluttering around his neck as if checking for his charm. He looked nervous, reaching into his pockets to frantically pull on a pair of gloves.

"It's okay." Fred smiled and took one of Ell's gloved hands.

"Sorry." El cringed. "I don't come to the city much. I mean, ever. And I don't *people* very well."

"Just stay close to me. My people are good, and they ain't gonna mess with you." Fred reached up and banged his fist against the door.

"No, they'll just leave me if I ever catch on fire," Ell mumbled.

The door opened before Fred could reply, and Lochlain was on the other side.

Lochlain pulled Fred into a fierce hug. "Hey! You're finally here! You're okay!"

Feeling Lochlain's arms around him was a pleasant sensation for Fred. He'd hugged Lochlain many times since his death, but to feel his warmth and the pressure of his embrace made him smile. "I'm fine."

"I was getting worried," Lochlain said, clapping Fred one more time on the back before releasing him. He looked around Fred to find Ell, and he was unable to hide his surprise. "This is your ghoul doctor?"

"Hi." Ell had shrunk back when Lochlain hugged Fred, and he remained a few feet away, hovering anxiously. "I'm Ell."

"It's nice to meet you, Ell," Lochlain said warmly. "I'm Lochlain Fields. Come on. Let's get upstairs."

Fred took Ell's hand again as they followed Lochlain inside. They went through the stockroom to a set of creaky stairs that took them up to the storage loft on the second floor.

There was a futon, countless boxes of files, and an ancient television that Fred had never seen turned on. A small kitchen area was off in the corner with a fridge and a sink. A narrow door to the immediate left led to a bathroom. The whole space was crowded by the boxes and smelled like lemon cleaner.

Robert was trying to push some of the boxes against the wall next to the fridge, but he stopped to wave. "Hey, Fred! Were you followed?"

"No," Fred grunted. "Might have tagged me with a watchman's spell, though."

"Come here. I can check." Robert frowned as he approached. He muttered an incantation to himself, waving his hands over Fred. He paused, his fingers catching an invisible thread, and he pulled until there was an audible snap.

"Fuck." Fred grimaced. "Bastards must have got me when I went back by my apartment."

"You're clear now," Robert assured him. He held out his hand, whispered a few words, and then blew a quick puff of air across his palm. "There. Sent their watchman's spell on a little joyride. They'll be tracking you all over the city for hours until they figure out they've lost you."

"Thanks."

"Hey, no problem." Robert gestured to the wards over the doorway and by the windows. "My strongest spells keep this building protected. You'll be safe here."

"What about you guys? Where you gonna stay?"

"At Robert's," Lochlain replied. "Same wards are up there, and you only went by my place, right?"

"Yeah."

"Good. Then that's where we want to avoid being."

"So, this is your mysterious ghoul doctor?" Robert asked, giving Ell a friendly smile. He offered his hand out. "I'm Robert, Lochlain's fiancé."

"I'm Ell Sturm." Ell extended his gloved hand and shook Robert's as quickly as possible before pulling away. "Uh…. Fred's boyfriend."

"Boyfriend?" Robert was shocked.

"Oh, *really*?" Lochlain grinned, glancing between the two of them excitedly. "Boyfriend, huh?"

Fred hated that he was blushing and couldn't stop it. He swung a thick arm around Ell's shoulders. "Yeah. Got a fuckin' problem with it?"

"No! That's great! I'm really happy for you." Lochlain did look genuinely pleased and more than a bit curious. Whatever he wanted to ask he kept to himself, instead saying, "While I can't wait to hear all the juicy details, we gotta get to business."

"Business?" Ell asked.

Lochlain gestured to the futon, and he sat down on one of the boxes nearby. Robert stood beside him, and he waited for Ell and Fred to sit on the futon before he began, "So, Robert and I did some digging, and we got a lead on the product you were hired to snatch."

Ell curled up against Fred's side, drawing his legs up and trying to keep as much distance between him and Lochlain and Robert as possible. Fred knew Ell was afraid of accidentally touching them, but he remained calm.

Fred pretended like it was totally normal for Ell to snuggle like this, and he curled his arm back around Ell's shoulders. "Yeah? So, what's the dirt, huh?"

"Those paintings were once the property of a Lord Collins, an eccentric Sage from the seventeenth century," Robert replied. "There was a full set of eight that he had commissioned, one for each Sagittarian holiday."

"Cute."

"Historians believe Lord Collins hid an ancient ritual within the paintings." Lochlain's brow wrinkled. "A ritual to awaken his patron god, Salgumel."

"Not cute."

"Salgumel?" Ell spoke up. "The god of dreams and sleep? But he's gone mad! If someone woke him up…. Come on, they'd have to be crazy. They'd…." He trailed off as he looked at everyone's somber faces. "What?"

"I guess Fred hasn't told you," Lochlain said slowly.

"No, because Fred keeps his mouth shut," Fred grumbled. "You're welcome."

"I appreciate you keeping my secret, I do," Lochlain said firmly, "but if Ell is going to be in your life, there's a few things he should know." He looked to Ell now. "I was murdered this past Dhankes over a job. There were very bad people trying to restore an ancient totem for Salgumel that had the power to wake him, and I was hired to steal a piece of it.

"Without that piece, my client was hoping the very bad people wouldn't be able to succeed. Unfortunately, things didn't quite work out, and they got it anyway. Long story short, too late, a very brave witch named Sloane Beaumont was able to destroy the totem once and for all."

"But," Robert prompted.

"But we always suspected it wouldn't be the last time someone tried to awaken Salgumel," Lochlain went on with a grimace. "If these paintings really have that ritual, Salgumel's followers are not going to stop until they have them all."

"Two of them are fuckin' toast," Fred scoffed.

"They still have the other two you nabbed," Robert pointed out. "Plus three of the other paintings have also been stolen and sold through the black market. One from an art college in Florida, one from an exhibit in Chester, England, and another from a private collector's home in Idaho."

"Which leaves one final painting," Lochlain said. "And it just so happens to be one of the items to be featured at the Archersville Rotary Club's Winter Auction next month."

"They said they needed the money," Fred realized out loud. "Those motherfuckers. They're going to try and buy the painting from the auction."

"Security must be really tight if they're opting to bid on the painting instead of trying to steal it," Robert mused.

"Or are they trying to conserve funds to hire another thief?" Lochlain suggested.

There was a long moment of silence broken by Ell's hesitant voice asking, "Can…. Can we go back to the part where you said you were murdered? Because you don't look like you were murdered?"

"A story for another time," Lochlain said with a wink. "Just trust me when I say I have been blessed by the gods."

"So, what now?" Fred frowned.

"Sloane and Loch are still gone and haven't answered any phone calls or texts," Robert said. "Last thing I got from Sloane was something about a waterfall made of wine and a temple of ancient erotic murals."

"They're gonna be gone for a while," Fred assumed.

"Most likely," Lochlain said cheerfully. "You two can stay here while the heat dies down. According to the news, the cops are busy looking for the culprit behind the fires downtown. No mention of the robbery."

"Hmmph."

"I'll keep an ear out for any jobs to snatch that last painting," Robert offered. "Be pretty smooth if we can get the job, steal it for ourselves, and then destroy it so the cultists can't get their hands on it."

"Will that stop them from performing the ritual?" Ell asked. "I mean, if Freddie already burned up two of the paintings, why would they bother going for the last one? Don't they need all of them?"

Lochlain perked up, catching Fred's eye and mouthing "Freddie" with a playful smile.

Fred glared.

"Not necessarily," Robert replied. "Lord Collins was pretty eccentric. And by 'eccentric,' I mean historians believe he might have transcribed his favorite sexual encounters in some of the paintings."

"So, they're either this guy's porn or a ritual to awaken an ancient god?" Fred scoffed. "Seriously?"

Robert held up his hands. "And with no way to know which is which, they're probably gonna go for the last one. The question now is are they going to try to steal it or actually bid on it."

"Oh!" Ell's eyes widened. "Why don't we do what Trip and King Blix did in episode twenty-four, season two of *Legends of Darkness*?"

While Lochlain and Robert stared, Fred racked his brain to recall the episode. "Wait, you mean when they fuckin' snuck into Baron Grappenhall's masquerade ball?"

"Yeah!"

"They dressed up as guests to infiltrate the party," Lochlain said, his memory jogged now and grinning slyly. "Oh, this could be fun. What better way to ensure the painting's safety than keeping an eye on it ourselves?"

"Or just stealing it," Robert drawled. "Why don't we go grab it before the charity takes place?"

"First of all, that's not as fun. Second of all, we'd need to find out where they're holding the items for the auction."

"I'm on it." Robert was already heading back to the stairs. "No planning any shenanigans while I'm gone."

"I will make no such promises!" Lochlain called after him. He turned back to Fred and Ell. "You guys need anything?" He eyed Ell's gloves and hat. "Is it warm enough in here?"

"Oh, I'm fine. I'm good." Ell smiled. "Thank you."

"There's not much food in the fridge, but there's a number for pizza by the sink."

"That's fine," Fred said. "Thanks."

Lochlain smiled sweetly at the two of them. "Can I just say how adorable you two look together?" He nodded at Ell. "Whatever you're doing, keep doing it. I haven't seen that big grump this happy in years."

"Really?" Ell perked up.

"Really really."

Whatever skepticism Ell had about Lochlain seemed to retreat, and he smiled. "Thank you. He makes me really happy too."

"He'd better." Lochlain winked. "He might be a tough ol' ghoul, but I can still take him if he messes this up."

"Thanks for the big vote of confidence, jackass." Fred snorted. "You done now?"

"Nope. We haven't even gotten to the good stuff yet," Lochlain teased.

"You gettin' none of the good stuff."

"Ah, come on. My best friend has a boyfriend for the first time in *years*? I wanna know everything."

Ell's cheeks pinked, and he cleared his throat loudly. "Uh, where's the bathroom?"

"It's that little door across from the kitchen." Lochlain pointed. "Shower and all that works if you guys need it, but the drain is backed up."

"Thank you." Ell scrambled to walk around Lochlain and maintain as much distance as humanly possible as he retreated.

Lochlain waited for the bathroom door to shut before he teased, "So, I was worried about you two sharing the futon, but I guess that's not gonna be a problem."

Fred rolled his eyes, and he ignored the urge to point out ghouls didn't need to sleep. He knew Lochlain was getting ready to start picking at him for more details any second now....

"So, you and Ell?" Lochlain grinned.

"Yeah?" Fred mumbled expectantly. "What?"

"You really do look happy," Lochlain said. "You look good too. Like, wow. Really good. You haven't looked this fresh since Lynnette brought you back. Whatever that Ell is doing, seriously tell him to keep it up."

"Will do."

"A little young, but he's definitely cute," Lochlain went on. "I'm assuming this is a recent development?"

"Very." Fred couldn't resist a little smile.

"How long have you been seeing him?"

"Not long. It's been kinda fast, all right? But it's good." Fred smiled again as that funny butterfly feeling made a return down in his gut. "It's real good."

"I'm happy for you. Really. I never thought you'd, you know...." Lochlain gestured vaguely. "See anyone."

"Ell's special."

"Well, maybe you can bring him as your very special date to the wedding?"

Fred scowled at the sudden turn in conversation. "I ain't even agreed on comin' yet."

"You're my best friend, and you love me," Lochlain said confidently. "You're coming."

"Maybe."

"Aw, come on, *Freddie*."

"I'll fuckin' think about it."

"Hey!" Ell came out of the bathroom. He'd taken off his hat, but the rest of his winter gear remained. He returned to his spot on the futon next to Fred. "I miss anything?"

Lochlain grinned. "Oh, I was just inviting you and Fred to me and Robert's wedding. We're still trying to settle on a date, but I would love for you guys to come."

"A wedding?" Ell gushed. "Oh! I've never been to a wedding before! That sounds amazing." He looked up at Fred. "We're going, right?"

Fred glared at Lochlain, who only beamed triumphantly in reply.

Asshole.

For a brief moment, just one quick second, Fred wished Lochlain had stayed dead.

CHAPTER 8.

AFTER BRINGING some extra blankets and a DVD player to hook up to the old television, Lochlain and Robert said farewell to head home for the day. Robert was going to keep working on finding where the items for the charity were being kept, and Lochlain was planning a grand caper to steal the painting during the event.

"Just imagine it," Lochlain was saying. "Me in a full tuxedo, drinking champagne, all the lights go out, and then poof! When the lights come back on, the painting has vanished!"

"Lochlain, I know you're a great thief," Robert began hesitantly, "but I'm not so sure—"

"A *blessed* thief!"

"I dunno…."

Their voices faded as the door shut.

Once Fred and Ell were alone, Ell peeled off his many extra layers and the charm that hid his horns with a sigh of relief. "Holy crap, I'm so glad they're gone."

"Nerves?" Fred wrapped his arm back around Ell and kissed his hair. He was enjoying the open affection, hungry for it in fact, and he was certain he was making up for lost time being alone for so long.

Ell, of course, had an entire lifetime of loveless solitude to compensate for.

"Yeah." Ell snuggled in close and held Fred's hand. "When you can hurt someone from just bumping into them, it's hard to relax around people."

"So, this means you don't really wanna go to the wedding?" Fred asked hopefully.

"No, I do!" Ell wrinkled up his nose. "I really do, I'm just… I don't know. I know it's risky, but I've never been to anything like that. I've never gone out to a movie or to a party before."

"No dates, huh?"

"Nope. Kinda goes with that whole not ever touching people thing. No dates, no prom, no dances, nothing."

"Right." Fred glanced around the room for a moment, and the gears in his mind turned. It wasn't safe to go out right now, but if he couldn't take Ell out on a date, maybe he could bring the date to him.

"Uh, since we're gonna be waiting for a while, do you wanna watch some more *Legends of Darkness*?" Ell wiggled in anticipation.

"Like you gotta ask." Fred smiled as Ell sprang up from the futon to set up the DVD player. It only took a few minutes, and they were right back to cuddling and watching the next season. Holding hands with a beautiful young man who had the sweetest lips while Fred watched his favorite show was a dream come true.

It was a wonderful way to pass the time, and it let Fred plot out the date he was going to have for Ell. Being sneaky was going to be difficult while Ell was there with him, but Fred had a plan for that too.

They made it to the end of the second season before Fred decided to make his move.

"You know there's a tub in the bathroom," he said.

Yup. Very subtle.

"I saw it." Ell quirked his brows. "What about it?"

"I just thought, maybe, you know, that you'd like to take a bath," Fred said casually.

Ell was definitely confused now, and he frowned. "Why? Do I stink?"

"No. You, uh, just seemed like you needed to relax."

"Don't you wanna watch the show?"

"No."

"Then what is it?"

"I'm trying to plan a surprise," Fred growled. "I wanna do something for you. A big first for you, okay? And I need you to go take a bath so I can get it ready."

"Oh… *oh*!" Ell blushed as understanding kicked in, and he planted a sweet kiss to Fred's lips. "Oh, Freddie. You're amazing! I'll go right now!"

Fred smirked as Ell hurried into the bathroom and slammed the door behind him. He was disappointed that the element of surprise was tainted, but he hoped Ell would still like what he had planned. He waited until he heard the water running and sprang into action.

He ordered an extra cheesy pizza and soda since they didn't have any tea, and he offered to tip well if they could deliver in under thirty minutes. He rewound the last episode he and Ell had watched and paused it right when the ending credits were about to play. Moving the boxes took some time, but Fred was able to create a big open space next to the TV. He kept four of the boxes out in the middle, two to serve as chairs and two stacked up to make a table.

Fred got a text that the pizza had arrived and hurried downstairs to retrieve it. He forked over a generous tip for the fast delivery and then rushed back inside.

He put the pizza on the makeshift table along with the soda. Searching the kitchen cabinets turned up no dishes except a cracked coffee mug, but he did find a variety of candles.

His search must have been making a lot of noise because Ell called out from the bathroom, "Are you okay?"

"Fine!" Fred jammed as many candles as he could together inside the mug to use as a centerpiece.

"Can I come out now?"

"In like, uh, one minute!" Fred brought the mug over to the table. He murmured a spell and then lit the candles with a snap of his fingers. He suddenly had the idea to use one of the extra blankets as a tablecloth, so he had to take everything off the boxes, place the blanket, and then put it all back.

Perfect.

"Ready!" Fred sat down on his box, watching the bathroom door. He felt weirdly anxious, and he was excited for Ell to see his surprise.

Ell stepped out with a shy smile, and Fred's jaw dropped.

Ell had taken off his charm, and his horns peeked out from his damp hair. He was wearing a flowery silk robe, several sizes too big, and nothing else beneath it. He'd tied the sash loosely and when he walked forward, Fred's eyes were treated to flashes of naked flesh from Ell's shoulder down to his hip and thigh.

Fred didn't even care where Ell had found the damn robe. He couldn't look away from the stunning vision of him in it, and it didn't register at first that Ell had clearly misunderstood his intentions.

"You… you did this for me?" Ell's eyes were wide as he looked over the candles and food. He blushed, suddenly wrapping the robe around himself tightly. "Oh! It's a date. A first date. You're, you're giving me my first date."

"Uh, yeah." Fred cleared his throat and forced himself not to drool. He was suddenly worried by the look on Ell's face. "Is it… is it not good?"

"No! It's amazing!" Ell insisted, sitting down on the box across from Fred. His cheeks continued to flush, and his neck was turning pink now too. "I just...."

"What?"

"I might have maybe sort of thought you were talking about... uh... another first."

The silky robe, the way Ell had come out wearing it....

Oh *shit*.

"No," Fred said quickly. "Not that I don't wanna. It's not that. By all the gods, I haven't wanted somethin' this bad in a really, really long time. Just, uh, this is somethin' that should be special. And, uh...."

"I like you, you like me." Ell nibbled a piece of pizza. "I mean, I really, *really* like you. Plus, we're boyfriends now. I think that's about as special as it gets."

"I don't want you rushin' into somethin' you're gonna regret."

"Rushing?" Ell actually laughed, and he reached over the table to take Fred's hand. "I've been waiting for a chance like this all of my life to be with someone I care about. My only regret would be not going for it while I could, you know?"

"Ell, we don't even know what I can do."

"We'll figure it out," Ell promised. "I don't care what we do, as long as I'm with you."

He looked so earnest and hopeful that Fred couldn't refuse, and his reservations crumbled. "Okay."

"Really?" Ell gasped.

"Yeah. We'll make it work, okay?"

"Absolutely." Ell was so excited that he looked like he was about to come flying off the box. "I have lube, I brought toys—"

Fred managed to choke on air.

"Hey, are you okay?"

"Good. I'm fine." Fred took a deep breath. "So. Yeah. After dinner. Eat your food, and I'll take care of dessert."

"Deal."

Fred had never seen anyone eat as fast as Ell did, laughing out loud when he abruptly burped after chugging nearly half the soda. "Mmm, very sexy."

"Excuse me." Ell grinned. "So, I might be kinda excited."

"I couldn't tell," Fred teased.

"This really is friggin' fantastic," Ell said, nodding to the candles and the pizza. "I was wondering what all the noise was, ha! It's so sweet." He beamed at Fred. "Thank you for an amazing first date."

"Eh, it's nothin'."

"No, come on! You made me a table!" Ell grinned sweetly. "I'm going to friggin' remember this night for the rest of my life."

"Good," Fred said, admiring the pretty way the candlelight flickered over Ell's face. He really was beautiful. Fred wanted to kiss him again, standing up and offering his hand.

Something sparkled in Ell's eyes, and he asked breathlessly as he took Fred's hand, "Does, uh, this mean it's time for dessert?"

"Almost." Fred pulled Ell up to his feet. He guided him a little closer to the TV so he could push play on the DVD to resume from where he'd paused it.

The ending credits of every *Legends* episode played the theme song, a slow and whimsical instrumental, but this version didn't have any of the words. It was only music and perfect for a first dance.

Fred guided Ell's hand up on his chest, and then he grabbed Ell's hips. He smiled as he rocked their bodies together, swaying gently to the beat.

"Oh, Freddie." Ell's smile was as bright as a shooting star. "This is… this really is perfect."

Fred smiled so hard that his cheeks hurt. "Yeah. It is."

Ell leaned his head against Fred's broad chest, humming softly as the music went on.

Fred carefully bowed his head so he could rest his cheek in Ell's hair, being mindful of his sensitive horns. He loved how they fit together, and he guided them through their simple dance. He'd never been much of a dancer, and he could remember practicing this little two-step with Lochlain when they were kids getting ready for a school dance.

He'd hated it, and he never ended up asking anyone to the stupid dance.

He was grateful for that lesson now, though, as he confidently turned him and Ell around in a lazy little circle. He rubbed Ell's back, and he closed his eyes. He was warm, happy, and he was actually disappointed that the song was so short.

Ell lifted his head to smile up at Fred. "That was wonderful, Freddie."

"You just wait," Fred promised. "I'm just gettin' fuckin' started." He hugged Ell's waist and lifted him up for a kiss. Ell's lips were perfect and soft, though a bit spicy from the pizza sauce.

"Mmm, Freddie." Ell sighed dreamily before wrapping his arms around Fred's neck. His kisses were firm, eager, pressing himself close with a new surge of confidence.

Fred held Ell tight, and he let himself get caught up in the deep kiss. The sleek fabric of the robe and Ell's firm body beneath it was incredible, leaving him wanting more. He playfully nipped at Ell's lower lip and carried him over to the futon.

It was difficult converting the futon into a bed while Ell was smooching on his neck, but Fred refused to let go of him. He had no idea what limitations of pleasure his ghoul body had, but he was going to push every single one of them tonight.

Giving up on fixing the futon, he sat with Ell in his lap. Ell's weight felt good on his thighs, and he reignited their kiss with a hushed groan. He wanted to take things slow, make it last, but Ell was positively frantic.

Ell was kissing him hard and fast, and he moaned when his hips rolled forward. "Ohh, oh, *Freddie*!"

Fred grabbed Ell's thigh and urged him to rock again. Fred's skin was tingling, and all of his discomfort was totally muted. "Mmm, come on, Ell. Nice and slow."

The robe did nothing to hide how hard Ell was, and he moaned again when his cock pressed into Fred's lower stomach. "Ohhh, yes… oh my gods… mmm, I can't stop, I just can't…!"

Fred couldn't believe the way Ell moved, apparently spurred on by some strong instinct as he ground roughly into him. Fred planted a firm hand on Ell's ass to guide him, and he cupped his cheek as their kiss deepened. He couldn't resist reaching up so his fingers could slide into his hair to brush over his horns.

"Freddie!" Ell groaned, his voice strained and hoarse in a way Fred hadn't heard before.

He definitely wanted to hear it again.

Stroking one horn firmly and squeezing his ass, Fred asked urgently, "Do you want me to touch you…?"

"Gods, yes!" Ell pleaded as his fingers dug into Fred's shoulders. "I need, I need you to touch me! Please!"

"Easy now." Fred kissed Ell firmly, rubbing his bottom as he loosened the sash of his robe. "I've got you."

Ell whimpered, his lips parted and panting hard. He was so worked up that he was shaking, and his bright eyes gazed in wonder at Fred as he whispered, "I trust you."

Not taking that statement for granted for a second, Fred slowly parted Ell's robe. He admired the reveal of smooth pale skin, how Ell seemed to tremble at the lightest touch, and he reverently caressed his palm across his lean stomach.

Still petting Ell's horn, Fred reached down to curl his thick fingers around his cock. The reaction was instant—Ell moaned desperately and clumsily bucked up into his hand.

Fred stroked him slowly at first, but he couldn't keep up with Ell's needy thrusts unless he increased the pace. He knew it would be over fast at this rate, but he didn't care. He wanted to make Ell feel good, and there was a new ache inside his own body demanding relief that he didn't know how to satisfy.

But he could take care of Ell. He could do this.

He jerked Ell off faster, focusing his thumb around the head of Ell's cock and teasing the tip of his horn as he tried to find the most pleasurable angle. When Ell sobbed, Fred kept going and growled encouragingly. "There you go, little one… come on… just like that…."

Ell looked lost, fucking Fred's hand erratically as he rolled his hips, begging, "I don't know what, I don't know what to do! Gods! I'm, I'm so close!"

"Just let go." Fred jerked him off faster and faster until his hand was practically a blur. "Just fuckin' let go and come… come for me, Ell…."

Ell threw his head back, moaning as his hips slammed forward. "There, there, I'm, I'm gonna—!"

The lights flickered, and the back of the futon suddenly dropped.

Fred went flat on his back, and Ell squealed as he fell forward on top of him, soon howling as he came. Fred never lost rhythm, stroking Ell through it and watching spellbound as a thick load of come pulsed over his shirt.

"Freddie, oh fuck, fuck, *fuck*!" Ell whimpered, his body still moving as he tried to hang on to every last second of pleasure. He was rutting against Fred's stomach, still hard and wet from just coming, and his face was scrunched up in concentration.

A deep wave of heat came over Fred that made his vision fuzzy and his limbs ache pleasantly. It wasn't quite the same explosion of bliss he'd known as a living man orgasming, but it was pretty damn close.

In some ways it was better. He was watching Ell wrestling with all of the new sensations, and the silk robe had fallen off his shoulder and made him seem infinitely more debauched.

Fred smoothed his hands down Ell's sides, holding him flush against his chest as he claimed a deep kiss.

Murmuring small little sounds of pleasure, Ell melted in Fred's thick arms. He kept on kissing Fred until he was no longer shaking, and he seemed to have caught his breath. "Mmm… wow."

"Yeah?" Fred grinned.

"Definitely wow." Ell wrinkled his nose. "Sorry about your shirt."

"It's fine." Fred grunted as he wiggled the soiled garment off, wiped Ell, and flung it over on the floor. "See? Problem solved."

"You are a genius."

Ell snuggled into Fred's bare chest, and he felt so hot that it was Fred's turn to shudder. There was a tug underneath Fred's ribs, fleeting but strong, and he smirked when he realized Ell was still hard.

"Need some more?"

"Oh please, yes, more of that—!" Ell squealed happily as Fred suddenly flipped them over and stretched him out across the bed. "Oh, Freddie!"

Fred kissed Ell again, and he groaned as Ell's hands slid around to cling to his back. He pushed up between Ell's legs, grinding down against Ell's hard cock. He tried to keep his big belly off Ell as much as he could, and he focused on pushing their hips together.

Ell's eyes closed as he gasped, arching off the bed and panting hard at what must have been an intense sensation. He didn't seem to care about Fred's size, groping every inch of him that he could reach and pressing close. "F-fuck… no, mm, I mean 'frig'… no, fuck, I definitely mean *fuck*! Fuck, that feels good!"

Fred turned his head to kiss his way down to Ell's ear, pleased at the way he writhed. Ell was so responsive to every little thing that he did, and it was a huge jolt to his ego. He knew part of it was certainly Ell's lack of experience, but that was no reason not to aim for total perfection.

He slid his mouth down Ell's chest, pushing the silk out of his way to kiss his collarbone, his nipples—

"Ahhh fuck!" Ell whined. "Freddie!"

Fred paused in his descent to lavish Ell's nipples with another round of kisses, lapping around each one and enjoying how quickly they stiffened. He sucked softly, and Ell's fingers were dragging across his scalp as he cried out in pleasure.

Ell was wonderfully loud, and every sweet sound only made the ache inside of Fred grow. He lifted his head to steal a glimpse at Ell, brightly flushed and wide-eyed, before ducking back to mouth along his stomach.

Ell scrambled to pull his arms out of the robe, fully bare beneath Fred now. He clumsily propped himself up on his elbows. "What, what are you doing?"

Fred stopped a breath away from Ell's cock, and he glanced back at him with a sly smile. "I was gonna use my mouth on you."

"Ohhh, oh… uh…."

"Is that okay?" Fred settled between Ell's thighs.

Ell was nodding before he could speak, his voice initially coming out in a much higher pitch as he said, "Okay, yes, please." He cleared his throat. "Yes, I would, I would like that very much."

Fred winked and then leisurely lapped at Ell's cock, enjoying the silky texture of his head and the heat of him. Ell trembled, and he carefully wrapped his mouth around him, sucking the first few inches down.

Ell flopped flat against the bed, his hands digging into the thin mattress with a shameless moan. "Oh, *Freddie*! Oh fuck…."

Fred could taste the first hint of precome, and he groaned, sucking harder—wait, he could *taste*. He didn't know if it was just his imagination or if it was an old memory clouding the moment, but he didn't want to lose it. He squeezed Ell's thighs as he swallowed him right down to the base of his cock.

Ell's hips jerked helplessly, his legs bending as he writhed. His cock hit the back of Fred's throat, and he started babbling as he tried to pull away, "Fred, I'm sorry, I'm so sorry!"

Growling low, Fred slid his hands under Ell and grabbed his ass. He lifted him right off the bed, dragging his body upward to take him deep down his throat.

Ell moaned, one of his legs awkwardly hooking over Fred's shoulders as he fucked his face. Fred kept him moving, guiding every thrust, and he could feel Ell's body shaking as his climax began to wash over him.

"I'm, I'm right there!" Ell gasped brokenly. "I'm sorry, I'm sorry it's so quick, I just can't, oh, ohh, ohhh! Fuck!"

A rush of hot come hit Fred's tongue, and he knew then that this was absolutely real. He could taste the heat, the familiar salt, and he nearly wept. He swallowed every drop, latched on to Ell's cock until he was sure he had taken all that he could.

Ell had covered his face with his hands, sobbing softly as his legs shook. "Freddie," he whispered, strained and breathless. "Oh, by all the gods…."

After returning Ell's hips to the bed, Fred climbed back up to claim a sweet kiss. Ell was still crying, and Fred was struck by a wave of guilt. Maybe he'd been too rough or this was too fast after all.

He wiped away Ell's tears, asking quietly, "Hey, are you okay? Was… was that too much?"

"No," Ell replied without hesitation with a firm shake of his head. "It was just, whoa, it was a lot. Going from nothing to all of *that* was really intense." He took a big breath, exhaling more calmly through his nose. "Wow."

Fred kissed his cheek. "Good?"

"So friggin' good." Ell laughed, and he reached up to cradle Fred's face. "I feel sort of numb and fuzzy and totally exhausted, and I've never been so happy. Thank you."

"Ain't gotta thank me," Fred said with a short grunt. "Just let me do it again."

"Oh, as many times as you want!" Ell grinned. "I mean, we didn't even get to use the toys I brought!"

Fred resisted the urge to ask which ones. "Don't worry. We will, little one."

Ell petted Fred's cheek, asking hopefully, "Did you enjoy it? I mean, did you get anything… you know, from it?"

"I got plenty from it. But no, my dick didn't do nothin' if that's what you're askin'."

"I'm sorry." Ell cringed.

"Hey, I ain't gotta get off to have a good time," Fred soothed. "I like bein' with you. I liked touchin' you and makin' you feel good."

"Oh, I feel *great*." Ell sighed with obvious satisfaction. "That was so good. It was better than anything I could have ever imagined. Kisses are still my favorite, but mm, that thing with your mouth? Close second."

"You just wait," Fred teased. "There's still plenty more I can do with my mouth."

Ell's eyes went wide for a moment as he was no doubt thinking over the many possibilities. He cleared his throat and aimed for calm when he replied, "Well, we'll just have to wait and see how our next date goes."

"We will, huh?" Fred rolled off Ell to stretch out beside him. He propped himself up on his elbow and laid his hand on Ell's chest.

"Uh-huh!" Ell put his hand over Fred's, tangling their fingers together. "I definitely deserve to at least be fed before putting out, my good sir."

Fred burst out laughing. "Fuck, I'll do anything you want, Ell. You just name it."

"Right now, could we just cuddle?"

"You got it." Fred turned on his back so Ell could burrow into his side like he had before. Fred reached out to snag one of the blankets and drape it over them, tucking Ell in close.

"You're so friggin' beautiful," Ell murmured, the excitement of the day finally taking its toll as his eyes fluttered shut.

Fred didn't know how to take the compliment, rebutting it with a simple, "Not as beautiful as you."

"Pffft." Ell ducked his head down.

"You are more beautiful than all the fairy rings glistening with dew in the early-morning light," Fred said quietly, quoting a scene from *Legends of Darkness*. "They are a sparkling chain of shining diamonds, an endless glittering field, and yet you are still more fuckin' beautiful."

Okay, sort of quoted.

"You're sweeter than a glass of elderberry wine after a unicorn has blessed the cup." Ell peeked up at Fred with a shy smile, continuing the speech. "One taste would never be enough to quench my thirst for you. I need you as roses need the sun to blossom, just as surely as the sun needs the kiss of the horizon to ascend every morning."

It was from Blix the goblin king's ill-fated declaration of love to Princess Daisy, and one of the most heartbreaking parts in the whole show when she told him she was in love with Trip.

Chuckling to himself, Fred kissed Ell's hair. "Fuck, you're awesome."

Although Daisy ultimately denied Blix's affection—a contentiously viewed decision by fans since Blix was by far a better match than that idiot Trip—Fred felt like his chances of a happy ending with Ell were looking pretty good.

There was an odd feeling of satisfaction resonating in Fred's bones, like he'd just finished a big meal. He nuzzled against Ell's horn, and he grinned when Ell squirmed.

"Mmm, sorry. I'll let you get some sleep."

"Well, I have a request for next time," Ell said, pausing to yawn. "After our next date."

"Yeah?"

"Could you take your pants off?"

Fred snorted a laugh. "Really?"

"Yes!" Ell said stubbornly. "It's not really fair if only one of us gets naked."

"Good point." Fred reached under the covers to unbutton his pants and slid them down along with his underwear. Once they were bunched around his ankles, he kicked them off onto the floor.

Ell's legs eagerly slid over his, exploring all the new skin as he snuggled in tight. "Mmm."

Feeling Ell's naked body pressed along the full length of his side was pretty damn nice. The odd tugging sensation down in his chest was back, but Fred ignored it. "This better?"

"Much better!"

"I'm guessing the rot don't bother you, huh?"

"Nope." Ell closed his eyes. "Mmm, I think I'm gonna doze off. You wore me out."

"I'd apologize, but I ain't really sorry," Fred teased. "Go on. Get some sleep."

"Good night, Freddie." Ell yawned. "Sleep sweetly."

"Night, little one."

"Thank you." Ell smiled sleepily.

Fred quirked his brows. "For?"

"For everything."

CHAPTER 9.

FRED WOKE up the next morning with a smile and Ell glued to his side. He didn't move yet for fear of waking him, happy to hold him and enjoy the tender moment.

He'd fallen asleep again, and he was definitely going to ask Ell about that because it was supposed to be impossible.

Tasting him last night was supposed to be impossible too.

Fred wondered what the true limits of Ell's magic were. Ell had said ghouls didn't have to come back once he was done healing them, but what exactly did that mean? Was Ell's true power a form of necromancy like he thought? Could he actually eat chocolate cake again?

His curiosity was crushed by a sudden realization—if Ell was truly resurrecting Fred, that meant a future where Fred wouldn't be able to touch Ell. After all, if Ell's touch was deadly to the living, then being alive was the last thing Fred wanted.

Shit.

One problem at a fuckin' time.

Downstairs, Fred could hear doors opening and closing. It was probably Robert opening up the jewelry store for the day. If he or Lochlain had any new information, he expected they'd be along shortly to share it.

Strange he hadn't heard from them yet.

Shit.

His phone was in his pants, and those were somewhere on the floor. The memories of how his pants had ended up there made him smile, but he needed to see if Lochlain or Robert had already tried to contact him.

Fred shifted his body to get up, but Ell didn't readily let go of him. If anything, Ell snuggled in tighter, and Fred became aware of something pressing into his side.

That was Ell's cock.

Fred chose to ignore it despite the hot flash of arousal coming over him. Robert was right downstairs, and Lochlain was probably with him. He and Ell really needed to get out of bed and put some clothes on.

Hoping to speed things along, he gently tapped Ell's back.

There, that should do it.

"Mmmph." Ell's hips rolled forward, his leg hooking over top of Fred's thigh as he struggled to get comfortable. He wiggled, fussed, and went still again.

Now his cock was digging right into Fred's hip.

Fred tried his best to remain calm. It was just his new boyfriend's dick, not a big deal. He wasn't going to be a creep, but he couldn't deny how nice it felt. He cleared his throat, well aware of the rush of desire stirring up inside of him.

"Hey." Fred patted Ell's back again more urgently. "Wakey wakey."

"Freddie." Ell murmured as his eyes slowly slid open, smiling sleepily.

"Good morning." Fred kissed his forehead. "Sleep good?"

"Mmm, yeah." Ell yawned. "So good. Mm, I'm not ready to get up yet." He suddenly froze, his eyes wide and all trace of sleep crumbling in the face of utter mortification. "Oh gods."

"It's okay," Fred began. "Used to happen to me in the morning—"

"I'm sorry!" Ell pleaded, trying to pull his hips away. "You're all super snuggly and comfy and I just woke up! I didn't mean to!"

"It's totally fuckin' normal," Fred soothed. He slid a hand down to the small of Ell's back to give him a reassuring hug. "You ain't gotta freak out."

"It's… it's okay?"

"Totally okay."

Ell's expression softened, and he relaxed once more in Fred's arms. He held Fred's shoulders, his cheeks pinking up as he leaned in to claim a kiss.

Fred was expecting a quick smooch, but Ell wasn't showing any signs of slowing down. His kisses were persistent, and Fred groaned as the most delightful tension quickly grew between them.

Ell slid his hands up Fred's neck and face as he tried to plaster every inch of his body against his. He deepened their kiss with a shy swipe of his tongue, and he moaned when Fred petted his horns.

Fred knew they should stop soon. Robert and Lochlain were probably gonna be up here any minute, and as thin as these walls were, they could probably hear exactly what was going on. It didn't help that Ell was feeling particularly vocal this morning.

He pried his lips away long enough to mumble, "Ell… we need to get up. We need to…."

Ell was looking at him with such raw want that Fred immediately forgot what was so damn important. He leaned in for another kiss, ready to get things going again. He was surprised when Ell suddenly pulled back after only a few more kisses.

"Ell, what's wrong?"

Ell's eyes were a spectacular shade of purple in the morning light, and his lip quivered as he asked, "Would… would you please… touch me?"

Ha, as if Fred would possibly refuse him.

"Fuck yeah." Fred dropped his hand down to tenderly cup Ell's cock. He watched as Ell bucked into his hand, listened to him groan, and he started to stroke him.

Ell's reaction was instant, passionate, and he whimpered. "Ah fuck… that feels so good… shit! Mmmph, *mmm*!"

Fred kissed Ell's neck, sucking just behind his ear, and he was amazed that he could taste his skin. Warm and clean, it was the most incredible flavor, and he backed off before he could leave any lasting marks.

"Freddie… mmm… can I touch you? Please?" Ell begged, his hand already gliding down Fred's chest and over his thick belly.

"Ell," Fred sighed. He didn't want to tell him no, but he didn't want to disappoint him either. "What I got down there ain't no more useful than tits on a boar hog."

"I don't know what that means!" Ell hissed stubbornly. He didn't stop until he was touching Fred's soft cock. "I just, I want to feel you too!"

Fred nodded, grunting as he went back in for a deep kiss. Being touched anywhere by Ell always felt good, and getting jerked off should have been fantastic. More than anything, though, it pissed Fred off. He hated that he was dead and couldn't do what the hell he wanted to do.

He wanted Ell so badly, and he wished he could give him everything he deserved….

"Fred!" Ell squeaked as his fingers clenched around Fred. "Fred! It's, it's—!"

"Huh?" Fred stared stupidly down at his cock in Ell's hand.

He was hard.

"Holy shit." He watched a single clear drop of precome oozing from the tip of his own cock. The heat inside of him had reached a boiling point, and he was *throbbing*. "How the fuck…?"

"I don't know! I don't know!" Ell hadn't resumed any movement, his hand frozen holding Fred's cock. "I just, I just started doing what you were doing to me! You're so friggin' hot, and I just wanted you to like this, and I don't know what to do!"

Oh, but Fred did, and he didn't give two shits about Lochlain or Robert or anyone else knowing what they were doing. He shifted his weight, putting Ell flat on his back so he could press on top of him.

"Freddie!" Ell gasped in surprise, his hands floundering and then bracing himself on Fred's broad shoulders. His legs awkwardly spread as Fred slid between them, and he stared down between them. "Freddie... you're really... *wow*...."

Fred shifted forward, grinding his hard cock down against Ell's and savoring his sweet moans. They were both wet enough that their lengths slid together easily, and Fred absolutely loved the slick friction. He had no idea how long this would last or if he could even come, but he was going to make the most of it.

He put his weight on one hand so he could reach down and grab both of their cocks, stroking them together as he claimed Ell's lips in a fierce kiss.

Ell's hips jerked up, and he whimpered against Fred's lips. He was trembling, and every few seconds he had to stop, catch his breath, and then he was kissing Fred again like there was nothing else in the whole world he needed more.

Fred stroked them faster and faster, loving the heat of Ell's cock against his own, and a new tension twisted up inside his body that he hadn't known in years. He'd had a taste of it when he and Ell had messed around yesterday and when they'd made out on Ell's couch, but this was so much stronger.

He was so hard that it hurt, and he had no idea what to do except to keep going. He knew Ell would not last long, not with the way he was twitching and crying, and he wanted to see him come.

Fred could feel how hard Ell was, his cock slick and writhing and *growing*—wait what was happening? Ell's cock was definitely bigger, longer, and Fred stole a quick peek down to see. He could swear that something else had just touched his hand down there, like another cock or a....

It couldn't be.

"Fred?" Ell whined sharply.

Fred had slowed down, and he picked the pace back up. "Hey, are you okay?"

"Fine! I'm just, *mmm*, please! I'm really close!" Ell whined again. "Please keep going, Freddie. Please!"

"Come on," Fred urged, growling low against Ell's throat. "Come for me, Ell."

"Freddie!" Ell moaned shamelessly, digging his fingers into Fred's back as his hips rose off the bed. His thighs shook against Fred's sides, freezing for one perfect moment of bliss before his entire body convulsed with an intense climax.

Sighing deeply, Fred stroked him through each dwindling shudder. "There you go… just like that… fuck, you're so fuckin' beautiful."

Another quick look revealed that whatever had been happening with Ell's cock had stopped, and it had returned to its normal size. He didn't find anything out of place that would explain what had touched his hand, but he did see his own cock was still annoyingly hard.

Fred didn't want to say anything and freak Ell out, but he definitely had some questions.

Ell's breathing was ragged, and he sobbed as he came down from whatever spectacular paradise Fred's strong hand had sent him off to. He kissed Fred's cheek frantically, groaning, "Oh, oh, Freddie… fuck."

"Good?" Fred smiled.

The questions could wait, he decided, as he was busy admiring Ell's flushed and grinning face.

"So good." Ell gasped as he flopped against the bed. He looked between them, his eyes wide as he said, "But you're, you're still, uh, you didn't… get off?"

"Don't think I can," Fred replied with a shake of his head. "It's okay."

"Well, we didn't think you could do *that*!" Ell gestured at Fred's erection. "Let me try!"

Fred thought he heard noise coming from the stairwell, but he couldn't think to argue when Ell grabbed his cock. "Mmmph. Fuck."

Ell's brow furrowed in concentration as he wrapped his hand firmly around the base and stroked upward. He tried twisting his fingers over the slick head, squeezing lightly before he slid back down to stroke him again.

Fred dropped to his elbows, and he gasped at the sudden explosion of pleasure. He could feel Ell's strong fingers, the ache of climax about to wash over him, and every muscle in his body was winding up tight. "Ell… oh… oh fuck…!"

"Freddie," Ell urged, nuzzling into the crook of his neck, "come on. I want you to… please… I just wanna make you feel so good!"

Fred curled his arms around Ell, grabbing his shoulder and digging his fingers into his hair. He was right there on the edge, but he couldn't focus. His brain kept telling him this was impossible, worrying about what it meant for him and Ell if he really did come back to life, what the hell was going on with Ell's dick, and he kept losing that last elusive push he needed to release.

He found Ell's horns, petting them to give himself something to focus on, and he heard Ell cry out. He couldn't identify the quality of the sound, asking, "This okay? Does, does it feel okay?"

"Good," Ell said quickly, his rhythm on Fred's cock faltering and trying to get back on track. "It's good! Keep going! Ohhh fuck, fuck, fuck!"

Fred kept rubbing and stroking Ell's horns, hissing softly as Ell's hand promptly sped up.

A glance between their bodies showed him that Ell was touching himself too. Fred bit his lip, watching intently. God, Ell was already hard again and working both of their cocks so fast. He looked back up to see Ell's face, his brow furrowed up and mouth open as he panted.

"Freddie… oh gods…." Ell's voice cracked, and he sobbed desperately. "I'm gonna… I'm gonna…." He jerked suddenly. "Fred? There's something, there's something wrong!"

Fred looked down and saw Ell's cock was doing that weird thing again. It was growing, turning *purple*, and there were two pointed appendages slipping out from fuckin' somewhere, and they were….

Tentacles.

"Holy fuck."

"Freddie? What do I do?" Ell demanded. "I don't, I don't know—"

"Does it hurt?" Fred asked.

"No."

"Does it feel good?"

"Yes?"

"Then don't stop." Fred kissed him hard. "Mmm, keep going. Come on."

Ell resumed stroking frantically, whining and squirming beneath Fred. The two tentacles slid around between them and then wrapped around both of their cocks, and Ell let out a moan that rattled the windows.

Fred couldn't believe this was happening. Ell had some sort of damn cock tentacles, and they were squeezing his damn dick. The pressure and heat were awesome, and he was so close that he wanted to scream. He kept playing with Ell's horns, kissing and nuzzling his hair, and he rocked his hips forward.

He didn't know if Ell had any control over the tentacles, but they were practically pulsing as they stroked his and Ell's cocks together. Ell's hands were now on Fred's shoulders, digging his nails in as the tentacles continued to slither and squeeze around them both. Nothing else Fred had ever experienced in his entire life, while either living or dead, could compare to this blissful sensation.

"Gods…. Ell…." Fred's eyes were tearing up. "I'm…."

"Freddie! I'm gonna come, I'm gonna come!" Ell howled as he spilled his load all over himself. His cock was long enough now that his come pulsed across his own chest and under his chin, and the two tentacles suddenly vibrated around them both.

There, *fuck*, that was the last bit of fuel Fred needed to push him through, and he roared. It was so loud, inhuman and deafening and—

"What happened?" Ell shrieked, pulling his hand away in a panic. "Did I hurt you?"

"No… you…." Fred was dizzy, trembling so hard he was worried he might collapse. His entire body was hot and hollow, completely drained and yet full of a deep and consuming satisfaction. He could hardly speak, and all of his limbs were incredibly heavy. "Oh, Ell… it's…."

"Shit!" Ell was nearly hysterical. "Just tell me! Freddie, what did I do?"

"You made me come."

"Wh… what?"

Fred was about to speak again when the door flew open. Robert and Lochlain raced inside with bright spells on their hands and shouting all at once.

"Fred? Hey! Are you okay?"

"What happened? We heard all of this noise—!"

"Get the fuck out!" Fred yelled, yanking the blankets up around him and Ell. "Ain't you fuckers ever heard of knocking?"

Ell squealed miserably and dragged a pillow over his head to hide his horns. "By all the friggin' gods, kill me now!"

Robert turned right around.

"Oh!" Lochlain grinned as he stared at the sight of them together in bed. "So, that's... okay, that's what all that was."

"Okay, time to go!" Robert grabbed Lochlain's shoulder and pushed him to the door.

"Wait, is that my robe?"

"Later! Sorry, guys! We'll, uh, we'll be waiting downstairs!"

Fred huffed as the door shut. He lifted the pillow so he could peek at Ell's flushed face. "You okay?"

"Can someone actually die of embarrassment?" Ell groaned dramatically. "Is that a thing?"

"Dunno. Don't think so." Fred grinned.

Ell burst out laughing and threw the pillow aside. "Oh wow! I can't believe they just, they just ran right in here!"

"Well, you know, we weren't exactly being quiet," Fred noted as he kissed Ell's pink cheek. "Especially you."

"I wasn't, uh, really thinking about that." Ell peered down at himself to get a good look at the mess. "I did it. I really did it! I made you come!"

"Fuck yeah, you did," Fred said, wishing he could hold on to this feeling forever. It was already fading, but there was a faint glow lingering. He wasn't in any pain, not at all, and he couldn't stop smiling.

But he had to ask....

"So, the tentacles?"

"Is that what that was?" Ell scooted into a sitting position and stared down at his groin.

The tentacles, if that's what they were, were gone now. Ell's cock was very human-looking and soft, and there was no sign of the tentacles.

"Pretty sure." Fred had seen a few in person, after all.

Ell slid his fingers around the base of his cock, frowning. "I don't understand. Nothing like that's ever happened before. Even when, uh, you know...." He cleared his throat. "When I was doing stuff with myself."

"Hey, it's okay." Fred rubbed Ell's thigh, trying to banish the images of Ell and that damn green tentacle dildo. "It was fuckin' hot."

"Really?" Ell perked up, and he smiled. "You... you liked it?"

"Hell yeah. Now I just gotta figure out how to make 'em come out again."

"Maybe it's like the Deverach!" Ell exclaimed.

"Huh?"

The Deverach were another one of the everlasting races, small goblin-like creatures with huge manes of tentacles on their heads.

"When I did my research trying to figure out what I was, I read everything I could find about the different magical races." Ell laid his hand on top of Fred's. "When the Deverach are, ahem, gettin' jiggy, their tentacles swell and special mating tentacles come out of these gills on their bellies."

"I don't believe it."

"What?"

"That you said gettin' jiggy."

Ell shoved him playfully. "Hey! I'm serious!"

Fred grinned. "So, we think you're part Deverach now?"

"No, I'm just saying this could be related to my Asran or Eldress heritage. We don't know how all the different races mated, you know. Maybe this is an Eldress thing that only happened because, well...." Ell's smile turned coy. "Because I was enjoying it so much?"

"Well, you know, there's only one way to find out." Fred kissed Ell's cheek sweetly. "Because I definitely wanna do that shit again."

"Oh, samesies. Big, *big* samesies. Sorry I didn't wait for our next date. You said it was okay, and I just sort of went for it."

"You ain't never gotta apologize," Fred said with a laugh. "Not for this." He scanned Ell's face, asking carefully, "Are you okay? It didn't hurt you to do any of that for me?"

"I'm great!" Ell insisted. "I mean, maybe a little sleepy, still a little weird about my tentacle bits I didn't even know I had, but super good."

"You're incredible, Ell." Fred kissed him sweetly, melting right into his arms and holding him close.

"Mmm, Freddie." Ell hugged Fred's neck and wrapped his legs around him as he laid back on the bed again.

Fred could feel a new wave of lust washing over him, and he resisted its pull. He reluctantly broke their kiss, giving Ell one last hug before sitting up. "Come on. Before you get somethin' else started."

"Me?" Ell blinked innocently.

"Yeah, you. Come on. Let's get a shower."

Ell stumbled into the bathroom, clearly more tired than he was letting on. Fred helped him get the water going and step into the stall, catching a glimpse of himself in the mirror.

He almost didn't recognize his own body.

Fred's skin was startlingly smooth, and there were no signs of any active rot. Some remaining scars still mottled his back and his thighs, but he looked like a completely different ghoul.

He looked... like himself again.

Jumping in the shower with Ell, he did his best to make it quick because he knew Robert and Lochlain were waiting for them. He resisted the urge to grope as he helped scrub Ell's back, though they did enjoy a long embrace beneath the hot spray. Soon enough, the slow drain was causing the water to pool around their ankles, and they got out.

Fred politely turned his back to give Ell some privacy so they could get dressed over by the TV, and he realized that he was in need of a new shirt. There was a small tap on his shoulder, and he turned around to find Ell was clothed and offering him a dark green tank top.

"Here. We really need to get you some more shirts," Ell said with a shy grin. "It might be kind of tight, but uhm, I think it'll look nice."

"Thanks."

Ell put on his charm and his horns vanished, and he smoothed his hands over his clothes. He was wearing a sweater that was baggy enough to pull the sleeves down over his hands and a big scarf to hide his neck.

"Why don't you use glamour to... you know." Fred pointed at his neck.

"Glamour charms don't grow on trees, you know. And well, I guess...." Ell touched the scarf. "I want to remember."

"Remember what?"

"To be careful who I trust." Ell smiled sadly.

Fred hugged him close, kissing the top of his head. "You can trust me, little one."

"I know." Ell hugged Fred's waist. "I trust you, Freddie."

"Ready?"

"Ready."

The borrowed tank top was definitely snug, but Fred didn't mind when he saw how Ell was looking at him. He took Ell's hand and led him downstairs. They found Lochlain and Robert hanging out in the front of the jewelry store.

"Hey," Lochlain greeted. "Took you guys long enough. Everything okay with the shower?"

"It was fine." Ell ducked his head against Fred's arm.

"Warm enough up there?" Robert asked, eyeing Ell's long sleeves and scarf. "I can adjust the heat."

"He's good." Fred felt Ell's hand clench in his. "Now, tell me you guys got something."

"We do, and we don't." Robert drummed his fingers along one of the cases. "The items for the auction might as well be on Xenon for all we know. I can't find any trace. Not even a receipt for what security company they're using to guard them."

"However," Lochlain chimed in cheerfully, "we do know the layout of the building where the charity auction is being held, the rotation of the security guards, and that the alarm can be neutralized if the power is flipped."

"You still wanna snatch the painting," Fred realized.

"Of course, I do!" Lochlain laughed. "Come on. You are talking to Azaethoth the Lesser's favorite thief, after all."

"Don't let that go to your head," Robert warned affectionately.

"Here's the deal." Lochlain clicked his tongue. "The charity is being held the day before the Winter Solstice. That's almost two weeks away. Sure, we may be able to find out where the painting is being held by then, but if we can't? We need to have a very clever, very sneaky backup plan to steal it from the auction."

Fred looked expectantly to Robert.

"He's right," Robert confirmed. "If nothing turns up about where the charity items are being stored, we'll have no other choice."

"Risky," Fred tutted. "Gonna be lots of people. Lots of eyes."

"Which is why I want you to come with me," Lochlain said. "I'll need a second man on this."

"Take Robert."

"Robert will be busy handling the power," Lochlain countered. "I need a second man on the inside with me."

Fred grunted.

"You can do it, right?" Ell asked quietly, giving him a nudge.

Damn if Ell didn't look real excited about the prospect of Fred committing a crime.

"I still got plenty of heat on me," Fred reminded them all. "I shouldn't be poking my head around in public."

"You won't be," Lochlain insisted. "Not until the night of the auction, anyway. That's more than enough time for the police to back off."

"This is so stupid."

"You haven't even heard my plan yet!"

"Let me guess," Fred drawled. "You want to wait until the auctioneer cracks his gavel and yells sold. Then you'll have Robert flip the power and grab the painting. You'll have me clear your exit with some commotion while the power is still out and zip right out the front door."

"Okay, well, I wouldn't use the front door," Lochlain said thoughtfully. "That would just be silly."

"Still no word from Loch or Sloane?"

"Nope." Robert clicked his tongue. "We will be on our own for this one."

"You wouldn't even really need to steal the painting, would you?" Ell piped up. He cowered when everyone looked at him. "I mean, uh, we need to destroy it, right? So, couldn't Fred just burn it up after Lochlain grabs it?"

"We'd have to get it off the venue grounds first," Lochlain replied. "With all those lovely shiny things floating around, they'll definitely have silencing wards up. Won't be able to cast a single spell inside the building."

"Uh…." Ell glanced up nervously at Fred.

"Disabling the silencing wards would take too much time, and someone would notice what we were doing," Robert said. "I wish it was that easy, though. If we could take out the wards, we could destroy the painting right then and there without Lochlain trying to make a daring escape."

"Not as much fun, though!" Lochlain pointed out.

"What if…." Ell squeezed Fred's hand.

"Ell," Fred warned. "You ain't gotta."

"It's okay," Ell said. "I really want to help." He took a deep breath. "What if I could cast a spell even with a silencing ward up?"

Robert and Lochlain exchanged a quizzical look.

"How?" Robert asked, definitely skeptical.

"Don't matter," Fred quickly replied. "I've seen him do it."

"I don't know any fire spells," Ell said, "but Fred could teach me! I could learn one in time for the auction!"

"You sure you wanna do this?" Fred frowned. "It's jail time if we get caught. This could go all kinds of bad."

"Not as bad as those crazy cultists getting their hands on that painting," Ell insisted. "I want to help."

"If you're sure…."

"I am!"

"Well, that settles it!" Lochlain declared with a clap of his hands. "Welcome aboard, Ell! I am very proud to be part of you committing your very first grand theft offense!"

CHAPTER 10.

"How DOES he do it?" Lochlain asked quietly, watching Ell repeatedly summon a small ball of light in spite of the silencing totem Robert had brought out.

Robert closed the store, and they had adjourned out back in the alley for a demonstration of Ell's magic. Robert was totally dumbfounded by Ell's resistance, and he kept trying to place the totem in different spots and challenging him to cast again.

Though a bit bored, Ell obliged and continued to summon the simple light spell Fred had taught him a few minutes ago. It did not escape Fred's attention that Ell was no longer using the spoken incantation and was only waving his hands to cast the spell.

He and Lochlain were leaning against the side of his truck, watching.

"I honestly don't know," Fred replied.

"Human?" Lochlain pressed.

"Eh, hard to say."

"Or won't say?" Lochlain frowned, scanning over Fred's shoulders and arms. "Don't think I didn't notice how much fresher you look. The rot… it's all gone, isn't it?"

"Pretty much."

"This morning when we busted in on you two," Lochlain demanded. "What were you guys doing exactly?"

"A gentleman doesn't kiss and tell."

"It's the fact that you've been kissing at all that interests me," Lochlain said. "I don't mean to pry, but I didn't think, ahem, things down in that particular department were functional for you?"

"They weren't," Fred confirmed. "Not until him."

"So, he can heal ghouls, resurrect dicks, and cast in the midst of a silencing totem without speaking the words of the spell," Lochlain mused. "Hmm. Is there anything he can't do?"

"Dunno yet."

"Do you know what he is? What he is really?'"

"I got some ideas," Fred said shortly, "but maybe you could just shut the fuck up and be happy for me for five fuckin' minutes."

"I am happy! I am!" Lochlain hissed, trying to keep his voice down. "But you have to admit this is a little crazy! Like, being brought back from the dead by a god crazy!"

"Hmmph."

"That kind of magic," Lochlain said warily, "could be dangerous."

Fred glared.

Lochlain was right, and he didn't even know the full extent of Ell's strange abilities.

Fred wasn't going to give him the satisfaction, and he snapped back, "We're all dangerous, aren't we?"

"Fair enough," Lochlain conceded. He reached out to squeeze Fred's shoulder, dropping his voice again. "If you're happy, I'm happy for you. I'm just worried about you. I don't want…."

Fred frowned as Lochlain trailed off, catching a glimmer of tears in his eye that he quickly wiped away. A wave of emotion surged up inside of him like a tidal wave, and he realized there were tears in his eyes too.

"I don't want to lose you again," Lochlain said firmly. "It was already my fault once. Not gonna let it happen twice if I can help it. I love you too damn much."

Fred wiped his face off on his arm, clearing his throat loudly. He and Lochlain didn't usually talk like this, and he couldn't keep his feelings in check. Lochlain was his best friend, and he knew that he loved him, but it had been so long since he'd actually felt it.

He tried to ignore it, mumbling grumpily, "So, you've decided to vet my new boyfriend because you're afraid I'm gonna die again… from what?"

"Too much sex?" Lochlain joked.

Fred snorted.

"Hey, anything is possible."

"We're fine," Fred assured him, watching Robert trying to sit the silencing totem right beside Ell's feet and telling him to cast again. "He thinks he's a descendant of the Eldress and the Asra. I dunno what he is for sure except that he's special, okay?"

"Would you let Azaethoth meet him?" Lochlain asked carefully.

"Yeah." Fred was surprised, and it took him a moment to recognize the question was a challenge. "Asshole. You ain't gonna think he's good enough for me unless your god gives him the okay?"

"He's your god too," Lochlain reminded him.

"Fuck you and him."

"Please allow me the courtesy of being a bit concerned when my best friend shows up with a new boyfriend who has very strange and mysterious powers we can't explain?"

"Fine. Be as concerned as you wanna be."

Ell yelped when Robert tried to place the totem directly on top of his head, backpedaling down the alley as he pleaded frantically, "Fred!"

"Hey, hey!" Fred sprinted toward Ell to intervene. He shook his head at Robert as he pushed his way in between them, shielding Ell with his broad body.

Ell cowered behind Fred, panting hard. "I'm sorry, I'm sorry, I'm sorry!"

"It's okay," Fred soothed as he turned around to hold Ell against his chest. "I got you."

"Hey! I'm sorry!" Robert retreated to Lochlain's side, concerned and equally confused. "I didn't mean to upset him. What's wrong?"

Ell was shaking, burying his face into Fred's shirt and on the verge of tears. "He was so close," he whimpered in a terrified whisper. "He almost touched me… if I hadn't moved…."

"What happened?" Lochlain had hurried over to Robert's side and grabbed his shoulders.

"I just tried to see if putting the totem in direct contact would have any effect!" Robert said urgently. "I'm so sorry, Ell! I wasn't trying to hurt you!"

"He don't like to be fuckin' touched," Fred growled. "You got it? Don't fuckin' touch him."

"Hello…?" an elderly man's voice called out, his thin frame popping into view as he hobbled around the corner of the alley. "Is the store open? The sign on the door said closed, but the moogle app on my phone says you're supposed to be open—"

"Sorry, sir," Robert said politely. "We were just taking a quick break. I'll be right there." He exchanged a small smile with Lochlain before leaving to let the customer in.

"So, no touching Ell. Got it." Lochlain's brow wrinkled. "Anything else you wanna tell me before we all decide to risk life and limb together on a dangerous heist to save the world?"

"Nope," Fred said curtly. "We're just ducky here." He nodded at the back door. "Go check on Robert. Make sure that old guy isn't gonna rob the place."

"Haha." Clearly not convinced, Lochlain sighed in frustration, but he chose not to push. "Yeah, sure thing."

Fred waited for him to go back inside before asking Ell, "You okay, little one?"

"It was so stupid," Ell gasped, angrily wiping off his face. "I shouldn't have freaked out. It was all my fault. I got too comfortable. I should have never let him get that close! I'm so sorry!"

"It's okay," Fred tried to comfort him. "No one got hurt—"

"But what if he had?" Ell demanded tearfully. "What if I wasn't fast enough…? I can't… I can't do this. I can't help you guys."

"What are you talking about?"

"The heist!" Ell cried. "I can't be in a crowd like that! I can't go on dates or go to a wedding or anything! I can't. I can't risk hurting someone! I can't do this! I just can't!"

Ell was nearly hysterical, and Fred didn't know what else to do except hold him. He rocked him until his sobs quieted, petting his hair and kissing his forehead.

"It's okay," Fred said. "I've got you."

"I'm sorry," Ell mumbled. "You're gonna need another new shirt because I've totally snotted all over this one. Ugh, I'm so gross."

"Ell, up until recently, I literally had parts rotting off. You ain't that gross."

"Heh, good point." Ell tried to smile, and his face was bleary from crying so hard. "I wish there was another way, but I'm too scared. You guys will just have to do the heist some other way."

"No, there's gotta be somethin' we can do," Fred insisted. "Come on. We got fuckin' magic. There has to be some kind of shield or fuckin' somethin' we can put on you."

"I've looked," Ell said sadly. "The only thing I ever found was a spell for something called stoneskin that created an invisible barrier from head to toe—"

"Let's do that!"

"You need to have the scales from a Vulgora." Ell pouted. "You know, the magical fish people that no one has seen in hundreds of years? Probably extinct? I mean, unless you believe in Fish Boy, and that there's a lost city down in the Marianas Trench—"

"Oh, really?" Fred grinned, suddenly sweeping Ell right off the ground and up into his arms. "Come on!"

"Where are we going?" Ell clung to Fred's neck.

"Field trip," Fred said as he carried Ell out to his truck. "I need a new shirt, and I gotta make a phone call."

"Ah, what are you talking about? Call who?"

"My second favorite ghoul doctor." Fred set Ell down in the passenger seat. He walked around to get behind the wheel, punching out a quick message in his phone. When he got an immediate reply, he smiled.

"Who?" Ell asked, confused and exasperated. "You mean Doctor York? I don't understand."

"You know she's not just a ghoul doctor. She's into selling lucky Asra feet and Eldress slick tea—"

"All of that stuff is fake!" Ell protested. "She asked me if I wanted a Faedra wing once!"

"Not all of it. Some of her stuff is legit."

"Like what?"

"Like the wind chime hangin' up by her front door."

"The wind chime?" Ell scrambled to get his seat belt on as Fred speedily pulled out onto the street.

"Yeah, that thing. She told me it was a gift from her great grandma."

"Freddie!" Ell pleaded, his knuckles white as he gripped the dashboard when they came to a sudden stop at a red light.

"It's a wind chime for Yeris." Fred reached over to squeeze Ell's knee. "For good weather and bountiful fishing."

"So?" Ell still wasn't obviously making the connection.

"It's made out of Vulgora scales."

"Holy crap." Ell gasped, holding his hands up to his mouth. "Are you friggin' serious?"

"Yup."

"Wait, did you already ask her about it?"

"I just texted her to make sure she's home. She lives out in the middle of nowhere like you."

"So, we don't actually know if she's gonna let us have it?"

"Not yet, but I can be mighty convincing."

"No," Doctor York said flatly.

"Come on, Doc!" Fred protested. "I even said fuckin' please and everything!"

"Not until you tell me why," she countered, calmly staring Fred down.

She was a frail woman with long gray hair and rainbow rhinestone glasses, and a strong wind might blow her over if she was ever without her thick cane. There were glittery flames painted up the side of it, sparkling like the gems in her glasses.

Her oddities business was run out of the front of her country cabin home, a short drive from where Robert and Lochlain lived at Professor Kunst's former property.

The cabin was packed with a variety of antique medical equipment, taxidermied animals set in ridiculous poses, and other bits of macabre and odd collectibles. There were also dozens of vials and bottles purported to hold rare magical ingredients, arranged neatly on packed shelves.

One was labeled as godly cerulean gel and was priced at over a thousand dollars.

There was a kitsch element to it all, and the rack of shirts with "I Saw Madam York's Oddities And All I Got Was This T-Shirt" stamped across them only added to it. It was at once dark, grotesque, and equally cheesy.

On the front door hung the wind chime in question, a dangling tangle of thin iridescent shells that made an eerie tinkling sound when a breeze came through.

Fred had never thought twice about the damn thing, certain he had walked by it dozens of times without a second glance. After having viewed it with a new level of scrutiny and a perception spell, he was confident that it was real.

The shells had a particular shimmer about them, and it reminded him vividly about feeling Azaethoth's divine touch. The shells were all very uniform and round, and Fred knew now it was because they were scales.

"You can't come barging in here demanding my very precious wind chime and not tell me why you are suddenly so very interested in it," Doc went on.

"Didn't you talk about throwin' it out because you hated the damn noise?"

"It was a gift, you know."

"I know, Doc," Fred said between clenched teeth. "It's kinda complicated, but I got a real strong feelin' that it's real."

"Of course it's real. Everything I sell here is completely authentic—"

"Then sell it to me!" Fred exclaimed. "You know I'm good for it."

"Not until you tell me why," Doc said. "There is so precious little of the everlasting races left here on Aeon. In these pieces are great power and the potential for even greater danger. I've kept this tiny bit safe for decades by hiding it in plain sight. Why should I give it to you?"

"Because we need it." Fred was getting frustrated, and he was struggling to control his temper.

He didn't want to blow up on Doc, but he didn't know how to explain what was going on without revealing Ell's secrets or that they would be using the scales for a crime.

Plus she would probably think he was totally nuts.

"It's okay," Ell said quietly, nudging Fred. "We can tell her."

"Eh...." Fred grunted.

"She's a friggin' ghoul doctor!" Ell argued. "She's not gonna rat us out!" He huffed, looking to Doc as he said, "The wind chime is for me. I need the scales for a potion to help Fred with a heist that could potentially save the world from a crazy cult who want to awaken Salgumel."

Fred cringed.

Yup. Totally nuts.

Doc looked thoughtful for a long moment, peering over her glasses at Ell and humming. She tapped her cane on the ground, saying finally, "Okay, you can take it."

"Wait, what?" Fred blinked in shock.

"Elliam has never lied to me." Doc shrugged. "He says the world is in danger, I'm obliged to believe him."

"What about me?"

"Perhaps if you had decided to tell me the truth, maybe I would have believed you too." Doc looked smug. "I suppose now we'll never know."

"Thank you," Ell said with a sincere smile. "For everything."

"Thank you for taking care of Fred," she replied. "He is a good man, you know."

"Don't you mean 'ghoul'?" Fred mumbled.

"I know," Ell said to Doc. He reached for Fred's hand. "I've never been so happy that you referred him to me."

"Ohhh," Doc cooed, looking over them with a bright twinkle in her eye. "So I see."

Fred couldn't quite explain it, but his face was hot. He was blushing, and that all needed to stop right now. "Look, I hate to rush off, Doc, but—"

"I know, you have to go save the world," Doc cut in with a wink. "Go on. Take the wind chime. Do what needs to be done."

"Uh, there's just one more thing."

"Oh, by all the gods, what now?"

Fred pointed at the rack of T-shirts. "Need one of them, please."

"Nineteen ninety-five plus tax."

"Sold."

One new shirt and magical wind chime richer, Fred and Ell said their farewells and headed back to the city. Ell held the wind chime close, and he was buzzing with excitement the entire way.

"This could really work," Ell was saying when they got back to the jewelry store. "The potion is supposed to last at least one whole night, and there's enough here for like, uh, a month? Maybe two?"

"Good." Fred held the back door open to allow Ell to walk in first. He hadn't seen any sign of Robert or Lochlain, and that was fine by him.

Once they were upstairs and the door was shut, Ell pounced on Fred. He kissed him passionately. "Oh, Freddie. I'm so happy."

Fred held Ell close, rubbing his back in slow circles. "Me too." The rush of emotions coming over him was still going to take some getting used to, but he didn't mind when Ell swooped back in for another kiss.

Once Ell had his fill of affection, he went off with a smile to open up his duffel bag. He kneeled and sorted through the books that he'd brought with him. The bag was so packed that he had to remove several other items in his search.

"What else do we need for the potion?" Fred sat on the futon to watch.

He ignored the bundled-up towel Ell set aside, having a pretty good idea of what was hiding there.

"Salt and water." Ell pulled out a weathered tome. "Ha! Found it. Finally." He hopped up with the book to explore the kitchenette.

"That's it?" Fred tried not to look at the towel Ell had left out.

"All the magic is in the scales." Ell dug through the cabinets. "The water and salt is basically a vessel to carry it into your body."

"Like a chaser for a shot?"

"I guess?" Ell shrugged. "I wouldn't know."

"Wait… you've never…."

"Uh, only nineteen, remember?" Ell came back to the makeshift box table with a bowl of water and some take-out packets of salt. He also had two spoons, holding them in his mouth as he quickly flipped through the old book.

"So, you just what? You've never had a single drink before?"

"No." Ell batted his eyes. "That would be against the law."

"So is healing ghouls," Fred reminded him with a grin. "Look at you now. You're getting to help out with a big ol' heist. We might just make a little delinquent outta you yet."

"No, the heist is different. It's to help save the world." Ell got flustered and raised one of the spoons as if to throw it. "You… you…! Shush!"

Although Fred was well aware of Ell's power, the idea of being threatened with a spoon was too damn funny. He snickered, softly at first, but soon so loud that he couldn't contain it.

Unable to focus on his work, Ell started to laugh too. He hung his head, groaning playfully. "Oh, you're so awful. I'm just, you know, trying to be good. I've always *tried* to be good."

"You're gonna make a fuckin' adorable crook," Fred teased.

"You're such a bad influence." Ell was still smiling as he scanned the book in front of him. "Now seriously, I've gotta work. This is important."

"Yes, sir." Fred winked.

Ell blushed anew, turning his attention back to the book as he mixed the salt into the bowl. He carefully plucked one of the scales off the wind chime and ground it between the two spoons.

"Can I help you with anything?" Fred offered. "Don't you need to cast a circle or something before you mix the potion?"

"Oh! I already did."

"Huh?" Fred blinked. He hadn't seen Ell call the corners or speak a single word of magic. "How did you do that?"

"What do you mean?" Ell blinked. "I just read the ritual, said the words in my head, and there it is." He shrugged off the amazing feat as if it was nothing special. "Now I just have to add in the scale, and it's done."

Fred watched Ell sprinkling in the crushed-up scales, now reduced to a fine powder and glittering as they fell into the water. "That's it?"

"This is it." Ell gave the bowl a quick stir and then lifted it up to chug. He grimaced, setting the emptied bowl down on the table.

"Feel any different?"

"Not really?" Ell frowned. "I did everything that the book said, and I've closed the circle. How are we supposed to know if it worked?"

"Go poke somebody and see if they rot?"

"Safely!"

"Hmmph."

"Oh! I've got it!" Ell jumped up and then scrambled back to the kitchen counter.

"What are you doing?" Fred's stomach heaved as Ell picked up a knife. "Ell?"

Without hesitation, Ell put his hand up on the counter and brought the knife down.

"Ell!" Fred shouted, far too slow as he leapt to his feet to intervene. He grabbed for the knife, and he found himself staring stupidly at a bent blade. Looking at Ell's intact and wiggling fingers, he realized that he was unharmed.

"Ta-dah!" Ell said cheerfully.

"For fuck's sake." Fred grabbed Ell's hand and kissed it fiercely. "We coulda figured out another fuckin' way."

"Why? This totally worked!" Ell beamed as he stood on his toes to kiss Fred's cheek. "I'm fine."

"Lucky you didn't lose a fuckin' finger."

"Don't trust my magic?"

"Hmmph. I trust you. I don't always trust the magic." Fred shook his head, bringing Ell's hand up to his lips for another kiss. He was glad that the potion worked, although he really did not like Ell's method of testing it. A sudden thought struck him, a return of something he'd worried about before and hadn't yet addressed. "If you actually heal me all the way back, we're gonna need some shit like this, huh?"

"What?" Ell's confused expression made it obvious that he hadn't come to the same conclusion as Fred had. "What are you talking about?"

"Your touch hurts people who are alive," Fred said slowly. "If you make me fuckin' alive, then your touch is gonna hurt me."

"Oh no." Ell's eyes widened, and he jerked away. "I, I didn't think about that! I've already healed so much, and it's just, it, it's like extra strong with you for some crazy reason, and, and—"

"Hey, hey. Take a breath, little one." Fred wanted to reach for Ell, but he didn't. "You touchin' on me doesn't automatically heal me, right?"

"Not exactly?" Ell frowned. "I'm not actually really sure. Every time I've touched a ghoul, I'm actively thinking about healing them. Like, I really focus my magic to make the rot go away."

"Okay. So, how about you don't do that?" Fred held out his arms. "I mean, I think I'm already pretty damn good right now, don't ya' think? Things are, you know, in workin' order."

"Yeah?" Ell hesitantly reached for Fred. He slid his hands up Fred's broad chest, sighing as Fred wrapped his arms around him. "I guess so. I… I really don't want to hurt you, Fred. When I touch someone… that rot doesn't go away."

Fred thought about Jeff, secretly enjoying the idea of that bastard decomposing.

"It's like with Doyle's mom," Ell went on. "Once I touch someone, there's no way to stop it. I am really, really scared—"

"Don't be," Fred insisted. "Listen to me, little one. We got this. All you gotta do is stop healing me. We could even let some of the rot come back just to make sure I'm dead enough, okay?"

"Freddie." Ell frowned, cupping Fred's cheek. "If we let you start rotting again, won't that hurt too?"

"Of course it fuckin' will." Fred smiled, and he picked Ell up to kiss him sweetly. It was soft, slow, and he loved how Ell's arms fit around his neck as they kissed. A familiar warmth was filling his chest and stealing away the breath he knew he didn't need, and yet he still had to gasp when Ell slipped his tongue inside his mouth.

Ell was a quick study, and his kisses had become passionate and heated, and he wrapped his legs around Fred to eliminate any increment of space between them. He was always frantic, as if he would simply cease to exist if he stopped kissing Fred, and it left Fred's head spinning and his body aching with need.

Yes, *need*. He needed Ell more than he'd ever needed anything. Yes, it was fast, maybe a bit insane, but he already knew he wanted to spend every day with this beautiful young man at his side. The jagged edges inside of him that had been sharpened from many years of loneliness were melting away, and in their places was a deep, resonating warmth he'd never known.

When they parted, Fred rested his brow against Ell's, whispering, "Look. Yeah, it's gonna hurt goin' back to rot, but not as much as never bein' able to do that again.

"Oh, Freddie." Ell hugged him tight. "Okay. We'll do it. I'll stop healing you. But only for a little while, okay?"

"Okay."

"Well, we know the potion works now at least." Ell grinned. "You know what this means, right? The heist is totally on, and we're gonna save the world!"

"That," Fred agreed, "and now I can take you out on a real date with real tables and shit."

"Yeah?" Ell's face lit up, and he wiggled excitedly.

"We can go to the movies, walk around a fuckin' park, do whatever you wanna do."

"What if… uh…." Ell's grin grew, and there was a hint of mischief gleaming in his eyes. "What if I wanted to go to a bar?"

"Really?" Fred barked out a short laugh. "And how do you think I'm gonna get your underage butt in?"

"You're a criminal," Ell said with an innocent bat of his eyes. "Surely you know some maybe possibly seedy place that isn't gonna ask for my ID?"

"Yeah." Fred smiled. "As a matter of fact, I do."

CHAPTER 11.

FRED AND Ell spent the rest of the day watching *Legends of Darkness*, waiting for the evening hour to arrive so they could go out on their date.

Fred was really looking forward to it, and he was surprised by how excited he was. He was still surprised to feel anything at all, but his emotions were growing exponentially. He knew it was all thanks to Ell.

The simple touch of Ell's fingers made him smile, and the way he snuggled against Fred's side was a new comfort he knew he couldn't live without now. They laughed at the same jokes, yelled at the show's frustrating twists together, and Fred had never experienced such a sense of peace.

It wasn't too long ago that Fred had considered letting himself go to the rot, and now he'd never felt so alive. What Ell had revitalized was more than just his decomposing flesh—Ell had healed his heart and become its very reason for wanting to beat once more.

Of course, there was the risk of Ell accidentally killing him if Fred became too alive, but Fred decided every relationship had its quirks.

Lochlain and Robert popped in during the marathon to keep them updated on the progress with the upcoming heist. Since Robert had still been unable to find out where the items were being held, their only choice was to steal the painting from the auction. The plan was relatively simple. Lochlain, Fred, and Ell would enter the charity as guests and wait for the painting to come up to the block.

They would have to keep an eye out for any suspicious activity, particularly potential cultists who could either be there to bid on the painting or perhaps conspiring to steal it themselves.

Per Lochlain, they would make their move when the auctioneer declared the painting sold. As silly as it was, up on stage during the bidding would be the only time the painting would be totally unguarded. When the gavel struck, Robert would turn off the power. Under the cover of darkness, Lochlain would snatch the painting right off the stage.

In what Lochlain described as a fit of genius, he would then remove the painting from the frame to pass off to Ell and Fred. Lochlain would make a flashy escape with the empty frame to distract the guards and any cultists.

Meanwhile, Fred and Ell would make a quick dash into the rear exit hallway and destroy the painting. They'd meet Robert outside in the alley and catch up with Lochlain at the jewelry store.

It all sounded so easy, and Fred was wary. There was a lot that could go wrong. The chances of the cultists trying to steal the painting for themselves were pretty high, and they were likely to clash. Considering what happened before, the risk of violence was great.

No weapons would be allowed inside the building, and the silencing wards would prevent any magic from being cast, but Fred didn't trust that the cultists wouldn't try to sneak something in. There was already a risk of the cultists recognizing him and Ell from their last encounter, and they were definitely not going to be happy to see him.

Especially that bastard Jeff, if he was even still alive.

Lochlain's only concern at the present time was picking out a tuxedo to show off at the charity. They needed to look their best to blend in with the rest of the fancy guests, and Fred wondered if Lochlain was more excited about the heist or dressing up for it.

"Enough of that," Fred grunted as he stood up, bringing Lochlain's monologue about satin lapels and shiny cufflinks to an abrupt halt. "You're in charge of disguises, okay? Done."

"What are you in such a hurry for?" Lochlain asked suspiciously. "You two got a hot date?"

"As a matter of fact, yeah."

"Public places probably aren't the best idea right now, my dear arsonist."

"We ain't goin' nowhere public," Fred replied. "We're going to Dead To Rites."

"That sleazy little dive behind Hollowed Grounds Coffee?" Lochlain scoffed.

"Aw, how romantic!" Robert exclaimed.

"Romantic?" Ell whispered loudly. "I can't tell if he's being sarcastic or not."

"It's where Lochlain and I met," Robert explained with a bashful smile. "The first time I was going to fence something for him, I wanted to meet in person, and well… it was sort of love at first sight."

"Except my darling Robert never told me," Lochlain teased. "Took me dying for him to finally spill."

"I used to think of it as the first date I was never brave enough to actually ask him out on," Robert confessed. "I do really love it, but eh, try not to touch anything. It'll probably be sticky. And make sure your glass is clean before you drink anything."

"Yeah, yeah, we got it," Fred snorted, shooing Robert and Lochlain to the door. "Now scram! We gotta get ready."

"Sure, sure!" Lochlain threw his arm around Robert's shoulders as they walked out. "We'll just be hard at work perfecting our ingenious plan to save the world while you two are sucking face in some bar—"

"Out!" Fred bellowed and shut the door behind them.

Ell pressed a hand to his mouth to stifle his giggles. "So, uh, is there actually something we could be doing to help?"

"Nope." Fred shrugged his big shoulders. "Unless Robert finds out where the paintings are being held, all we can do is fuckin' wait."

"Does that mean we should get ready to go?"

"I'm ready now."

"Aren't we supposed to dress up for a date?" Ell gestured at Fred's oddities shirt. "Or are we like, uh, blending in?"

"Blending in," Fred confirmed. He smirked and bowed his head to smooch Ell's cheek. "When this bullshit is over, I'll take you somewhere real fancy."

"Oh, like more-than-one-fork fancy?" Ell beamed.

"Damn right."

"And you'll wear a shirt that has buttons?"

"Whatever you want."

"You're on, mister." Ell hurried back over to his duffel bag. "I'm gonna at least put on another shirt. I don't think unicorns and rainbows is the right look going to a scary bar."

"It's not that scary," Fred said with a chuckle.

"Really?"

"Eh." Fred considered the question more seriously. "Okay, okay, maybe a little." He shrugged. "But I don't think there's been any murders there lately."

"*Lately?*"

"Yeah."

"Well…." Ell stood up straight, throwing his shoulders back. "Don't worry. I'll keep you safe."

"Ain't a doubt in my mind." Fred smiled. "You're one tough babe. Just like Princess Daisy."

"Yeah? Except I'm smart enough to totally go for the goblin king, you know." Ell bit his lip as he slowly pulled his colorful shirt up over his head. Aiming for sultry, he twirled the shirt around his finger with a wink.

Fred was instantly charmed, looking over Ell's bare chest with an appreciative grin. He'd expected him to run off to the bathroom to change, but this was much better.

Ell was still a little awkward, his seductive twirling suddenly flinging the garment off from his hand and nearly hitting Fred with it. "Shit, sorry!"

"It's okay." Fred didn't mind at all, and the air felt charged despite Ell's clumsy efforts. The desire between them was becoming palpable, and all Fred wanted to do was get his hands on Ell. He wanted to repay him for each and every smile, all the laughter they'd shared, and the simple bliss of no longer being alone.

He couldn't believe how this shy young man could inspire such an intense wave of emotion, and he was immediately drawn to him.

"Which, uh, which shirt should I wear?" Ell asked quietly, holding up a few different ones.

Fred reached not for the shirts, but to touch Ell's face. He didn't think this sweet boy had any clue how he really made him feel. "You'll look good in anything, you know."

"Awww!" Ell pressed into Fred's palm, turning his head to kiss his wrist. "You're so sweet."

"Nah, just tellin' the truth." Fred loved how soft Ell's skin was, and he couldn't resist leaning in for a kiss.

"Mmm, you're ridiculous," Ell mumbled, kissing back softly. "Like, goblin royalty level ridiculous."

"Uh-uh," Fred grunted, sliding his fingers through Ell's hair and wrapping his arm around his little waist. He kissed him more deeply, and he savored how Ell melted in his embrace.

"Hmmph, thought this part was supposed to come after the date," Ell huffed, pulling back to catch his breath.

"Didn't stop us before."

"Come on," Ell huffed, clearly flustered and bopping Fred with one of the shirts. "You're supposed to be helping me get dressed."

"Technically, you started it."

"Me?"

"Lookin' all pretty and stuff," Fred teased, ducking his head to kiss Ell's neck. He could feel him tremble and then heard him gasp, and the urge to take him right back into bed was strong. He was getting hard, and just that was almost enough to rob him of his senses.

Five years had come and gone, but even when there was still blood running through his veins, no one had ever made him feel like this. He wanted to give Ell everything he had, to take care of him, and more than wanting to save the world, he wanted to keep Ell safe.

He kissed Ell and swallowed back a moan, exhaling sharply when they finally parted.

Ell's eyes were purple, wide and shimmering, and his smile was as bright as a thousand suns. He had dropped the shirts except a blue one with clouds plastered across the front, holding it up as he tried to catch his breath. "Uh, so, uh, this one?"

"Good, that's good," Fred agreed, stepping away so Ell could put it on. "Real good."

They managed to behave long enough for Ell to finish getting dressed, and then they went downstairs, walking hand in hand out to Fred's truck.

"I'm so friggin' excited!" Ell said as he got buckled in the passenger seat. "My very first bar!"

"This place ain't exactly glamorous," Fred cautioned, "but the drinks are strong, and the food is decent. Well, it used to be anyway."

"As long as you're with me, I don't care about the rest." Ell's smile faltered. "I mean, you were joking about the murder thing, right?"

"Eh…."

"Freddie!"

"Just stay close."

Dead To Rites was an old funeral home that had fallen into disarray and been turned into a bar. The chapel was crowded with chairs and tables instead of pews, and drinks were served from the converted pulpit. The walls of the viewing rooms had been knocked down to make room for pool tables and a jukebox.

It was sticky, dirty, and reeked of cigarette smoke and rotten flowers. The patrons were as rough as the building, but the general atmosphere was surprisingly mellow. The thrum of rock and roll music was only broken by fits of raucous laughter and the occasional crack of billiard balls.

Above the bar hung a crude effigy of Azaethoth the Lesser, his twisted dragon where the Lucian star would have been. There were flowers, stale peanuts, and emptied shot glasses left as offerings at his clawed feet. As the patron god of tricksters and thieves, his was a fitting visage for a den of crooks.

Fred doubted that Azaethoth even knew this shrine existed but was certain he would love it.

Ell's eyes were about to pop out of his head when they arrived and he took in the new surroundings. "Holy crap bunnies, look at this place! Wow!"

"Not too bad, right?" Fred grinned, bringing Ell to the Sage's table by the bar.

It was a lone square table set with old high-back chairs and a lush chaise that was likely original to the building.

One of the tall chairs had been dragged over to the end of the bar right behind the table, currently occupied by a lone redhead with curly hair. His head was down, he wasn't moving, and Fred thought he heard snoring.

"This is just like when Blix went to the tavern in the enchanted forest pretending to be a peasant!" Ell was practically bouncing as he plopped down on the narrow end of the chaise. "This is great!"

"Yeah, except we're not hiding any crowns in our cloaks," Fred teased as he sat next to him. His bulk easily took over the dainty piece of furniture, but he didn't mind the closeness.

"Is this like your special spot?" Ell rubbed his hand over the edge of the table. "It's a lot cleaner than the other ones. Not that I'm judging. The rest, well, they do look… sticky."

"This is the table for Sages." Fred nodded at the stocky bartender. "That guy there? His name is Jackie Cheese. Him and his brother, Ashtray, run this place. They're both Sagittarians."

"Wait. His brother's name is Ashtray?"

"Ashley, Ashley Trey. Ashtray. That guy's name is actually Monterey Trey, but they call him Jackie Cheese."

"I thought my name was weird!" Ell laughed, cuddling up against Fred's side. He made sure there was not an inch of space between them, and he slid his hand under the table to squeeze Fred's thigh.

"Elliam, right?" Fred recalled, eagerly leaning into all the sweet touches. The abundance of affection was very addictive, and Fred was more than happy to reciprocate. Jackie waved at him, and he waved back.

"Elliam Jimantha Sturm," Ell said, shrinking in on himself with a shy grin.

"What?" Fred scoffed. He saw Jackie coming around the bar toward them and said, "Hold that thought."

"Hey, Fred," Jackie greeted as he walked up to them, throwing out a meaty hand to shake Fred's. "How goes it?"

"It goes."

"Looks like it's goin' pretty good." Jackie smirked at the two of them snuggled up together.

"I ain't got no complaints," Fred replied, pulling his arm back to slide around Ell's shoulders. He could feel him fidgeting and tugged him closer. "This is Ell. He's with me."

"Hi," Ell said, waving hesitantly.

"I'm Jackie." Jackie offered his hand to Ell. "Nice to meet you, Ell."

"Oh! Um…." Ell took a deep breath before reaching out to shake. "Uh, ditto!"

Fred tensed when their hands touched, but he was instantly relieved when Jackie didn't start to rot. The potion was a complete success.

"If you're a friend of Fred's, then you're a friend of mine." Jackie smiled, looking back to Fred. "You want your usual?"

Since Fred's death, the usual was a cup of boiling hot coffee. Although he wouldn't drink it, it helped not draw attention to himself.

After all, everyone in a bar always had some sort of drink in their hand.

This time, however, he decided he was going to try something different.

"Nah, not tonight," Fred replied. "Let me get one of them boozy hot chocolates."

"Really?" Jackie was surprised.

Although Fred had never outright told Jackie what he really was, Fred was pretty sure Jackie knew, so the order was certainly unusual for him.

"Yup. And whatever he wants." Fred jerked his head at Ell.

"All right. What'll you have?" Jackie asked, smirking slyly at Ell. It was obvious he knew Ell wasn't old enough to be here, but he was still willing to serve him.

"Uh." Ell glanced helplessly at Fred.

"Strawberry daiquiri," Fred suggested, recalling Ell's penchant for fruity sweets.

The redhead at the end of the bar let out a particularly loud snore that drew all their attention.

"Is that guy okay?" Ell's brow wrinkled.

Jackie shook his head. "Don't worry about him. That's pretty normal. He won't bother you none. So, the house hot chocolate and a strawberry daiquiri? Comin' right up." He gave a quick salute and then headed back to the bar.

"Wow!" Ell gasped as if he'd been holding his breath. "I can't believe I couldn't think of what to order. I mean, I guess I've never ordered a drink before, and, wow! I touched him! We actually touched and nothing happened! I'm freaking out."

"Ell, it's okay—" Fred cut in gently, trying to comfort him.

"I'm gonna get us caught just like when that peasant recognized the goblin king's cologne—"

"Hey, hey! It's okay." Fred grinned. "We know that potion works, and I promise we ain't gettin' busted."

"Are you sure?"

"Very sure."

"Okay." Ell sank down against Fred's side in relief.

"So, how many drugs were your parents on when they named you?"

"Aw, come on!" Ell laughed. "It's not that bad. They just really wanted me and my brother to have unique names!"

"Shit. What did they name him?"

"Tedward Beauseph."

"For fuck's sake."

"Well, hey! What's your name?" Ell stuck out his tongue. "What's 'Fred' short for? Frederick?"

"Nothing. It ain't really my name. My name's Farrokh."

"Oh, that's right. Your mother was Tauri! Huh. What's your middle name?"

"I don't have one. It's just Farrokh."

"I was kinda hoping you at least had a super weird middle name."

"Nah, just plain ol' boring Farrokh, I'm afraid."

"There is nothing boring about you," Ell said with an unexpected burst of passion, taking Fred's hand with a sweet smile. He became self-conscious and stammered, "You know, I just, I just mean you're special. To me. You're very special to me."

"You're special to me too," Fred said quietly, bowing his head to kiss Ell's brow.

"Yeah?" Ell perked up.

"Yeah." Fred's chest was tight, and there was a distinct thump. "Real fuckin' special."

Jackie was back with their drinks, carefully setting down Fred's spiked hot chocolate and Ell's icy daiquiri. "All right, here you guys go. Holler if you need anything."

"Thanks." Fred took a deep breath as he grabbed the handle of the mug to raise it for a sip. He was prepared to taste absolutely nothing, and then—

He jerked away, startled.

"What's wrong?" Ell frowned, and his brow furrowed with worry. "Are you okay?"

"It's hot," Fred said dumbly. "I just burned my fucking mouth. It's hot, and it's fucking sweet. I can taste the chocolate, the fucking *chocolate*, the cream, the fuckin' booze. I usually order boiling hot coffee, but this…."

"Coffee? Because you couldn't feel anything else?"

"Yeah. I could kinda feel it if it was real hot, but I sure as fuck could never taste it." Fred reached out to touch the side of Ell's glass, and he laughed when he could feel how icy cold it was. "Fuckin' hell."

"Here's to you, Farrokh," Ell said cheerfully, picking up his glass and tapping Fred's. "To feeling hot and cold and all sorts of fun things."

"To feeling all the damn things," Fred agreed, lifting up his mug by the handle. He wasn't sure how much he could drink—where did it even go?—but he couldn't resist a few more sips of rich chocolatey booze. He smiled fondly as Ell slurped at his daiquiri.

And kept going.

And going.

"Hey, Ell? Maybe you should—"

The glass was empty.

"Wow, that was good!" Ell licked his lips. "Like, wow. Oh, can I have another?"

"Of course." Fred waved at Jackie and pointed at Ell. "Maybe try to slow down and taste this next one, huh?"

"Oh! But I did taste it! And it was *good*."

Fred noticed that Ell's cheeks were already turning pink, and he couldn't stop smiling. "So, Elliam Jimantha, you like strawberry daiquiris, huh?"

"Farrokh, I think…." Ell hiccuped. "I think I love them."

"Yeah?" Fred laughed. "Good. I'm glad."

"This is really awesome. It's like something out of a friggin' movie. I didn't think places like this were real."

"Places like what?"

"Seedy taverns!" Ell hissed as if he was trying to keep his voice down but failing. "Dark and shadowy hotbeds of criminal activity!" He clammed up when Jackie came over to drop off his daiquiri and retrieve the empty glass. "Thank you!"

"Here ya go," Jackie said seriously, winking at Fred. "You know, those strawberries are from the shadowy hotbed's organic rooftop garden."

"Ah!" Ell squeaked. "I didn't mean to say that… it's just…! I think it's a very nice bar! I swear!"

"Easy, kid!" Jackie laughed. "Hey, it's a joke! Whew! Lighten up!"

"It… it was?" Ell stared.

"Hey, but the strawberries really are organic." Jackie grinned. "Enjoy!"

"Thanks, Jackie," Fred said, chuckling as Jackie left to return to the bar.

"I'm terrible at this!" Ell snatched his drink and took a big sip. "It's super obvious I've been a friggin' hermit for years and have no idea how to people, isn't it?"

"Little bit," Fred teased. "Don't worry about it. Just have fun." He patted Ell's knee to help reassure him. "You like the drink? You can try somethin' else if you want."

"Thanks, but I really like these daiquiris. What about you?"

"Huh? Me what?"

"What did you like to drink?" Ell asked, gesturing to Fred's cup. "You know, before you went on your, ahem, big coffee kick."

"Beer," Fred replied longingly. "I really liked fuckin' beer. There was this one chocolate stout that used to come out every winter. Like a seasonal thing. Fuck, I coulda bathed in that shit, it was so good."

"Well, it'll be out soon, right? Maybe you can try to taste one?"

"Yeah. Plenty of other things I'd rather be tastin' right now, though."

"You mean me, right?"

"Yup."

Ell grinned. "Good. Because I already know exactly what I want to do after our date tonight."

Fred kissed Ell's cheek. "I ain't sayin' we need to leave early, but I am sayin' that I'm lookin' forward to it."

A scruffy patron brushed by their table on his way to light a candle at the shrine for Azaethoth. He said something under his breath, perhaps a small prayer, before returning to the pool tables.

Ell was watching him curiously, and he asked, "Is that guy a Sage?"

"Doubt it," Fred replied. "When people are down on their luck, I figure they're willing to try just about anything."

"There really aren't that many of us, are there?" Ell frowned. "And everybody thinks we're crazy. They think it's all a joke."

"Fuck 'em." Fred snorted. "We know."

"Do you really think the gods are all sleeping up in Zebulon?" Ell asked wistfully, gazing up at Azaethoth's monstrous visage. "Or do you think some of them are still awake somewhere?"

"Not all of them." Fred hesitated. "I've been meaning to tell you somethin'. It's pretty important. I care about you, and I trust you. That's not an easy thing for me to do, and I think you oughta know…."

"What is it?"

"About Lochlain. And him comin' back to life."

The redhead's slumber had been disturbed by the other patron coming over to visit the shrine, and he groaned loudly as he lifted up his head. "Jackie? Hey. Just one more."

"Water," Jackie argued. "You need to go home and sleep it off."

"I don't need to sleep nothin' o-fahfah because I am totally fine," the redhead protested. "I'm so very…." He had turned his head to glance behind him, and he froze when he saw Fred and Ell sitting at the table.

Ell noticed him staring, and he waved shyly.

The redhead screamed.

Ell jumped, startled, and he clung to Fred. "What the frig?"

"What the *fuck*?" Fred scowled. "Hey, buddy! The fuck is your problem?"

"Gotta go, gotta go so fast! Nope, don't want none of that!" The redhead was up, stumbling to the door. He hesitated, looked back at Ell, screamed again, and then bolted outside.

"Hey! What the fuck was that about, Jackie?" Fred demanded.

"That's just Ollie." Jackie shrugged, oddly calm for having a hysterically screaming patron. "He does that sometimes."

Fred noticed none of the customers seemed to be that bothered either. He hugged Ell, asking, "Hey, are you okay?"

"That was friggin' crazy!" Ell squeezed Fred's arm. "Like when Trip forgot to wipe off his feet when he went inside the gremlin's house and they all screamed at him! Wow. Wait, what were we even talking about?"

"I was gonna tell you about Lochlain."

"Oh! Yeah. I've been wondering about that." Ell leaned in close with wide eyes. "What really happened to him?"

"Well, Lochlain went out to a party on Dhankes and met this guy Sloane Beaumont a few hours before he was murdered."

"Wait, the same Sloane Beaumont who destroyed the Salgumel totem you guys told me about?"

"That's the one. See, it turns out that Azaethoth the Lesser was a really big fan of Lochlain's."

"The Azaethoth the Lesser? As in, the god?"

"You just relax and sit right there, Elliam Jimantha. I'm gonna tell you a fuckin' tale that's even crazier than the season four finale of *Legends of Darkness*."

"How are you gonna beat Trip finding out his long-lost brother is actually the one who left him the magical book because he was plotting to kill him so he wouldn't have to share their wealthy uncle's inheritance?"

"Heh. You'll see."

In great detail, Fred shared with Ell the exciting story of how Azaethoth took over Lochlain's body in his quest for revenge, culminating in the dramatic battle in which Sloane was gifted a sword of starlight to kill Tollmathan, the god who had murdered Lochlain and was trying to summon Salgumel to bring about the end of the world.

Ell had many questions, and Fred did his best to answer them all. When the epic tale was finally complete, Ell was silent for several moments as he visibly struggled to absorb the new information.

"So." Ell paused to gulp the last sip of his daiquiri. "The friend you told me about, Loch, is not Lochlain's twin, but he's actually Azaethoth the Lesser living in a ghoul copy of Lochlain's body. Sloane, the private investigator, is his lover, and he's a Starkiller because he friggin' killed a god?"

"Yup."

"Holy crap. I'm gonna need another drink."

CHAPTER 12.

FRED TOLD Ell he could have as many drinks as he wanted to, and that turned out to be only one more.

That was all it took for him to sway in his seat and for his speech to slur. Fred cut him off and urged him to eat something, but even two orders of extra cheesy fries weren't enough to ease Ell's turbulent stomach.

Despite Ell's protests, Fred paid the tab and helped him up from the table. They'd been having such a nice time, but there wasn't any point in staying if Ell didn't feel well.

They made it outside to Fred's truck before Ell got sick, and Fred rubbed his back while the fries and strawberry daiquiris got acquainted with the parking lot pavement.

"I lied," Ell wailed miserably between bouts of heaving. "I hate strawberry daiquiris. I *hate* them!"

"I'm sorry." Fred sighed. "I shoulda made sure you drank water or somethin'."

Ell retched again. "No water. Ugh, no anything ever."

Fred wished he knew a spell to help sober Ell up, but that was college kid shit he never learned. He would have to do it the old-fashioned way and let Ell spill his guts. "Come on. Let's get you some food."

"*Ugh*, I don't want food. I don't want anything except the sweet embrace of death to take me."

"Trust me. I'm stoppin' for cheeseburgers and fries—"

"Please! For the love of Great Azaethoth and all that is sacred to the old gods, no more fries!"

"Okay, just some burgers."

"I'm sorry I messed up our date," Ell fussed as Fred got him in the truck. "I was having so much fun. Even when that drunk guy screamed at us. And I wanted to do the sexy stuff that comes after a date."

"You didn't ruin anything," Fred promised. "It was your first time drinkin'."

"You're not mad?" Ell asked pitifully.

"Nope." Fred got in behind the wheel.

"Not even because we can't do the sexy stuff?"

"Not even a little." Fred cranked up the truck and then eased out into traffic to avoid jerking Ell around. "Let's get you some grub."

Ell managed to keep the burgers down and then passed out on the drive back to the jewelry store. Fred carried him inside, all the way upstairs, and lovingly tucked him into bed. After putting on another DVD of *Legends of Darkness*, he joined him and soon fell asleep himself.

The next morning, Fred woke up with Ell clinging to his side as usual. He smiled and gently reached down to pet Ell's hair.

He heard his phone buzzing and found it on the floor. It was a text from Lochlain.

How'd the date go? :)

good

Fred decided that was a fine reply. He scowled when there was an almost immediate text back.

That's it? Just good? Where are all the juicy details?!

Fred rolled his eyes.

it was fine

Robert and I are getting ready to come over. We'll be sure to knock this time haha! Want us to bring you guys anything?

Thoughtfully glancing at Ell, Fred typed another message out.

cabbage, rosemary, tomato juice. and soup in a cup. chicken flavor

He paused and then added one more.

please

Who's hungover?

who do u think

Ha! Hope he had fun! On our way!

Fred set his phone down, turning his attention back to cuddling Ell. He eased onto his side to face him, and Ell buried his face in Fred's chest.

"Never drinking again," Ell blearily mumbled, speaking directly into Fred's shirt.

"Awww, come on," Fred teased. "Not even one?"

"Never. My head hurts so friggin' bad."

Fred rubbed his back. "Mm, I've got the cure comin'."

"I wanna throw up. A lot. But that will make my head hurt more. But it also might make me feel better. But also worse… ughhh…."

"Trust me. I've got just the thing."

"I'm so sorry I messed up our date." Ell sighed. "I feel awful. And like, extra awful because I got so sick. I'm still trying to…." He paused. "Wait. You did tell me that Azaethoth the Lesser is hanging out in a ghoul copy of Lochlain's body, right?"

"Sure did."

"All that really happened?"

"Yup."

"I'm gonna go back to sleep."

"Go ahead."

Fred kept caressing Ell's back with soothing strokes, and he smiled when he felt him relaxing as he drifted off again. He held him until he heard a soft knock at the door and carefully peeled himself away to answer it.

"Hey," Lochlain greeted from the other side. He offered him a grocery bag. "Ell okay?"

"He's okay," Fred replied. "Rough night."

"But you guys had fun, huh?" Lochlain grinned.

"We had a nice time." Fred realized he was smiling too. "Finally told him about Azaethoth."

"Oh?" Lochlain was surprised. "How'd he take it?"

"Pretty well. Wants to meet him, so I guess you can have your stupid godly seal of approval."

"Hey." Lochlain frowned. "You know I only said that because I'm concerned."

Fred scowled.

"Fine. Go take care of your little lush. I'll be downstairs if you need anything else."

"Thanks."

"I'll get your measurements later."

"For what?"

"For your tuxedo, of course," Lochlain said with a grin, brightening back up. "It's a black-tie event. I'll need Ell's too."

"Ugh."

"It's gonna be great. See you later."

"Bye," Fred grunted. He closed the door, brought the bag over to the kitchenette, put the cold items away, and then went back to bed.

Ell was still asleep, but Fred didn't mind. It was easy to relax and enjoy the snuggling, and he was able to doze back off too. He woke again when Ell wiggled around and fussed grumpily.

"Good morning," Fred said.

"Morning," Ell mumbled, opening up his eyes with a groan. "Oh, I feel awful."

"It's okay, little one. I got just what you need." Fred kissed his forehead. "Stay put."

"Did I already say I'm never drinking again? Because I'm never drinking again."

"You did." Fred got out of bed and headed over to the kitchenette to prep the groceries.

"I really had so much friggin' fun, though," Ell called out. The sound of his own voice apparently hurt his head because he spoke much more softly when he said, "It was a great second date. Except the part where I threw up."

"That part was okay too." Fred poured water into the soup and heated it up with a softly whispered spell, but he drained out most of the liquid.

"Really? Even though I'm now on the brink of death as we know it?"

"Promise." Then, in a tall glass, Fred mixed up the cabbage, the juice, and rosemary. He whispered another spell to blend it together and heat that up too.

"What's that?" Ell lifted his head and sniffed the air cautiously.

"Soup and hangover juice," Fred replied, bringing the food over for his inspection.

Ell made a face, but he sat up to accept the juice. He took a sip and made an even bigger face. "Ugh, that's nasty."

"Drink up."

After swallowing a few more gulps, Ell switched over to the soup. "The noodles are kinda crunchy."

"They're supposed to be." Fred ruffled Ell's hair. "It'll help soak up all that crap in your stomach."

Ell took a few more bites, closed his eyes, and exhaled slowly.

"Better?"

"The room isn't spinning as hard." Ell managed a weary smile. "Thank you for taking such good care of me."

"That's what boyfriends do." Fred got the television going, sat back next to Ell, and watched him eat. He could smell the savory aroma of the noodles, the sweet herbs in the broth....

Damn, he missed eating.

"Do you want some?" Ell asked politely.

"I'm good."

"You're drooling."

"Yeah, well. I can't eat. You know that."

"You could try it!" Ell argued. "Your ghoul body would just absorb it, but maybe you could taste it like you did with the hot chocolate."

"No."

"Come on." Ell had a mischievous look in his eye, casually setting down the juice and his cup of soup. He pinched a small bit of noodles and dangled them in front of Fred's face.

"Quit." Fred swatted at his hand.

"Just try it!" Ell tried to push the noodles into his mouth.

"Hey!" Fred laughed as he grabbed Ell's wrist. "Don't you start."

Quickly transferring the noodles to his other hand, Ell jumped in Fred's lap and tried again. "Just one little teeny, tiny taste!"

"Stop it!" Fred laughed harder as he tilted his head back away from the wiggling noodles. "Thought you were sick? On the brink of death?"

"I'm feeling better! Now try these damn noodles!"

Fred curled his arm around Ell's waist and deftly swung him back on the futon beside him.

Undeterred, Ell got right back in Fred's lap. He lost some of the noodles as he made another attempt to feed him.

"Stubborn little shit!" Fred couldn't stop laughing, trying to push Ell away and groaning as a single noodle managed to make it in his open mouth.

"Ha! Victory is mine!" Ell cried triumphantly.

Fred flopped back against the futon and groaned as he clutched his chest. "Poison! I've been poisoned! Trip! Brave hero Trip! Avenge me!"

"Oh shush," Ell scolded, poking Fred's ribs. "You are not Lord Farris from *Legends of Darkness*. It was just some soup."

Fred finally gave in to the bit of food in his mouth and chewed. It was strange at first, but it was like riding a bike.

Chew, chew, chew, swallow.

And there....

"I can taste it," Fred said dumbly as he sat up. "I can fuckin' taste it."

"Here!" Ell offered him the juice. "Try this!"

Fred took a sip and nearly gagged. Yup, that was the stuff. It made sense with the way he'd been able to taste Ell's kisses and the boozy hot chocolate—and *other* things—but he hadn't thought to try food.

"How is it?" Ell asked.

"It's…." Fred shook his head, searching for the right words. "It's crap. It's cheap fuckin' crap, but fuck if it's not fuckin' amazing."

Grinning, Ell swooped in for a kiss. "What else do you want to taste? What do you like? Oh! Maybe we could get that beer! And cake! We could get you a big chocolate cake!"

"Right this second?" Fred smiled, cupping Ell's cheek and kissing him deeply. He let it linger, and he could feel Ell tremble as he pulled away. He kept their foreheads pressed together as he whispered, "All I want is you."

"Oh, Freddie," Ell sighed, the soup forgotten as he slid over to straddle Fred's hips. He hugged his neck and kissed him more earnestly.

Fred turned and pushed Ell down against the bed, sliding a hand up his shirt to stroke his side. As eager as Ell responded, Fred was hit with a pang of guilt. "Hey, are you really feeling okay?"

"Huh?" Ell's face was red as he unclasped his necklace to reveal his horns. "Okay for what?"

"For you and me… for the…." Fred paused. "The sexy stuff."

"Mmm, well, uh." Ell ran his hands through his hair and over his horns. "I'm feeling pretty good right now."

"No more puking?"

"I'm not gonna barf, I promise!" Ell pleaded. "I wanna do the sexy stuff that we were gonna do last night!"

Fred snorted.

"Come on." Ell batted his eyes and rubbed Fred's shoulders enticingly. "It's not like we had anything else that we needed to do today, right?"

"Well, we do need to work on that fire spell. If you're gonna incinerate the painting in a pinch, you're gonna need some practice."

"Yup. Totally. We should do that."

"Yeah."

"Okay, so show me!" Ell kissed him firmly. "Tell me what to do."

"The spell is called *urolus*." Fred grunted when Ell's teeth began to nibble on his throat. He swept his hand beneath Ell's shirt to tease his nipple. "You gotta picture the fire in your mind, focus on the complete and total destruction—"

"Mmm, got it." Ell dragged his teeth over Fred's jaw. "Urolus!"

The cup of soup on the coffee table promptly turned to ash.

"What in the actual fuck?" Fred stared in shock at the fine black powder left behind.

"There. I learned the spell." Ell grabbed Fred's cheek to bring him back so he could claim a kiss. "Mmm, now come on! I want you!"

Unable to resist the desire building between them, Fred chose to forget about Ell learning a spell in seconds or being able to burn something up without even touching it for now. The crush of Ell's hot mouth against his own was a fine distraction.

Ell managed to fling his shirt off in between bouts of their frenzied make-out, and Fred's soon joined it. When Ell's cock pressed against him, Fred grabbed him through his pants and squeezed.

Ell's responding cry was the stuff wet dreams were made of—soft and breathy, yearning for more.

"Fred," Ell moaned, shoving his pants down and bucking up into Fred's hand. "Please, I want you so bad!"

Fred wrapped his thick fingers around Ell's cock and stroked him. "Easy. I've got you."

"I want… I want more!" Ell's brow wrinkled up, and he panted haggardly as he twitched. "I want…."

"Like this?"

"Mmm… mmmph!"

Moving his hand faster didn't seem to help, prompting Fred to ask, "Tell me what you need."

Ell blushed, whining as he grabbed Fred's hand. His eyes were turning that spectacular shade of violet as he begged, "Please. I want… I want this."

"You want…?"

"You. Fingers. In me."

Fred's brain shut down momentarily.

"Freddie?"

"Yes, fuck yes," Fred said. "Just give me a second." He kissed Ell. "You stay there, and I'll be right back."

"What are you doing?"

"We need, you know… supplies."

"Lube?" Ell was already out of Fred's lap and headed over to his duffel bag before Fred could reply. He picked up the bundled-up towel. "I've got some."

Fred tried not to stare at the towel too hard.

Ell got back in Fred's lap, setting the towel next to them. He reached inside—not yet revealing what toy was lurking within—and presented Fred with a bottle of strawberry-flavored lubricant. "Will this work?"

"Absolutely." Fred grabbed Ell and stretched him out in the middle of the bed, whisking his pants and underwear off. Once he had Ell naked, Fred paused to admire him and was surprised by a strange thump in his chest.

Ell was stunning.

With the sunlight pouring in from the window, Ell's horns and hair were practically glowing, and he looked absolutely divine.

"What is it?" Ell laughed nervously. "Why are you staring at me like that?"

"Because you're beautiful," Fred replied.

Ell smiled bashfully, and he patted the space next to him. "Come on. Show me how beautiful you think I am."

Fred stripped out of his pants and then kneeled between Ell's thighs, bowing his head for a passionate kiss. Ell's legs wrapped around him and made him shiver, their hands roaming down every inch of each other's bodies. He turned his head to catch Ell's throat with a teasing little bite. "Just you wait, little one."

Ell squealed happily and groaned as Fred began to smooch down his chest and stomach. "Mmm, Freddie… what are you doing?"

"Trust me," Fred said, licking coyly up the shaft of Ell's cock. "There's somethin' else I wanna taste before I get my fingers in you."

"Freddie?" Ell gasped. "You're… you're gonna… down there?"

"Uh-huh."

"Oh, by all the gods…."

"Is that okay?" Fred asked, parting Ell's thighs wider.

"Yup, that, so okay, so good, so very good! Oh—!" Ell's voice cracked when Fred's tongue first lapped over his hole. "That, yup, that, that, that! More of that please!"

Pushing Ell's hips up, Fred smothered his face between his cheeks as he hungrily licked and sucked. He lavished Ell's hole with long strokes of his tongue, lapping around it in wide circles.

Ell tasted warm, hot, and Fred couldn't get enough. He ignored his own aching cock for now, occasionally grinding down into the bed for relief. He wasn't worried about getting his nut—all he wanted was to make this good for Ell.

Fred thrust his tongue forward with firm strokes, sliding his thumbs inward to gently pull at the tender skin around Ell's hole. He could feel him opening up, and he pushed his tongue in, growling low.

One of Ell's legs came up on Fred's shoulder, his back arching off the bed as he groaned. He kept on panting and crying out, offering a long stream of breathless praise, "Yes, Freddie! You feel so good, so damn good! I love it! Please don't stop!"

His words dissolved into incoherent moaning, and Fred glanced up to see Ell was jerking off. Fred watched Ell's feverish stroking before diving down to push his tongue back inside of him.

"Mmm, close," Ell whimpered, his heel hitching along Fred's spine. "Ah, mmm, so friggin' close! I'm—oh! Freddie!" His voice was now shrill with alarm. "The things! The tentacles!"

Fred stopped to look, and he could see two small purple tips emerging from just underneath the base of Ell's cock. He gingerly bumped one with his nose. "Huh. So that's where them things come out from."

"What, what should I do?" Ell had frozen.

"They feel good, right?" Fred boldly ran his tongue over the tentacle tips.

Ell gasped, and the tentacles grew, unfurling from somewhere deep inside of his body. They were now as long as his cock, and he wrapped his trembling hands around them, giving himself a little squeeze. "F-fuck… yeah. They feel really, really good."

"Then keep on touchin' 'em." Fred licked from the base of the tentacles back down to Ell's hole. "You look fuckin' sexy as hell playin' with yourself like that."

"R-really?" Ell squeezed again, and the tentacles suddenly curled around his cock. "Oh fuck. Oh gods." The tentacles were jerking Ell off, working together in firm strokes, and Ell was sobbing. "That, oh *fuck*!"

"Fuck." Fred couldn't believe what he was seeing, and wow, it was *hot*.

"Freddie!" Ell pleaded. "I'm so cl-close! Please! Do the thing, do that thing again!"

Fred obediently dropped down and thrust his tongue back into Ell's hole. It only took a few licks before he heard and felt Ell climax. Fred was coming right with him before he even knew what was happening, his cock pulsing across the sheets beneath him as he kept licking and sucking at Ell's hole.

"Mmm, Freddie!" Ell patted the top of Fred's head. "Mercy!"

"Mmmph, sorry." Fred kissed Ell's thigh and wiped his mouth off with the back of his arm. He watched the tentacles release Ell's cock and then retreat back inside of him. Now that he was looking for them, Fred could see two tiny slits that at first glance appeared to be big pores.

"Wow." Ell flopped against the bed with his limbs splayed out in all directions. He was glistening with sweat and flushed down to his chest. "Friggin'… *wow*."

"Uh-huh." Fred grinned. "That was fuckin' awesome."

"Did you see what I did? My tentacle thingies? I could, like, I could actually control them. And I did *that*."

"I definitely saw, and it was the hottest thing I've ever fuckin' seen." Fred pulled himself up to snag a kiss.

"It was so friggin' good. And oh! That thing with your tongue!"

"Yeah?"

"That's really, *really* nice."

Fred chuckled. "Mm, so you like havin' your ass eaten out?"

"Ew! Don't say it like that!" Ell covered his face with his hands.

"Why? What's wrong with eating out your ass?"

"You make it sound all nasty!" Ell protested as he laughed. "Come on. There has to be some other way to say it."

"Mm, visiting the butt buffet?"

"Ugh!"

"Tushy tasting?"

"You're making it worse." Ell dropped his hands with a smirk. "You're so lucky you're cute."

Fred smooched Ell's cheek. "I'm glad you liked it. You still wanna do the, ahem, other thing? The finger thing?"

"Oh, definitely," Ell confirmed with a big grin. "As long as you promise not to call it something gross."

"No such promises."

"I was planning to get to that part, you know. I didn't mean to come so fast! It just, well, it just felt so good, and then my tentacle thingies were really into the tongue stuff."

"Tentacle thingies? Is that what we're callin' them?"

"Yes. Because you'd probably call them something icky."

Fred grinned.

"Don't you dare."

"I won't, I won't." Fred slid his fingers up into Ell's hair to pet one of his horns. "I am lookin' forward to seein' them again."

"Yeah?" Ell's eyes fluttered, his lips parting in a soft gasp. "Shouldn't take long."

Fred kept stroking around the horn's base, tracing where it erupted from Ell's scalp. "You just tell me when, and I'm all yours."

"What about now?"

"Already?" Fred barked out a laugh.

"Is that okay?" Ell pouted. "I'm just, well…." He gestured at his erection. "He has a mind of his own, you know."

"I've got you." Fred rolled off Ell onto his side, reaching for the lube. He slicked up his fingers, and the overly sweet scent of artificial strawberries filled his nose.

"What do I do?" Ell asked, still flat on his back and watching Fred intently. "Should I move, should I… what will make this good?"

"First of all, relax." Fred scooted close, urging Ell to turn on his side so Fred could press up against his back. "Let me take care of you. We'll go slow, okay?"

"Okay." Ell took a deep breath. "I trust you, Freddie."

Fred bowed his head for a kiss, holding it sweetly as he reached between Ell's legs. He found Ell's hole, still soft from his mouth, and he swirled the lube around it. Only after he was sure Ell was good and wet, he pressed in the tip of his finger.

Ell shivered, tensing immediately.

Fred pushed in a little deeper, and he only made it halfway before he met resistance. He shifted his weight, slipping his arm around Ell's shoulders so he could reach up to pet his hair. "Hey, you gotta relax."

"Trying," Ell whispered earnestly. "Feels weird. Good-weird. Just… different than what I'm used to. I have toys, okay? But this, this is just different."

"Do you want me to stop?"

"No! No, please keep going! I'm okay!" Ell took a deep breath. "I can totally do this."

Slowly, Fred thrust his finger. He waited until some of the anxious energy left Ell's body before pressing deeper. He took his time, carefully rocking in and out, and he was now able to fully insert a single digit.

Ell dropped his head back, moaning. "More... please...."

Fred paused to get more lube, maybe too much, and his fingers were dripping when he touched Ell's hole again. He pressed two inside now, and he watched Ell for any signs of discomfort.

Though his forehead wrinkled briefly, Ell let out an excited cry. He lifted up his leg, arching his ass up and grinding on Fred's hand. "Oh, by all the gods... oh, Freddie... oh fuck!"

Ell twisted his body over, pushing back until he was flush against Fred's chest. Fred cradled him close, slipping his arm around him and rubbing his stomach as his fingers continued to steadily pump in and out of his tight body.

His cock was unbelievably hard again, slipping between Ell's thighs. Ell squeezed his legs together, and Fred pushed forward with a lusty groan. Ell's skin was so hot, and the friction was incredible. Fred thrust in time with his fingers, delighted when Ell rocked back to meet him.

"There," Fred growled huskily. "Just like that... you're doing so fuckin' good." He sucked at Ell's shoulder, kissing up his neck and mouthing through his hair to get to his horns. "Feel good? You okay?"

"Good." Ell kneaded at the bed in front of him. "Mmmm, so good... oh, Freddie...."

Fred kissed the tip of his horn.

"Oh! Fuck!"

Fred kept his fingers thrusting inside of Ell's slick hole, stretching his other hand down to grab Ell's cock while continuing to suck at his horn. He was like a conductor at a symphony, using his entire body as an orchestra to bring out an opus of pleasure from Ell's writhing body.

Ell had given him his life back. Maybe it wasn't quite the miracle of Lochlain's resurrection, but Fred sure as hell felt alive. He could taste. He could smell. And by all the gods, the things he could feel—the silky sensation of Ell's most intimate parts against his fingers, the hot dribble of precome down his knuckles as he stroked him, and the click of his horns on his teeth as he kissed them.

Though these physical pleasures were mind-blowing all on their own, it was the intangible bliss that Fred found most exquisitely priceless. He could laugh again, he could smile, and he could hold this gorgeous creature in his arms knowing he was the source of it all.

There, as the rest of the world vanished around them, Fred could feel it....

His heart beat.

"Oh! Freddie!" Ell's tentacles were out now, one of them curling around his cock and the other sliding down to grab Fred's. "Mmm, yes!"

The grip of the tentacle was intense, and it tugged at Fred's cock between Ell's thighs as he kept thrusting. The one on Ell's dick had all but pushed Fred's hand away as it feverishly stroked, and Fred was left clutching Ell's hip as he tried to keep up. He fingered Ell's hole faster, and when he slipped in a third, Ell's entire body convulsed.

"Freddie!" Ell sobbed. "Coming! I'm coming!"

Fred worked him through his orgasm alongside the tentacle, moving his hand in tandem to wring out every last tremor of bliss. The squeeze of Ell's thighs around his cock and the tentacle's pulsating grip was too good to resist, and Fred's heartbeat throbbed in his cock as he came.

The erratic thumps dwindled as his orgasmic tremors left him, and he withdrew his hands to wrap his arms around Ell's waist. "Mmm, Elliam."

"My full name." Ell panted, grinning goofily. "Mm, must have been really good."

"Very good," Fred promised.

He didn't even know how to tell Ell how much this meant to him, how much *he* meant, and he hoped Ell could tell by the way he held him and kissed him that he was the most precious thing in the world to him.

"Your tentacle thingies are hot as fuck."

Not exactly romantic, but he did mean it sincerely.

"Thanks." Ell laughed. "Your thingies are hot as fuck too."

Fred chuckled, and he kissed Ell's shoulder.

"Is that what sex is like? Not that what we did isn't sex, but you know... uh, sex as in... going all the way?"

"Sort of." Fred struggled to answer. "It's different, but it's still good. You get to share yourself with another person. It's pretty cool."

"Pretty cool, huh?"

"Yeah, especially when you care about them. Like how I care about you." Fred hesitated. He'd never been good at this. "That's what makes what we do fuckin' special. Because… you're special to me."

"I would have taken anything you gave me, you know." Ell smiled. "This is so much more than I ever thought I could have. And the sexy stuff, well, that just makes it even better."

"I know just what you mean."

"Wanna snuggle and watch more *Legends*?"

"Sure. Unless you need more sexy stuff."

Ell pretended to think about it. "Mm, well, I guess I can wait. I mean, we do need to think about conserving our strength to save the world soon."

A flicker of dread settled in Fred's stomach, and his smile dipped. "Yeah, I guess we do."

As if sensing his anxiety, Ell cuddled closer. "But hey, that day isn't today, right? We still have plenty of time."

Fred snorted.

"Hey. What's with that face? Are you worried about the heist?"

"Yeah."

"Don't be," Ell said cheerfully. "Lochlain's got a really good plan, and we're gonna kick crazy cultist butt."

"And how many heists have you been on again?"

"Hey! Come on. What could possibly go wrong?"

"In my personal experience," Fred grumbled, "a whole fuckin' lot."

"Right." Ell cringed. "Death is pretty much the worst thing ever, but hey!" He grinned. "Look on the bright side."

"What?"

"Chances of that ever happening again are super slim!"

"I feel better already."

CHAPTER 13.

THE DAY of the auction had finally arrived.

The preceding days were a blur of reviewing blueprints, tuxedo changes, and plenty of steamy intimacy. Though they hadn't taken the very final leap in their love life, Fred was enjoying showing Ell everything else he had been missing out on.

Fred wasn't in any hurry. They had time.

And yet, time was such a fickle thing.

It had passed slowly for Fred since his death, dragging by in a miserable agonizing fog, but now it seemed to be zipping by in a blink. All too soon, they would be back in danger's crosshairs.

Though their mission was most noble, Fred didn't like that Ell was at risk.

Not one fucking bit.

He knew that getting the painting was important. It would hopefully deny a bunch of crazy assholes the chance of waking up Salgumel, who would certainly destroy the world.

That was fuckin' bad.

But Ell getting hurt….

Also bad.

Fred wished like hell that their pocket god would return to help, but neither Azaethoth nor Sloane were returning any prayers, messages, or phone calls. They were still off doing gods knew what in other worlds, leaving Fred and the others to go into this armed with only their mortal wits and magic.

Plus whatever the hell Ell was.

Ell seemed excited about the heist, and he was very vocal about being eager for a chance to help defend all of mankind. In private, to Fred, he also shared how much he was looking forward to participating in his first criminal caper.

He was up bright and early that morning and tried to drag Fred up with him right away. "Good morning! It's heist day! Wake up! It's time to get up!"

Grumbling, Fred went totally limp. He knew Ell couldn't move him. "It's too damn early."

"It's never too early to save the world!" Ell grunted as he struggled to move Fred. "Come on!"

Fred waited for Ell to stop pulling and then tugged on his arm, easily catching him off guard and sweeping him back into bed.

"Hey! No!" Ell laughed, kicking wildly. "It's not bedtime! It's wake up, take a shower, and get ready for heist time!"

"Technically, this is your fault," Fred accused. "I didn't used to sleep, you know. You brought this on yourself."

Ell groaned. "Freddieee!"

"Five more minutes."

"I'll touch your thing in the shower," Ell offered coyly.

"Mmmm…." Fred pretended to be lost in deep thought.

"With my mouth."

"I'm up."

Their shower was long, hot, and Fred knew exactly where to touch and pet to get Ell off in moments. The first climax would be quick to take the edge off, and then Fred would drag the second one for as long as possible.

Coaxing the tentacles out took some time.

Fred had learned that Ell had to be really worked up for the tentacles to make an appearance, although Ell claimed that he enjoyed their intimate time even without them. Fred saw it as a challenge, and he took great pride in being able to coax the tentacles out, and he loved how hard they could make Ell come.

His own ability to orgasm was intermittent, and that was fine. Even as a living, breathing man, it would have been impossible to keep up with Ell's insatiable appetite. There had been some times when no matter what they did, Fred wasn't able to finish.

When Ell daintily slipped down onto his knees to take Fred into his mouth as promised, however, there was no force in all of the universe that could stop Fred from coming.

After Fred had returned the favor and earned a visit from Ell's tentacles, they got out and put on the first season of *Legends of Darkness*. They'd finally made it through the entire series, and now it was time to start it over with director's commentary on.

Ell ate a quick breakfast and then cuddled with Fred on the futon, trading suggestions for what they could order for lunch. Since Fred could taste now, Ell was determined for them to share meals together. While Ell used his phone to sort through local take-out menus, Fred checked his messages.

Lochlain and Robert would be on their way later that afternoon. Robert would drop Lochlain off with the tuxedos and tickets to the auction while he went ahead to prepare cutting the power at the venue. They'd go in, mingle, and wait for the painting to come up for bidding.

Once it sold and that gavel came down, it was game on.

After they'd eaten and Fred had thoroughly enjoyed rekindling his love for egg rolls, Ell made another batch of his stoneskin potion. He waited until they knew Lochlain and Robert were on the way to drink it, and he had all the evidence cleared away by the time Lochlain was knocking at the door.

"Ding-dong!" Lochlain was wearing a black tuxedo and had slicked his hair back. He had a small case and a pair of garment bags. "Who's ready to play dress-up and commit some crime?"

"Me!" Ell waved from the futon.

Fred rolled his eyes. "All right. Let's get this over with."

"Aw, come on!" Ell laughed as he got up to grab his bag. "This is seriously the best part!" He kissed Fred's cheek before hurrying off to the bathroom to change.

"He's going to make an adorable little felon," Lochlain said with a wink.

"Robert got his tuxedo on too?" Fred grunted.

"No. You know I did try to get him one, but he didn't want it."

"What's the fuckin' point? He's gonna be sittin' in a van."

"But he could sit in a van and also look amazing," Lochlain pointed out.

Fred sighed and chose to move on. "Any idea what time the painting is going up?"

"It's one of the last items, scheduled for eight o'clock."

"What the fuck are we supposed to do until then?"

"Drink champagne, be fabulous, pretend to be filthy rich...." Lochlain glanced over Fred's shoulder as the bathroom door opened. "Enjoy the scenery."

Fred turned around to see Ell, and his jaw hit the floor.

Ell was a gorgeous vision in a soft pink velvet tuxedo, the top of his white shirt collar still undone allowing the scar on his throat to show.

He had the bow tie and matching cummerbund in his hands, grinning sheepishly. "Sorry, I didn't know how to put this part on."

"I think you look great just like that." Lochlain reached out to adjust Ell's collar, but he paused before actually making contact. "May I?"

"Uh, s-sure."

Fred watched cautiously. Even though Ell had taken the potion, it still made him nervous for anyone to get too close.

"Lochlain?" Ell flinched as Lochlain continued to unbutton his shirt a few inches. "Really? That much?"

"Yes, that much!" Lochlain insisted, now reaching for the case he'd brought with him. Inside was a selection of jewelry, and he picked out a long golden chain with a piece of rose quartz. "Here."

Ell hesitantly pulled it over his head, certainly being mindful of the other necklace he wore. The glittering chain dangled between the open folds of his shirt, drawing attention to the thin sliver of bared flesh.

Fred unconsciously licked his lips.

"Perfection," Lochlain declared, now turning his attention to Fred. "Go on! Get changed. Then it's your turn to get sparkly."

Fred stepped into the bathroom. Lochlain had a good eye for fashion, and he wasn't surprised to see his suit was black on black and a perfect fit. After putting it on, he came back out. "There. Done."

"Wow," Ell gushed, clasping his hands together. "Freddie... you look, you look friggin' amazing!"

Fred's face grew warm. "Thanks."

"Why, Freddie," Lochlain teased, batting his eyes. "You are positively radiant."

"Shut up."

"Come here." Lochlain took Fred's hand and shoved a glittering pinkie ring on. "There. Now you look nice and rich."

"Does this mean we're ready to go save the world?" Ell asked.

"Yes," Lochlain confirmed with a sly little wink, "and looking gorgeous as hell while we do it. Let's go!"

Downstairs they went, the trio opting to take a taxi to the venue and leave their personal vehicles behind. Fred was more than aware that his old truck would be way too recognizable should they encounter any of the cultists they'd run into before.

He held Ell's hand on the way over, enjoying the simple comfort of their fingers intertwining. Lochlain had no problem filling the drive with his usual chatter and joking around with Ell, but Fred was quiet.

The trip was giving him a chance to reflect on the last few weeks with Ell and what he hoped for the future. He wanted a life with Ell, no matter what that meant, and any chance for their relationship to grow was contingent on tonight's success.

After all, it would be pretty hard to build a life together with the end of the world looming over their heads.

Tonight had to be perfect.

He had to protect everyone, especially the man he loved.

Loved....

There it was.

That was the word for that strange tightness in his chest, the warmth taking up residence inside his once cold body, and for the way his heart beat anew whenever Ell was with him....

He had fallen in love with Ell.

It was fast, yes, but Fred knew he was hopelessly and madly—

"What is it?" Ell asked suddenly.

"Huh?"

"You're staring at me with the funniest look on your face." Ell smiled brightly. "Are you okay?"

That smile was fuckin' everything.

Fred smiled back, and he gave Ell's hand a squeeze. "It's nothin'. I'll tell you later." He glanced up as the taxi came to a stop. "We're here."

The auction was being held at the Williams Building, a historic monstrosity that was once a hotel before it was gutted and transformed into a conference center. It was set up for the glamorous evening with spotlights, a red carpet, and valets at the ready to open their doors.

Lochlain got out of the taxi first, and the valet offered a hand to Ell to assist him. Fred used the other passenger-side door to exit and then walked around the cab to offer Ell his arm.

Ell was staring up at the brightly lit building with wide eyes. "Whoa."

"Remember," Fred said quietly, "you're filthy rich. You see stuff like this all the time."

"Right!" Ell blinked out of his stupor and took Fred's arm. "Sorry! It's just so friggin' cool!"

"Cool, huh?"

"Very friggin' cool."

Ell did his best not to look completely starstruck once they were inside, but he failed miserably. He couldn't stop staring at the chandeliers, the lavish wallpaper, or the fancy finery of the other guests.

It was charming to see him so awed, and Fred grabbed some champagne from a passing waiter. "Here."

"Oh! Is this the bubbly juice kind or the alcohol kind?"

"Pretty sure it's alcohol kind. You ain't gotta drink it, but just hang on to it."

"What for?"

"You look like Trip did when he first went to visit the goblin kingdom."

"Oh." Ell nervously took the champagne. "I swear, I'm trying not to look crazy. It's all just so pretty."

"It's okay." Fred guided Ell through the crowd. "We're gonna lay low, blend in, look around a bit. Just be chill."

"I can be chill." Ell held his head high. "So very cool. Chill as the Ice King. Yeah, I got this!"

Despite Ell's obvious excitement, no one seemed to pay them much attention. There were enough people here that they could easily blend in. Fred saw Lochlain chatting up some of the other guests, his natural charm in full effect as he told some ridiculous story about being a real estate mogul's sole heir.

Fred chose to focus on Ell and enjoy how tickled he got over the smallest things. Being able to safely brush by someone was downright thrilling for him, cheese trays were the most amazing thing he had ever seen, and he simply could not stop smiling.

"This is the best thing ever," Ell announced over a large plate of crackers and dip he had taken from a waiter. "I mean, I know we're waiting for the auction thingies, and this is all very super important, but I'm having so much fun!"

"I get it," Fred said. "You ain't never even been to a party before. This is a big deal. With that potion, we can do this kinda stuff more often."

"I can't wait." Ell munched on another cracker. "Mmm, have they started the auctions yet?"

"Yeah." Fred caught Lochlain's eye from across the room and saw him nod. "Almost time." He winked. "When you're done with your third course, we should probably head over."

"Fine." Ell pouted, protectively clinging to the plate. "It's gonna be in that big fancy ballroom, right?"

"Yeah." Fred paused when another familiar face caught his attention. He grabbed Ell's arm, dropping his voice as he said, "Don't freak out, but we got company."

Even with the side of his face bandaged up, it was definitely Jeff. He hadn't seen Fred or Ell yet, and Fred hurriedly steered Ell to the ballroom to meet up with Lochlain.

"Company?" Ell gulped down the last of his food and handed off the empty tray to a passing waiter. He glanced over his shoulder, and he squeaked when he also got a glimpse of Jeff. "If he's here, that means—"

"Others probably are too," Fred cut in.

"Oh *fuck*," Ell hissed.

"It's fine," Fred promised, patting Ell's back as they slid through the crowd. "Everything is chill."

People were gathered in the lavish ballroom at the front of the stage where a chatty auctioneer was rambling out a string of bids on—Fred's best guess—a gilded chamber pot.

Lochlain was with his cluster of guests, still chatting as the bids soared, but he must have recognized the urgent expression on Fred's face because he excused himself to join them.

"What's wrong?" he asked.

"That asshole who shot me is here." Fred swung his arm protectively around Ell. "We ain't alone, if you know what I mean."

"Hear that?" Lochlain spoke to Robert through his earpiece. He listened for a moment. "There's no sign of anything going on outside for now. We stick to the plan."

"All right, ladies and gentlemen!" the auctioneer called out, drumming his gavel along the edge of his podium. "If I may have your attention, we're about to begin bidding on the next item. Lot four-oh-one, I repeat, this is lot four-oh-one.

"This is one of the rare and tantalizing paintings personally commissioned by Lord Collins in 1669. Named for the ancient Sagittarian holiday of Dhankes, he called this one *Ever Grateful For the Throbbing Splendor of Dhankes*."

Fred's jaw tightened.

"Shall we start the bidding at ten thousand dollars?" the auctioneer called. "Do I hear ten thousand for this lovely piece of priceless art?"

"Fifteen!" a voice shouted out, its owner pushing his way to the front of the crowd.

It was Jeff.

"Well," Fred muttered, "we know now that they wanted the money to buy the paintings."

"We do?" Ell asked.

"Why else would they bid on it?" Fred pointed out. "If they were gonna steal it, they wouldn't fuckin' bother."

"I'm going up," Lochlain said quietly. "The side door you need is right over by the stage. Leads into a hallway and outside—"

"Yes, into the fuckin' alley where Robert is gonna be waiting for us," Fred grumbled. "We got it."

Lochlain clapped his hand on Fred's shoulder and winked at Ell. "See you two on the other side."

As Lochlain slinked his way toward the stage, the bidding became incredibly fierce. It was in the hundreds of thousands now, and Fred was delighted to see Jeff panicking.

"Cultist piggy bank musta run out," Fred noted, watching Jeff get outbid for the final time and leave in an angry huff.

"Maybe he won't bother us?" Ell asked hopefully.

"They want it bad enough, they're gonna try. We gotta be quick." Fred saw Lochlain hovering a few feet away from the stage as the bidding came to a close. "You ready?"

"Ready." Ell took a deep breath and stood up straight.

"Sold!" the auctioneer bellowed, raising his gavel to swing it down with a deafening crack.

The lights went off, and several guests screamed and gasped in confusion. Fred held on to Ell as they got jostled by people rushing, trying to use their cellphones as lights to move around.

"Uh, ladies and gentlemen!" the auctioneer called. "Please remain calm! We'll sort this out soon!"

Lochlain brushed by Fred, Ell gasped, and then Lochlain was very loudly clearing his throat.

"Ahem!" Lochlain was grinning like a fiend when the lights came back on, holding the picture frame under his arm. "I'm sorry for the inconvenience, but this is coming with me."

"Security!" the auctioneer screamed. "Someone get security in here right now! Call the police!"

"Is that really what we're going to do here? All I want to do is borrow it! For a very long time!" Lochlain kept the frame tilted so at a glance no one would see that the painting was gone.

That was nearly folded in Ell's bleeding hand—wait, why was Ell bleeding?

"What happened?" Fred asked worriedly, looking over the small cut.

"Lochlain caught me with the frame, but I'm okay!" Ell insisted.

"Let's go." Fred grimaced. He knew this meant the potion was wearing off, and they needed to get out of here. He swung his arm around Ell and walked very purposefully toward the exit as Lochlain continued to taunt the crowd.

"I really don't think it's worth two hundred thousand whatever it was you were going to pay!" Lochlain was saying. "It's very ugly."

"Drop the painting, sir!" a security guard demanded as he rushed up to intercept Lochlain.

"Ah, there's my cue!" Lochlain turned and dipped out of sight with a whole team of security guards now hot on his tail.

Fred and Ell made it to the side door and then slipped out into the hallway. As soon as the door shut behind them, Fred urged, "Go on! Toast it!"

"Got it!" Ell stared at the painting. It burst into flames, crumbling to ash between his fingers. "Ha! We did it! We did it, Freddie!"

"Fuck yeah!" Fred swept Ell into a heated kiss, swinging him around in the air. "My fuckin' hero!"

Laughing, Ell hugged Fred and kissed him eagerly. "Ha! We're both heroes! Just like when Trip and the Goblin King saved the unicorns by getting them the magical jam to cure their horn fungus!"

"Yup. Just like that, except less sticky." Fred set Ell back down and grabbed for his hand. "Mmm, let's get goin'. Robert should be waitin'."

"We really did it! We saved the friggin' world!" Ell exclaimed as they rushed through the exit door together. He pumped his fist in the air, laughing, "We're heroes! We're amazing! We're—!"

"We're fucked," Fred said flatly.

It was not Robert waiting for them.

It was Jeff.

There were at least a dozen men with him. They had the street blocked, guns drawn, and Jeff was glaring at Fred and Ell both furiously.

Ell's celebratory cheering ended abruptly, and he clung to Fred's arm. "Oh no."

"Well, well, look who it is," Jeff sneered. "The ghoul who just won't fuckin' die and his little bitch." He turned his fury on Ell, snapping, "I don't know what the fuck you did to my face, but I'm definitely gonna get some payback for this."

Fred pushed Ell behind him, flexing his fingers and hissing a spell to call upon a raging inferno. He would burn all of them to a crisp, every last one of them! They would be absolutely roasted.

Except....

There was no fire, no burning—only the click of the guns being aimed right at him and Ell.

It had to be the silencing wards. They weren't far enough from the building to negate its effects.

Shit.

The door they had exited through could only be opened from the inside, so there was no way to get back in.

Shit.

"Where's the painting?" Jeff demanded. "We know your little buddy only got away with the frame. Very clever, by the way."

Fred didn't say a word, dread pulling at his stomach as he tried to put together how they already knew that. He hoped Lochlain was safe.

And where the fuck was Robert?

He was supposed to be here in the alley waiting for them. Something had to have gone seriously wrong, and now all Fred could focus on was getting Ell out of here safely.

"Ell," Fred warned, "no matter what happens—"

"Freddie." Ell squeezed Fred's arm. "No, you can't do this!"

"Listen to me," Fred snapped. "Stay behind me, okay?"

"No!" Ell tried to pull Fred back against the door. "I still have the stoneskin potion, I'm safe—!"

"It's wearing off! Now stay back! I'm going to—!"

"Shut up already! We'll take the fuckin' painting off your corpses!" Jeff roared, waving at the other men. "Waste these fuckin' idiots!"

"*No!*"

It was Ell who screamed as the bullets fired, and Fred grimaced in pain as they pierced his skin. The agony was new, fiercely hot, and black fluid poured out of his chest.

Fred staggered to one knee, his arms still up in an attempt to shield Ell. Another barrage of bullets slammed into him, making his whole body spasm and jerk. More fluid gushed out of his mouth, warm and thick.

No, not just fluid. It was blood. It was bright red blood gushing out of his body. This wasn't supposed to be happening. This wasn't right.

Fred could hear Ell crying, and he wished he could tell him how much he loved him.

"Stop it!" Ell screamed angrily, lunging forward at the gunmen. "Stop it right now! You're killing him! Stop!"

Fred was too weak to grab him, and he watched in horror as Ell ran right at the cultists. He tried to yell, but he kept choking on his own blood and could only gurgle, "Ell… no…!"

Bullets were hitting Ell, but he didn't stop.

He kept going.

Fred couldn't tell if he was hurt or not, staring as Ell began to glow with a brilliant light. It was prismatic, all of the colors and somehow none of them at the same time, totally enveloping Ell and blinding Fred.

The cultists scattered, and they tried to flee to the street. A magical wall came up to block them off, trapping them inside the alley. The very ground beneath their feet was trembling, the streetlights exploded with loud pops, and Ell's desperate screams became a monstrous roar.

All of the cultists' faces began to turn black, viscous fluids spilling out from their eyes and mouths as they rotted from the inside out. They were putrefying in mere seconds, their bodies collapsing in wet heaps with only their clothes left behind in slick pools on the ground.

Fred saw something glittering, a quick flash of silver catching the bright aura exuding from Ell's body. He knew it was Ell's necklace because now he could see his horns—but they were bigger.

Way fuckin' bigger.

They had grown into massive twisting branches, arching up from his head and glowing bright white with a dazzling halo of stars hovering above them. It was both terrifying and beautiful in the midst of the oozing destruction.

As the last body fell in a sopping puddle, Ell turned to face Fred. His eyes were such a vivid shade of purple that it hurt to look at them, and the stars in his halo were pulsating with violent sparks.

"Ell…." Fred whispered.

He could have never imagined that he would see him in such a state. Ell had killed those men, completely destroyed them, and his lips were twisted up in an eerily satisfied sneer. There was not a trace of the sweet young man Fred knew, something hateful and vile now wearing the face he loved so dearly, and Fred's heart ached.

His beautiful and precious Ell looked like a monster.

Fred suddenly collapsed, and Ell snapped out of his strange spell. He ran over to Fred's side, grabbing his shoulder and frantically shaking him.

"Oh! Fred! No, no, no!" Ell sobbed, trying to pull Fred into his lap and pressing his hands against his chest. "No! Wait! You can't die!"

Fred stared up at Ell, his vision blurring. He could see that Ell's horns had shrunk back down and the halo of stars was gone, but he couldn't focus on his face. He could feel Ell's magic rushing through him, but he was cold, clammy, and slipping away.

It still didn't make any sense. He was a ghoul, and mortal weapons shouldn't have been enough to wound him like this. Then again, ghouls weren't supposed to be able to bleed either.

Or laugh.

Or feel their hearts beat.

Or fall in love with beautiful boys with horns.

"It's okay." Fred coughed through another splash of blood. "Ell… it's okay. I love you."

"Huh?" Ell's eyes widened and immediately filled with fresh tears as Fred's words sank in. "Oh no! Don't you *dare*! You don't get to say that and friggin' die on me! I love you! I love you too, you big friggin' jerk!"

"Oh, Ell." Fred groaned in pain, the magic working through his skin and deep inside of his body. His muscles and skin were being ripped apart and pulled back together, and it was so painful that he began to scream in agony.

"Hold on!" Ell pleaded. "Please! I'm almost done! Don't you do it! Don't you friggin' die!" He held Fred close and pressed a fierce kiss to his lips.

There was an intense flood of energy, and Fred found he had the strength to reach up and touch Ell's face. He kissed him hard, not even caring about the rich taste of blood between their lips. All that mattered was hanging on to this moment for as long as he could.

The pain was leaving him, a final pulse of magic washing over him from head to toe. He clung to Ell, terrified that he might somehow vanish away in a cloud of stars, and he whispered, "I love you, Ell."

"I love you." Ell whispered back, sniffing softly. "Oh, Freddie, I love you so much…." His eyes fluttered, and his hands clenched around the lapels of Fred's jacket. "Freddie, oh, I'm sorry…."

"Ell?" Fred patted Ell's cheek, and his stomach twisted when Ell's skin turned cold. "Are you okay?"

"I'm just so…." Ell's eyes rolled back, and then he fell forward.

Fred scrambled to sit up and grab Ell so he could pull him into his lap. "Hey. Hey! Come on now. You don't get to fuckin' save me and then try and die on me. Hey! Who's the jerk now, huh?"

Though he was breathing, Ell didn't respond. He was limp, freezing cold, and trembling all over.

Fred couldn't summon a warming spell so close to the building because of the silencing wards. He had to move. He stood, sweeping Ell into his arms and then heading out of the alley. He had to get somewhere safe and fast.

As he reached the dumpster near the end of the alley, he was startled by *Jeff* suddenly bolting out from behind it.

Son of a bitch!

Fred watched him flee out into the street and then vanish out of sight. He'd worry about that bastard later.

All that mattered right now was saving Ell.

Headlights flooded Fred's vision, and he snarled as a big van pulled up right in front of him. The tires made a wet squelching sound as it ran over the puddled remains of the cultists. It was so close that Fred could have kicked the bumper.

"Hey there, strangers! Long time, no see!" Lochlain popped his head out from the passenger side, sporting a bloody cut on his forehead and a cheeky grin. His mirth vanished when he saw the state of Fred and Ell, asking anxiously, "Oh, by all the gods… what happened?"

"No time," Fred growled as he hurried over to the sliding door. "We've gotta fuckin' go! Now!"

CHAPTER 14.

"I TRIED to stay parked in the alley, but there were two security guards out there taking a damn smoke break!" Robert hit the gas, speeding back to the jewelry store. "I had to leave before they started asking questions!"

"What took you so fuckin' long to get your ass back here?" Fred demanded as he took off his jacket to wrap around Ell. He tried to keep Ell's horns hidden in his lap, but he wasn't sure if Lochlain or Robert had already seen them. "We almost fuckin' died!"

Ell was still unconscious and trembling, ice-cold to the touch.

"I'm sorry!" Robert cried, jerking the wheel hard as he took a turn too fast. "I saw Lochlain almost get hit by a car, and I stopped to get him—!"

"Yes, yes!" Lochlain cut in. "I zigged when I should have zagged, no big deal! Now—" He snapped his head back to look at Fred. "—what the hell happened to you guys? Was it the cultists?"

"Yeah," Fred growled. "They shot me up, and…." He trailed off, faced with the reality of having to tell Lochlain and Robert what Ell had done.

He didn't even fully understand what he had seen.

"And?" Lochlain pressed urgently.

"And…." Fred didn't want to lie. "And Ell took 'em out. Okay? They're all dead except that Jeff fucker. He ran the fuck off. Ell saved my fuckin' life. And him healing me hurts him, all right? He needs to get warm."

"Okay. What can I do?"

"Help me get him warm," Fred pleaded.

Lochlain immediately took off his jacket to pass it back to Fred.

Fred wrapped it around Ell, and he summoned all of his magic to put into the warming spell. He closed his eyes as he held Ell against his chest, whispering in his ear, "Come on, baby. Come on, Ell. I love you. Do you hear me? I fuckin' love you."

Feeling a hand on his shoulder, Fred looked up to see Lochlain offering him an encouraging smile. A rush of new energy pulsed through Lochlain's touch, and Lochlain was also holding Robert's hand.

They were both funneling their magic into Fred to help power his spell, and he could feel Ell's shivering subside. He still hadn't woken up, but his breathing didn't seem as labored. He looked almost peaceful.

"Is he gonna be okay?" Robert asked.

"He will be," Fred insisted, not sure who he was trying to convince more—himself or Robert. "I've seen him fall out like this before. I just gotta keep him warm and let him rest."

Lochlain looked like he had a thousand questions, but he said nothing. He continued to share his power all the way back to the jewelry store, and he was there to open the doors for Fred to pass through as he carried Ell upstairs.

"Do you need anything?" Lochlain asked, watching Fred get Ell bundled into bed.

"No." Fred realized he probably sounded harsh, and he tried to soften his tone when he added, "No, thank you. I'm good. I'm just gonna try and get him warmed up, okay?"

"I saw his horns," Lochlain said quietly.

Fred froze, glancing over his shoulder at Lochlain. He kept his expression neutral even as his guts tried to clench up. "And?"

"He's been using a glamour charm," Lochlain went on. "We'll have to get him a new one."

Fred was relieved that Lochlain seemed to be taking his discovery so well, and he nodded. "Yeah. He don't like people seein' 'em."

"Fred." Lochlain's voice indicated he was struggling with what he wanted to say, and he fell silent.

"What?" Fred grunted impatiently.

"What is he?" Lochlain blurted out.

"I already told you, I don't know." Fred's temper flared. "Can we talk about this later? Like, oh, I don't know, how about fuckin' never?"

"Fred, I'm sorry—"

"The painting is fuckin' history, and so are all those fuckin' nutbags—"

"Yeah, how? Did you see what happened to them?"

"Who cares?" Fred ignored the vivid memory of the cultists melting into puddles.

"I care because I saw a bunch of weird piles of empty clothes and no people. Can you explain that? How did he do it?"

"The world has been fuckin' saved again. What else fuckin' matters?"

"You! *You* matter! I'm trying to save you now!" Lochlain hissed, clenching his hands in frustration.

"Save me?" Fred's heart dropped into his gut. "Save me from Ell? You really think he's dangerous?"

Lochlain's silent glare spoke volumes.

"He's the man I love, and you ain't gotta worry about anything else." Fred turned his back on Lochlain and gritted his teeth. "Now get the fuck out."

"Fred—"

"We'll be gone as soon as Ell wakes up."

"Come on!" Lochlain pleaded. "You've gotta see that this is a little crazy!"

"What I see is you carrying about five tons of guilt about lettin' me burn, and now you're lookin' for any fuckin' chance to save me to make yourself feel better," Fred barked, whirling around to face Lochlain.

Startled by Fred's vicious words, Lochlain took a step back. "That's not true."

"No?" Fred scoffed. "Keep tellin' yourself that."

"Whatever." Lochlain hung his head. "I'm going. We'll talk later when you've calmed down." He started to walk out, but he paused. "I'm sorry, Fred. I'm just worried. I love you."

Too angry not to say anything he might regret, Fred turned back around to check on Ell. He knecled beside the bed and then gently placed his hands on his chest as he whispered the warming spell to soothe the lingering trembles.

The door shut, announcing Lochlain's departure, and Fred kept his attention focused on Ell. He did his best to ignore his anger and stretched out on the futon beside him to hug him close.

He could feel an awkward jerking in his chest, now recognizing it as the erratic presence of his heartbeat. Yelling at Lochlain must have stirred it up, and he grumbled in frustration.

His growl must have been particularly loud because he felt Ell stirring.

"Mmm… Freddie?" Ell's eyes fluttered open, and there was a flash of purple before they faded back to blue.

"I'm here." Fred stroked Ell's hair, his irritation quenched by a flood of relief. "I'm right here."

"Oh, Freddie!" Ell groaned weakly. "Are you okay? What happened?"

"You don't remember?"

"No." Ell looked afraid, and his hands twisted into the front of Fred's shirt. "There were all these men in the alley, and I saw the guy with the face I messed up, uh, Jeff or whatever, and they were going to shoot us."

"Hey." Fred rubbed Ell's back. "It's fine. We're safe now."

"Freddie," Ell whimpered as his eyes glistened. "I don't know what I did, but… but it feels like I did something awful." He burst into tears, pleading desperately, "Tell me! Freddie, tell me, what did I do?"

"You saved me," Fred replied firmly, wiping at Ell's cheeks. "You fuckin' saved my life. That's what you fuckin' did."

Ell began to sob, and Fred held him as tightly as he dared. He hated to see Ell so distressed, and he didn't know if the truth would help or upset him more. He kissed his horns, petted his hair, and wished he knew what the hell to say to make him feel better.

Ell seemed to have some ideas.

After he wiggled out of the jackets bundled around him, Ell pushed himself back into Fred's arms and kissed him. It was hot, deep, and his hands were on Fred, roaming urgently across his chest and his thick belly.

The touch of Ell's lips lit a fire inside of Fred's loins, and he crushed Ell against his chest. All he could think about now were those terrifying moments when he thought he was going to lose Ell before he got to tell him how much he loved him.

He was angry with Lochlain for ever suggesting that this precious soul could be a danger, and he kissed Ell with everything he had. Their bodies desperately pressed together, Ell grinding close, and Fred rolled him over on his back as the kiss continued to heat up.

Moaning softly, Ell spread his legs and hugged Fred's shoulders. Fred turned his attention to Ell's throat, sucking along the tender skin there as Ell began to pant loudly. Fred pulled back before he could leave a mark, but he grazed his teeth along Ell's jaw as he made his way up to his horns.

He could hardly believe how they'd shrunk back down after seeing them in their grander form before. He kissed each one, listening to Ell gasp. He didn't care what Ell really was. It didn't make two fucks.

Ell wasn't any more of a monster than he was, and Fred loved him so much.

"I remember," Ell whispered, his voice hoarse, his fingers clinging to Fred's back. "Freddie, I remember…."

"What?" Fred asked worriedly.

"That you…." Ell's face was a brilliant scarlet, blotchy from crying and their intense passions. "You said you loved me."

"Yeah?" Fred smiled. He was glad the memory was a happy one. "Probably because I did."

"Wanna know a secret?" Ell shyly bit his lip.

"Sure."

"I love you too." Ell pulled Fred back in for another hot kiss.

Heart pounding, Fred eagerly kissed back. The rapid thump in his chest was going to take some getting used to, but he never wanted it to end. He rolled his hips, groaning when his cock met Ell's, and they were both so hard. Even through their pants, the friction was so good, and he kept going, setting a slow and pleasurable rhythm.

Though Ell was clearly weak from exhausting his powers earlier, his patience was lacking. He kept bucking up against Fred, squeezing his legs around his waist and trying to increase the pace.

"Hey, hey," Fred grumbled affectionately, nuzzling Ell's cheek and trying to calm him down. "What's the hurry?"

"I wanna do it," Ell said. "The sex stuff. All of it. Right now."

"Wait, what?"

"I wanna do it, Freddie."

"Uh." Fred's brain shut down.

"I love you." Ell's hands held Fred's face as he pressed a sweet kiss to his lips. "I love you so much. I don't wanna go another second without knowing what it's like, what it would be like to finally make love to you."

"Ell." Fred hesitated. "We don't have to do this right now. You were literally unconscious just a few fuckin' minutes ago. We can wait."

"I don't want to," Ell said stubbornly, already fighting to peel himself out of his clothes. "The goblin king never got a chance to get his happy ending. He kept waiting until it was too late, but not me! I'm ready."

"Fuck, Ell." Fred watched as Ell stripped down in seconds, now fully naked and staring up at him expectantly. He did his best to think clearly and ensure he was using the right organ to make this decision.

It wasn't that he didn't want to. He and his cock were in full agreement that they *definitely* wanted this, but he was worried. He didn't know if he could do this. He'd been able to do all kinds of other physical things with Ell, but this would be the ultimate test.

He met Ell's beautiful bright eyes, and he knew there was no way he could refuse. They were going to make love, and Fred was going to do everything he could so Ell's first time would be incredible.

Although he had no idea if Great Azaethoth or any of the other gods could hear him, he said a quick prayer anyway for this to be perfect.

"I'll make it so good for you." Fred sealed his promise with a kiss. He began to undress, aided by Ell's very impatient fingers until all of their clothes were strewn across the floor.

Ell was trembling with excitement as he kissed Fred's broad shoulder, completely revitalized by their brewing passions. Fred couldn't help but notice how small and vulnerable Ell seemed now, anxiously wiggling beneath him and looking up at him like he'd hung every star in the sky.

"I've got you," Fred swore, reaching for the bottle of lubricant. He was surprised by how hard his hands were shaking as he fought to get it open, and the fresh scent of strawberries filled the air as it gushed over his fingers.

Ell giggled, and he tried to clasp a hand over his mouth to stifle the sound.

"Yeah, yeah, very funny," Fred griped, rolling his eyes playfully. He reached down to rub his fingers up against Ell's hole and slowly slid one inside.

"Mmm, sorry. It smells really nice, though!" Ell was still laughing, but his lips parted with a sharp gasp when Fred pressed a second finger inside of him. His lashes fluttered, and he let out the most delicious moan.

They'd done this before, many times, and Fred knew exactly how to curl his fingers to make Ell's thighs quiver. He sought out that sensitive little spot within, pushing against it with firm strokes as he sucked along Ell's collarbone.

Ell's responding cries of pleasure were a sweet symphony of sound, and he couldn't stop talking, rambling urgently, "There, there, that's it, right there! Oh, Freddie! Yes, yes, yes, that's it! Please don't stop, don't stop, don't stop—!"

Fred never tired, relentlessly pounding his thick fingers in and out of Ell's wet hole. He could tell by the way Ell was twitching and begging that he was close, and he wanted to get him off quickly. Knowing Ell's insatiable libido, this was just going to be a warm-up, something to soften the edge before they got to the main event.

Before they made love.

Such flowery language would have once made Fred grimace, but nothing else he could think of felt right describing what they were about to do.

"I love you," Fred whispered, bowing his head against Ell's shoulder.

"Love you, I love you too!" Ell groaned as his tentacles slipped out, immediately curling around his cock. They stroked him quickly, matching the frantic pace of Fred's probing fingers.

Fred took a deep breath, and he twisted his wrist to take Ell over the edge. Ell's entire body jerked in reply, and he zeroed in on that angle and sped up. "Ell, come on, baby. Fuckin' come for me."

"Uhmmm, *mmmph*, Freddie!" Ell cried out, his hips pushing down on Fred's hand as he clawed at his back. He was absolutely writhing as his body clenched around Fred's fingers, his breathy whimpers turning into deep, desperate moans. "Yes, oh, ohhh, yes! Yes! *Yes!*"

Fred rocked Ell through each powerful shiver of his orgasm, seizing his lips in a hard kiss that was almost too rough. Their teeth clicked before he readjusted to kiss him more sweetly, murmuring, "There you go... just like that...."

Ell moaned happily, humping Fred's hand to wring out the last few divine twitches his body had to offer. The tentacles were lazily jerking him off, sliding around in his come. "By all the gods, I love you, Freddie."

"Love you too." Fred gently withdrew his hand. He studied Ell's flushed and come-dazed expression, and he hated himself for being so worried, but he had to check. "You sure you're okay for this? Not too tired?"

"I feel wonderful," Ell laughed. He stretched his arms out above his head with a gleeful squeal before clinging to Fred's neck. He was beaming radiantly, grinning as they kissed again.

Fred noticed that Ell's tentacles hadn't fully retreated yet. That was unusual as they usually slipped back in fairly quick, and he figured Ell had to be really turned on. Fred couldn't resist scooting down so he could run his tongue over them.

"Oh!" Ell squeaked in surprise.

"Is that good?" Fred asked, lapping over the base of the tentacles and then up the shaft of Ell's cock.

"V-very good. Please… do that? Keep doing that." Ell dug his fingers into Fred's scalp, holding him there between his thighs.

Fred was happy to give Ell whatever he wanted, and he sucked one of the tentacles into his mouth. He grunted as it grew, sliding deep into his throat. He reached for the other, wrapping his fingers around it and Ell's cock, stroking them together.

Ell's hips jerked up, and he moaned brokenly. "That, mmm, that right there! Please, Freddie! More, mmm, more of your mouth!"

Fred liked a challenge, but he wasn't sure just how much he could stuff inside his mouth. The tentacles were tapered at least, and he slid the second one over to push in alongside the other. He sucked them both, his lips stretched wide to take so much on, and he grabbed Ell's ass to lift him up off the bed.

Ell gasped, draping his legs over Fred's shoulders and then rolling his hips, fucking Fred's mouth with his tentacles. He was shy at first, trembling, but he found a rhythm and thrust faster. "Oh, ohhh, oh, fuck!"

The tentacles were slick and wet, a pleasant contrast to Ell's cock, and they slipped in and out of Fred's throat with ease. He squeezed Ell's ass, encouraging him to keep going. He could see Ell was stroking his cock, his other hand slapped up against the wall to keep his horns from hitting it. He was an absolutely divine vision, lost to taking his pleasure from Fred.

"Freddie! I'm, *mmm*, I'm gonna come!" Ell warned.

Fred grunted, sucking harder and faster, giving the tentacles everything he had. When Ell cried out sharply and shivered, the last thing Fred had expected was for his throat to be filled with a hot load from the tentacles.

That was new.

He swallowed it down—it was hot, sweet, thick—and he grunted in surprise when he got a second splash. He took it all, gently lowering Ell's body back down to the bed. He pulled off the tentacles and then licked his lips. He actually felt buzzed, a heady rush that echoed the distant memory of taking a really strong shot of liquor. "Wow."

Ell was limp, flushed, and he couldn't stop panting. "That, that was, just, yeah, *wow*."

"Still feeling good?" Fred kissed Ell's thigh, nuzzling there. "That was pretty intense. We ain't gotta—"

"Now, Freddie." Ell grabbed Fred's cheek and lifted his head until their eyes met. "Right now."

"All right, little one." Fred took a deep breath. "You got it."

This was it.

He sat up to grab more of the lube, and he was more cautious as he squirted some in his palm. He stroked his hard cock, leaning back on his knees as he gazed down at Ell. "Fuck, you're beautiful."

Grinning bashfully, Ell pressed his hands over his face, and it only added to his allure. He was still damp and blushing from coming moments ago, but his cock was already hard again, slick and glistening against his stomach alongside the lingering tentacles.

From his toes to his tentacles to the horns on his head, Ell was stunning. Beyond that, he had a kind heart, with a wonderful sense of humor, and Fred had never felt so loved. Seeing Ell like this, open and waiting for him, made Fred's heart pound so fast that the room spun.

"Hey." Ell peeked through his fingers, prodding Fred to get back on top of him by hooking his legs around his waist. "You're beautiful too, Freddie," he said as he cupped Fred's face in his hands. "I love you so much."

"I love you too." Fred knew he would never get tired of saying those words. "You wanna do it like this…?"

"Yeah. I wanna be able to see you."

"Whatever you want. I wanna make this so fuckin' good." Fred tried to quell the rush of nerves buzzing through him as he got himself lined up. His heart thumped as the head of his cock slid in effortlessly, and he gasped from the intensity of their bodies joining for the first time.

"Oh fuck." Ell inhaled sharply and grabbed on to Freddie's forearms to brace himself. "Oh, Freddie… by all the gods…."

Fred grunted, blown away by how hot and tight Ell's body was clinging to his cock and making him shudder. Nothing had ever felt like this, and he leaned down to pepper Ell's cheek with soft kisses as he pushed a little deeper.

Ell's brow scrunched up, his senses clearly warring over the intense feeling of being filled. It was difficult for Fred to tell if it was from pain or pleasure or some heady mixture of both. When Ell moaned, it was loud and gasping, and his head twisted back into the pillows.

"Breathe for me," Fred said, burying his face against Ell's shoulder. "Nice and slow, okay? You're doing so fuckin' good… you feel so fuckin' good…."

Ell panted frantically, and he cried out when Fred slid in another few inches. "Fuck! You're so big! Mmmph!"

Immediately halting, Fred asked, "Are you okay? Are you hurting? Fuck, do we need more lube?"

"It's okay!" Ell insisted. "I can take it! You're not going to hurt me. Please keep going!" He pushed himself down clumsily, trying to take more.

"Hey! Mm!" Fred groaned, his cock plunging deeper. He could feel himself throbbing, blown away by the snug squeeze of Ell's hole. It was beyond perfection, and a strong shiver rolled over the back of his neck and all the way down his spine.

"Please." Ell sounded almost frantic now, clinging to Fred's shoulders and continuing to wiggling impatiently. "Freddie!"

"Easy." Fred tried not to get too carried away, and he placed a firm hand at Ell's side to help keep him still. It would be so easy to slam forward, but he didn't want to hurt Ell. With patient strokes, he went on thrusting until Ell had taken every last inch of him. "Gods…."

"Is it in now?" Ell whimpered.

"Fuck yeah." Fred slipped his arm beneath Ell's back as he slid in and out, savoring the slick friction on his cock and trying not to bust on the spot. "There, Ell… you did it, little one."

Ell arched into Fred's strong embrace with a happy moan, his legs falling apart as he submitted to the passionate rhythm. "You feel so good. Mmm, you feel so fuckin' good."

"So do you," Fred murmured, kissing the soft words from his lips. A shock of energy zinged over his tongue as they kissed, and his body was flush with a tingling heat.

It was like nothing he'd ever felt before, and he didn't know if it was because he was a ghoul or if it was from Ell. Whatever the cause, he didn't want it to stop. He kept kissing him, moving his hand down Ell's thigh to guide his leg up to his waist.

Smiling blissfully, Ell moaned, "Ohhhh, that… that… that's good… so good…." He kissed Fred passionately, clinging to his neck and trying to eliminate any space between them.

Fred could feel the tentacles pressed between them, squirming around Ell's cock. He kept their bodies moving together with steady thrusts, rolling his hips with every ounce of grace that he could summon. It had been a very long time since he'd done this, but he was determined to please Ell. He changed the angle often, determined to find what Ell liked the best.

"There, that! *That*!" Ell gasped.

"Here?" Fred held his hips in place, pushing forward again.

"Yes!" Ell shouted as Fred focused in on that spot and soon had him trembling. "Harder, Freddie… please, I need more. I need more!"

Burying his face into Ell's chest, Fred arched his back and plowed forward. Their skin slapped together noisily, and he was worried he'd been too rough.

"Ohhh my gods!" Ell howled, eagerly digging his heels in Fred's back. "Yes! Just like that! Come on, please!"

Fred could never say no to Ell, and he reared back to slam into him again. He propped himself on his elbows as he sped up the tempo of their lovemaking. Even as he pounded into Ell, he knew that's exactly what this was.

He wanted to give Ell everything he'd never been able to have, trading fierce kisses and hot puffs of breath. He loved him so much, and the temperature between them was absolutely soaring now. Ell was moaning and wailing with every deep thrust, and Fred couldn't look away.

Ell's expression was morphing between openmouthed groans of pleasure and delighted little smiles, grinning deliriously as he announced, "Freddie, I'm gonna come! Oh! Fuck, I'm gonna come!"

Hearing that only made Fred work harder, throwing his weight behind his slams and feeling Ell jerk beneath him from the force. He moved his weight onto one arm, reaching up to grab one of Ell's horns to keep him from scooting up the bed. "Come on, baby! Come on!"

Ell came the moment Fred's fingers twisted around his horn, screaming triumphantly, "Yes! Oh *gods*! I love you, I love you so much!"

Fred could see tears in Ell's eyes, watching them flash purple as his thighs squeezed his waist. The clench of Ell's hole around his cock was all too much for him to resist, and the tension in his muscles wound up and immediately snapped. His cock unloaded fast and hard, and he smothered a roar against Ell's lips.

He fucked them through every last intense quiver, wrapping his arms around Ell tight as they kissed. He finally slowed down when he felt Ell twitching, giving one last lazy thrust. He could feel how wet Ell was from taking his come, and how easily his cock slipped in and out made him ache. His heart was miraculously thumping so strongly that he could feel it in his ears, and he whispered, "I love you."

"I love you too." Ell breathed out shakily, his face blotchy and red and unable to stop smiling.

Fred smiled back, but he noticed his eyes were stinging. He touched his face, staring dumbly when he saw his fingers were wet.

He was crying too.

"Are you okay?" Ell reached up to wipe Fred's cheeks. His brow wrinkled with worry. "Was it bad?"

"No," Fred assured him. "It was fuckin' perfect. You were amazing. It was… it was just a lot for me." He took Ell's hand, and he guided it over his heart so he could feel its steady pounding.

"Oh, Freddie." Ell sighed, smiling brightly up at him. He kept his hand there until the pulse finally began to fade, sliding his arms up to hug Fred. "Thank you. Thank you for everything."

"Thank you," Fred replied. "You did more than just give me my life back. You gave me a fuckin' reason to live."

Ell's lower lip began to shake. "Freddie, my gods… you can't say super sweet stuff like that right now! I'm going to cry again!"

"Sorry. I just love you, Ell. So fuckin' much." He kissed him gently.

"I love you too. Thank you for this, for being so patient with me…." Ell cringed. "I hope I was, you know, okay."

"You were fuckin' amazing." Fred adjusted his hips to pull out with a low grunt. He reached down between them, pausing to stroke Ell's retreating tentacles before gingerly petting Ell's slick hole. "Are you okay? Did… did I hurt you?"

"No." Ell shook his head. "I might be a little sore, but uh, yeah, I'm good. I'm so very good. It was wonderful. It was so much better than I thought it would be."

"Good." Fred smooched his cheek. "Mm, I'm gonna get up, get us cleaned up, and order some grub from that all-night Chinese place so you can eat before we crash. Sound good?"

"Or," Ell suggested coyly, "we do all of that but instead of going to bed—" He grinned. "—we do the sex stuff again?"

Fred laughed. "By all the gods, I've created a fuckin' monster."

"Only a little one!" Ell pouted.

"Elliam Sturm, I promise that I will make love to you every fuckin' chance I get."

"So, that's a yes?"

"Goddamn right it is."

The world had been saved, the cultists were vanquished, and Fred made love to Ell two more times that night before they finally went to bed. They traded little kisses and whispers of love before finally drifting off in each other's arms. Ell fell asleep first, clearly exhausted, and Fred watched over him with a happy smile.

He caught himself looking at Ell's horns, always beautiful, though quite small compared to the spectacular display he'd seen before in the alley. He didn't understand Ell's transformation, and though it bothered him that Ell couldn't remember what had happened, he decided that it didn't matter.

Ell wasn't dangerous. He was the sweetest soul that Fred had ever known, and he was the best thing that had ever happened to him.

He loved Ell.

No matter what.

CHAPTER 15.

"WHAT IF they don't like me?" Ell asked anxiously.

"They're going to love you," Fred promised as he parked in Lynnette's driveway, noting that Sloane and Azaethoth were already here.

Milo's car was also here, but that was expected. He and Lynnette were practically living together now, and he figured they would make it official soon. Lochlain and Robert hadn't arrived yet, which was odd given Lochlain's usual punctuality.

It had been two months since the heist at the auction, and tonight all the members of the so-called Super Secret Sages Club were getting together to celebrate Galmethas, a holiday named in honor of the god of kindness, Galmelthar. Though they weren't an official coven, it was traditional for Sages to gather in groups to perform cleansing and purification rituals.

Ell and Fred had remained inseparable since the night of the heist. Ell couldn't remember what he'd done to the cultists, and Fred was glad he didn't ask. He didn't know how to explain what he'd seen to himself, much less how he would try to tell Ell.

Any heat from Lochlain's showy theft had died down, as had the search for the elusive arsonist who had destroyed the city's beloved dog park.

Since that prick Jeff was still out there, Fred moved into a new place on the edge of town. He would miss his familiar neighbors, but being safe was more important. He even made sure there was a small yard and flower boxes hanging outside the windows for a certain someone because he wanted to ask that someone to move in with him.

The risk of Jeff returning for revenge was great, but Ell had made it clear he didn't want to abandon his beloved country home. He stayed over with Fred every night except for once a week when he and Fred would go back to his place to get more clothes and check on his plants. Fred was working up the courage to ask Ell to come live with him permanently, but he wanted to make sure Ell knew it was because he really wanted him to and not just because he was worried.

To be honest, Fred wasn't sure who he was more concerned for—Ell or any of the poor bastards who would be stupid enough to come looking for him.

In any case, Fred was glad Ell's powers were now back to normal.

Well, as normal as healing the dead and wounding the living could be.

To ensure that Fred wouldn't come back to life completely and risk Ell's touch harming him, Ell stopped all of Fred's healing treatments. Fred had expected new spots of rot to appear, but none did. It was as if he was frozen right on the cusp of life and death, and as long as he could remain with Ell, he didn't care about his heartbeat coming and going.

With the help of the stoneskin potion and a new glamour charm, Ell was brave enough to venture out more into public. They went to the movies, the mall, and all the other places Ell had always wanted and been too afraid to try. There were only so many scales left, however, and Ell went back to wearing gloves and scarves to help keep himself from accidentally touching anyone.

After all, Ell had reasoned, they weren't likely to find any more scales, and he needed to come up with other ways to be safe without sacrificing his newfound freedom.

For tonight's celebration, though, Ell had chosen to mix up more of the special potion.

The last thing he wanted to do was accidentally hurt the famous Starkiller and enrage his godly mate. He was already clearly distressed with the prospect of meeting an immortal in the flesh.

"How can you be so sure?" Ell groaned. "He's a god! An actual living, breathing god! Am I dressed okay? Do I look like a normal person?"

Fred looked over Ell's vest and T-shirt combo, dressy but not too uptight, and he nodded his approval. "You look great."

"Are you sure?"

"Very sure." Fred leaned in for a quick kiss.

"But you look really nice!" Ell still fussed. "You're wearing a jacket!"

"With no tie," Fred pointed out, "and I'm wearing jeans." He took Ell's hand and gave it a squeeze. "You're fine. Potion?"

"Yes!" Ell pulled the small bottle out of his pocket and chugged it down. He made a face. "I'm sorry I'm so nervous. It's just been so crazy trying to meet them, and now that it's here—"

"You're freaking out?"

"Tiny bit."

The last few times Fred thought Ell was finally going to meet Azaethoth and Sloane, something had always managed to come up. Ell had met everyone else in their small circle of friends except that very elusive couple.

Either they were busy with a new case or Azaethoth had decided to whisk Sloane away for another spontaneous trip. The pair had missed Lynnette's Winter Solstice party because of some magical porno temple they'd found.

Fred knew Ell had been relieved when those other plans fell through, but there was no getting out of it now.

Ell was holding on to Fred's hand for dear life, clinging close as Fred led them to the front door.

Fred knocked, and then he turned once more to reassure Ell, "Hey, it's gonna be okay. I fuckin' promise."

"O-okay." Ell's responding smile was hopeful but strained.

Lynnette opened the door, hugging them both excitedly as she greeted, "Hey, guys! Love the vest, Ell! Come on in!"

Fred ushered Ell in front of him with a strong hand on his waist to keep him moving. Ell was dragging his feet as they followed Lynnette into the kitchen. Something smelled like lemons, common for cleansing rituals and foods for Galmethas, and Milo and Sloane were seated at the kitchen table.

"So, Galgareth's day is the Winter Solstice," Milo was saying. "And today is hers too?"

"No," Sloane laughed. "Today is for Galmelthar, totally different god."

"Well, if they didn't want people to get confused, they should have given them different names!"

"That's him?" Ell whispered frantically, gawking at Sloane. "That's the Starkiller?"

"Yup, that's him," Fred confirmed.

"Wow. So, that's what a Starkiller looks like."

Fred didn't think Sloane looked much like a Starkiller. He was just an average guy in Fred's opinion. It was hard to believe that man right there could summon a sword of pure starlight with the power to kill a god.

Maybe it had something to do with those big eyebrows.

"Yo!" Milo waved at Fred and Ell with a big smile. "Welcome to our fancy purification party, dudes!"

"Hey!" Sloane said, turning his attention to Ell and Fred. His face lit up, and he got to his feet to greet them.

Fred noticed Sloane was already swaying a little and counted at least three empty bottles of wine on the counter.

Sloane shook Fred's hand first. "Good to see you, Fred! Wow! You look fantastic!"

"Thanks." Fred gestured to Ell, who was staring in awe up at Sloane. "This is Elliam Sturm. Ell, this is Sloane Beaumont."

"Hi!" Sloane took Ell's hand, smiling warmly. "It's nice to meet you, Ell. I've heard so much about you—"

"You really killed a god?" Ell blurted out.

Fred cringed, but Sloane just laughed.

"Yeah, I did." Sloane's smile never wavered, though Fred swore it was a bit strained. "I've been told you're pretty amazing yourself. Healing ghouls? That's freakin' incredible."

Ell appeared ready to faint receiving such a compliment from a Starkiller.

Fred wrapped his arm around his shoulders to steady him. "Ell is the best at what he does. None fuckin' better."

"All right, boys and girls!" Lynnette called out, lining shot glasses filled with yellow liquid along the edge of the counter. "One of the most important parts of Galmethas is taking on some intense purifying action. This is not just about a cleansing of the home, but a deep cleansing of your own body."

"Is this the part where we all drink until we puke?" Milo asked suspiciously.

"You don't actually have to drink until you puke." Sloane chuckled. "You're just supposed to drink enough to flush out your system."

"Which Sages traditionally make a lemon beer for!" Lynnette explained. "But I fucked up the beer, so we're having boozy lemonade instead."

"Is there a nonalcoholic option?" Ell sounded hopeful.

"Of course!" Lynnette smiled, removing one of the glasses to replace it with one that had a pink liquid inside. "Here. The pink lemonade is totally safe."

Everyone took their glasses and raised them in a toast as Lynnette declared, "Through our stomachs to our hearts, may Galmelthar bless all our parts!"

Ell grinned at the cute expression, and he sipped his pink lemonade as the others went back in for another round of shots. Fred could taste the alcohol's burn and the bite of fresh lemons, and he briefly wondered if he could actually get drunk off this.

Of all the things he and Ell had tried—and oh, they'd tried a *lot* of fun stuff—intoxication hadn't been on the list.

"You dared start the holiday festivities without me?" Azaethoth's booming voice suddenly roared, the sound filling the kitchen and violently rattling the windows. "Me! Azaethoth the Lesser, brother of Tollmathan, Gronoch, Xhorlas, and Galgareth! The son of Salgumel, he who was spawned by Baub, the child of Zunnerath and Halandrach, they who were born of Etheril and Xarapharos descended directly from Azaethoth himself!"

"Shit!" Ell yelped, cowering back more with every word toward the door with Fred chasing right after him. "Oh no! Were we not supposed to do that? That's him? That's Azaethoth the Lesser? He sounds so angry!"

"Ignore him," Sloane said flatly. "He's being dramatic."

Azaethoth appeared then, his arms crossed and pouting defiantly at Sloane as he said, "Aw, come on, my sweet mate! You never let me have any fun!"

"We've been celebrating since the sun came up," Sloane scolded. "Don't get fussy about a few shots you missed out on, Mr. 'Mortal Libations Don't Affect Me.'"

"That's why I had to go get some *immortal* libations!" Azaethoth argued. "How else can I properly honor my aunt?"

"Loch—"

"I guess she's technically my great aunt, but I'm not really sure. It's very difficult to track a family tree when your relations can spawn on their own—"

"Hey, Loch—"

"My love, I can't help it that I got lost! Do you have any idea how difficult it is to navigate all the worlds between worlds? Especially when you're looking for another god's hidden stash—"

"Hey, *Azaethoth*!"

"Yes, my gorgeous mate?"

"Listen, right now there's someone I want you to meet." Sloane grabbed Azaethoth's hand to steer him over to Ell and Fred. "And you'd better behave yourself!"

"Mmmm, I love it when you get so aggressive." Azaethoth sighed adoringly as his tentacles unfurled from his arms and dragged Sloane into a close embrace.

"Will you hold on for one damn second—" Sloane's protests were silenced by Azaethoth's lips, giving in to a very passionate kiss.

Ell's quaking fear had now morphed into blatant confusion. He cleared his throat before he asked quietly, "That's... that's an old god?"

"Yup." Fred smirked. "That's him."

When Azaethoth's tentacles began to wander, Sloane frantically smacked them away and tried to straighten himself out. "Ahem! Right! So, this is Fred's friend, his ghoul doctor. His name is Ell."

"Hello, little mortal," Azaethoth said, eyeing Ell curiously. He stepped right into Ell's space, and his eyes turned into a hazy pool of stars. "Aren't you an interesting little creature?"

Fred was hit by a sudden surge of panic. He didn't like how Azaethoth was looking at Ell, and he hated how Lochlain's fears bubbled back up to the forefront of his mind.

Save me from Ell? You really think he's that fuckin' dangerous...?

"He's my boyfriend," Fred said firmly, hugging Ell close to his chest.

"Oh!" Azaethoth blinked, and his eyes returned to normal. He grinned and bopped Ell's shoulder with one of his tentacles, teasing, "You two must have discovered a way to mate! How exciting! I want to hear everything!"

"Oh!" Ell blushed furiously. "I don't... uh...."

"Uh-uh! Come over here and drink your immortal libations," Sloane ordered firmly, grabbing Azaethoth's arm and tugging him over to the kitchen counter. "Don't ask people about their sex life. It's rude."

"Can I tell people about ours?" Azaethoth asked hopefully. "Because the way you took all of my seed this morning and still wanted more was absolutely—"

"No!" Sloane roared. "Not appropriate!"

Ell had wilted in relief to no longer be the topic of conversation and hugged Fred's waist. "Is he always like that?"

"Always," Fred said, bowing his head to press a kiss into Ell's hair. "You doing okay?"

"I'm okay!" Ell smiled. "I don't know what I was expecting, but they're both just… I don't know. They're both so nice. Kinda got myself worked up for nothing."

"Not for nothin'," Fred insisted. "It's a big deal meetin' a god. Ours just happens to be a bit of a pervert."

Ell laughed. "Just a bit, huh?"

"Okay, a lot."

There was a knock at the door, and Lynnette called out, "Fred? Can you get that?"

She was busy stirring something on the stove while Azaethoth and Sloane were doing more shots with Milo. There was a purple bottle on the counter that hadn't been there before. Whatever was inside was glowing as Azaethoth poured himself a cup.

"No problem." Fred kissed Ell's cheek before leaving him to go answer the door.

It was Lochlain and Robert.

Robert's arms were full of cupcake trays, and he was apologizing profusely, "I'm so sorry we're so late! Someone told me the oven was preheated and it wasn't, and I'm sorry it took forever!"

"I already told you that I thought it was on!" Lochlain groaned. "I made a mistake! I said I was sorry!"

"Hey." Fred ignored their squabbling and moved aside to let them into the house. He and Lochlain had made up since their fight, as in they'd decided to act like it never happened and not ever speak of it again.

Lochlain remained supportive of Fred's relationship with Ell, and he hadn't said another word about what he'd seen the night of the heist. Robert didn't mention anything either, and Fred wondered if he even knew.

Not that he was going to fuckin' ask. The whole thing was better left alone.

After Fred shut the door, he followed Robert and Lochlain back into the kitchen where everyone was exchanging hugs, kisses, and swipes of tentacles from Azaethoth. Ell had positioned himself in the corner, awkwardly sipping at his drink as he watched them.

Fred put his arm around Ell's shoulders. "Hey, you okay?"

"Yeah!" Ell smiled shyly. "It's like when the goblin king went to court for the first time, and he didn't understand any of the human customs. He just, you know, hung back and observed, trying to learn."

"Until Trip came over and started talking to him," Fred recalled.

"Yeah, that's you," Ell agreed with a brighter grin.

"Me?"

"Yeah! You're my hero!"

"Thought I was the damn goblin king."

"Tonight, you're Trip."

"Dammit."

"Hey!" Ell grinned. "This means you get your happy ending."

"I already did," Fred promised him, leaning in for a sweet kiss.

As the night wore on and the drinks flowed, the party began to take its toll.

At some point, Ell's pink lemonade got switched out for the boozy yellow kind, and Lynnette insisted that she had no idea what had happened. Milo drank so much that he got sick and had to go to bed.

Robert would have followed him had it not been for eating an entire tray of his own cupcakes that helped forestall any vomiting. Lochlain took him over to the couch to doze for a bit while Sloane and Azaethoth got totally hammered.

Fred had never seen a drunk god before, and it was pretty damn funny watching him explore Lynnette's kitchen cabinets and start rearranging things based off some damn cooking show he loved.

Lynnette was quick to correct him, waving a spoon around that may have been the very one Fred's soul had been once bound to.

Ell rarely engaged with anyone else, but he was confident enough to take a seat at the kitchen table and listen to the conversation.

Azaethoth took the lead often, excitedly sharing his naughty adventures with Sloane exploring the hidden worlds. Sloane derailed him when the details got too graphic, hoping to spare the remaining guests and himself from the embarrassment.

After Azaethoth's latest attempt to explain how they tried to recreate some of the dirty murals and how flexible Sloane was, Lynnette cut in.

"Okay! Enough of that! It's time to cleanse the house!" she announced, finally attending to the contents of the pot that had been boiling all evening. She spilled a lot, and she was giggling as she poured the steaming liquid into small bowls.

"Ready!" Sloane grabbed a bowl.

Milo emerged from the bedroom, still looking a bit green. He stared at the bowls in horror. "Oh, is that food? Because…. Ugh…." He put a hand over his mouth. "Food is the enemy."

"No, sweetie," Lynnette soothed. "This is a brew of rosemary, lemons, and a bunch of other magical stuff to help clean the bad energy out of the house. It's like magical 409." She handed him a bowl. "You can help Robert cleanse the living room from the couch."

"Mmm, meh, okay." Milo accepted the bowl and then walked unsteadily in that direction.

"Sloane!" Lynnette ordered, surprisingly firm despite how much she'd had to drink. "You go with Ell and cleanse the front of the house. Fred? You're with Lochlain. You've got the back."

Fred growled.

"Does that mean you have the honor of accompanying me?" Azaethoth asked her with a bat of his eyes.

"It means you have the honor of staying in the kitchen and drinking with me while they cleanse the house!" Lynnette laughed as she passed out the rest of the bowls.

"Wait! Wait! I should do something!" Azaethoth said, his tentacles flailing around him.

"Like what?" Sloane wobbled until he had to grab the edge of the counter to steady himself.

"In honor of my aunt, I can bless everyone with a cleansing ward!" Azaethoth lurched forward, smacking Lochlain right in the forehead with his tentacle. "There, my dear mortal, you've been blessed!"

Lochlain nearly fell over, laughing as he touched his face where Azaethoth's tentacle had landed. "Thank you, O' Blessed Trickster!"

Lynnette was next, but she took it much better and didn't even stumble. Azaethoth briefly dipped away into the living room to bless Robert and Milo. When he returned, he was headed right for Ell.

Ell closed his eyes, and Fred held his breath.

Fred had no idea what Azaethoth might feel when he touched Ell with his divine flesh.

Lochlain apparently still had his own concerns as well because he was watching Ell and Azaethoth like a hawk.

"You've been blessed!" Azaethoth declared as he bopped Ell. He paused and tilted his head. His eyes filled with stars, and he leaned very, very close to Ell. "How curious…."

Ell became panicked, and he squeaked, "I'm, I'm part Eldress. A-and maybe a little Asra, and—"

"Ah!" Azaethoth smiled and backed off. "That explains it! Now! Where was I?" He came at Fred next to give him a tentacle bop. "There! All the mortals have been blessed!"

"Let's go!" Sloane cheered, clumsily looping his arm through Ell's and stumbling with him toward the front door. "Eldress, huh? That's crazy! I thought they all died…."

"Uh, bye, Freddie!" Ell waved. "Be right back!"

Fred waved back, and he tried not to worry. He knew there was no one safer for Ell to be with than a Starkiller, and they didn't seem to be too shocked by Ell's confession.

Then again, everyone was also very drunk.

"Shall we?" Lochlain said, offering Fred a flashy smile.

Fred rolled his eyes and stepped through the back door into the yard. He had the bowl of lemon water, doing his best to think pure thoughts as he dipped his fingers into the bowl and flicked the liquid around the yard.

Lochlain followed right on his heels, and Fred said nothing. He and Lochlain hadn't spoken much since the night of the heist. Sure, they'd been friendly enough, but this was the first time they'd been alone together.

Lochlain fell into step beside him, asking, "So, Ell is part Eldress, huh?"

"And some Asra." Fred grunted. "He believes some of the everlastin' people stayed here on Aeon. Had kids and shit."

"Huh. I guess that explains why he can't be silenced."

"Yup."

"And the horns."

"Those too."

"So, have you decided if you're coming to the wedding?"

"You still think Ell is dangerous?" Fred countered immediately.

"No." Lochlain shook his head. "If Azaethoth has given him his blessing, then you have mine." He held up his finger. "But I still reserve the right to inflict severe bodily harm should he break your heart."

"Hmmph." Fred snorted, flicking some of the water in Lochlain's direction. "Whatever."

"So, does that mean you're coming?"

"When is it?"

"Next month," Lochlain replied with a hint of annoyance. "Didn't you get the invitation?"

Fred vaguely recalled balling it up and putting it in the trash. "No."

"Liar," Lochlain accused affectionately. "It's the first of March. You and Ell are both invited, just so we're clear."

"Was that before or after he got your godly seal of approval?" Fred griped.

"Before."

"Hmmph."

"I'm sorry," Lochlain said sincerely. "Really. For ever doubting him or you. You guys are great together."

Fred eyed him suspiciously.

"And yes, I'm still going to worry," Lochlain went on, "but it's only because I love you so much. You're my best friend, Fred. But I am really happy for you. I mean it."

Fred decided that was as good of an apology as he was ever going to get, and he pulled Lochlain into a crushing hug. He waited for Lochlain to start gasping for breath before letting go, muttering, "Love you too. Jackass."

"Let's get back in and finish cleansing our bodies," Lochlain said. "I think there's one more pitcher of lemonade left!"

Fred hadn't experienced much more than a passing buzz from the alcohol, but he still enjoyed tasting it. Back inside the kitchen, they found Sloane reciting some sort of poem to Ell.

"And in our hearts, we carry that spark, of the gods and goddesses above," Sloane was saying. "And we sleep, we dream their dream, and will always feel their love." He bowed as if finishing off a grand performance.

"That's so beautiful!" Ell gushed, swaying back and forth as he clapped. "It's the most beautiful thing I've ever heard!"

"Oh, come on!" Sloane laughed. "It's from *Starlight Bright*! It's a kid's book! Like, my favorite kid's book ever!"

"I'll try to find a copy!" Ell said. "I would love to read it!"

"My love," Azaethoth purred, wrapping his tentacles around Sloane's waist and hugging him to his chest, "I simply adore when you recite poetry. It fills me with such desire for you…."

"I fill you with desire when I open the fridge," Sloane teased as he stroked his coils with a wink. "Mm. You're ridiculous."

"Ah, yes, ridiculously in love with you, my sweet Starkiller."

Ell turned to pull Fred into a clumsy hug, burying his face into his broad chest with a long sigh. "I don't know if I'm cleansed, but I'm definitely drunk."

Fred saw Sloane and Azaethoth making out, and Azaethoth's tentacles were definitely going down the back of his pants. He could hear new retching sounds from the living room, and there was no telling if it was Robert or Milo. Lynnette shook her head with an affectionately annoyed sigh and was reaching for a bucket from under the sink.

"I think it's time for us to go." Fred grimaced.

"Farewell, dear mortals!" Azaethoth declared, dragging Sloane over to the kitchen counter. "I believe my mate is in need of some very *intimate* cleansing. Happy Galmethas to you both!"

"By all the gods, you're so disgusting." Sloane laughed and pulled away from Azaethoth to wave. "Happy Galmethas, guys!"

"Happy Galmethas!" Ell said, leaning heavily on Fred as he waved goodbye to everyone. He stumbled when he started to walk to the door, and Fred was quick to pick him up.

He shifted Ell in his arms, grunting a quick goodbye to everyone. He caught Lochlain's eye before he walked out, and he allowed himself to give him a friendly nod.

Things weren't the same between them, and maybe they never would be, but they were getting better.

Fred could live with that.

"Did you know that Milo is gonna move in with Lynnette?" Ell hiccupped as Fred set him down in the passenger side of his truck.

"I figured," Fred replied, checking Ell's seat belt.

"People do that, you know. When they're dating."

"Yeah." Fred shut the door and walked around the truck to get behind the wheel. As he cranked it up, Ell's hand rested on his knee.

"Freddie."

"Yeah?" Fred paused, turning to look at Ell.

"I want…." Ell's eyes were wide, and he was clearly nervous. He took a deep breath. "I want you to move in with me. But wait, like, at your place. I wanna move in with you, at your house."

"Really?" Fred's heart fluttered to life, beating hard and fast.

"Really!" Ell fidgeted with the seat belt. "I wanted to ask you like, well, forever ago! But I was scared, and I know you really wanted me to meet Azaethoth, or Loch, or whatever his name is—"

"Wait, huh?"

"I heard you and Lochlain," Ell confessed. "When you guys were outside? You asked him if he still thought I was dangerous—"

"Hey, hey," Fred cut in sharply, reaching for Ell's hands. "Listen to me. I never thought you were fuckin' dangerous. Never. That was Lochlain's bullshit head trip because he was worried about me, okay?"

"Really?" Ell squeaked. He sounded as if he was about to cry.

"Really." Fred kissed Ell's palms, his fingers, and then held his hands against his cheek. "Ell, I love you. I never needed anybody's fuckin' approval for that."

"But what I did before," Ell asked quietly, "the night of the heist…?"

"You saved me," Fred insisted. "That's all I give a fuck about. I'm sorry you heard that shit with Lochlain, but I'm telling you now that I love you. I love you more than anything, and I don't give a fuck what any fuckin' god thinks."

"Oh, Freddie!" Ell scrambled to get free of his seat belt. He surged into Fred's lap and held him close. "I love you so much. I just want my happy ending, Freddie. I wanna live happily ever after with you."

"And we will, Ell," Fred promised, drawing him in for a deep kiss. "Just me and you."

"Does that… does that mean you want us to move in together?" Ell blinked and rubbed at his eyes.

"Fuck yeah," Fred said without hesitation. "No offense, but you know your place is fallin' the fuck apart."

Ell laughed.

"And mine, well." Fred smiled. "It's only home when you're there, you know."

"We're really gonna do it?" Ell hiccupped. "We're gonna live together?" He made a face. "Okay, and we're totally talking about this again when I'm sober too."

"Hey, it's the best way to take care of you," Fred teased with a little wink. "Who else is gonna watch all of *Legends of Darkness* with you with the director's commentary on, huh?"

Ell laughed, hiccupped again, and then groaned.

"Or hold your hair back?"

"I'm not gonna puke!" Ell protested. "You know, maybe. Very strong maybe."

"I love you." Fred kissed Ell's forehead.

"I love you too." Ell smiled. "Take me away, my goblin king. Back to our home."

"Wanna stop for burgers or somethin'?" Fred asked kindly. "Might help your stomach."

"Oh gods no. Just home. I want home, blankets, bed, and you."

"Sounds like a very happy ending to me."

EPILOGUE

IT WAS a very happy ending….

Until the day of King Grell and Tedward Sturm's wedding.

Since meeting Ell, life had been one adventure after another living in Archersville, and Fred had made sure that he and Ell only watched from the sidelines. He knew he wouldn't be much help against twisted cultists, guys with godly souls, snarky cat people, or old gods stomping around, and he didn't want Ell in danger.

Or risking anyone else, for that matter.

Ell was dangerous, even if he would never intentionally harm someone, and Fred was secretly grateful that Ell still preferred the comfort of their home over going out into the world. Not that they stayed there all the time—they ventured out for special occasions like weddings and a few brief meetings of the Super Secret Sages Club.

As the months went on and the cultists persisted, Fred's mind would always return to the night of heist….

Fred refused to let himself think about it, and he would always banish the memory as quickly as he could.

It didn't matter.

He loved Ell, and he knew that Ell would never hurt anyone.

When Fred had learned that the cultists' latest plot was to lure out the Kindress, Fred didn't think anything of it. Even when Ell started having nightmares about people drowning right around that time, he chalked it up to what he and Ell had been seeing on the news.

It was nothing.

The cultists were once again stopped thanks to Sloane and the rest of their special club—plus a few honorary, albeit temporary, members—and soon Ell's awful nightmares stopped too. The whole ordeal also brought an end to Ell ever leaving their home.

Ell had sworn not to do it again due to a close call with a rude man that happened while he and Fred were out shopping during all that mess. The man didn't think Ell was moving fast enough and had pushed him out of the way. Ell had been hysterical with guilt knowing how close he'd come to hurting someone.

They'd run out of the magical scales months ago, and Ell didn't think it was right to risk anyone's safety over some strawberry poofs— even assholes at the local grocery store.

That changed when Ell's estranged brother, Ted, and future brother-in-law, King Grell, came to visit to invite them to their wedding.

The meeting had been its own unique experience, especially that Grell guy, and Fred couldn't recall a more awkward evening. Neither Ell nor Fred was dressed, as they had been occupied in bed, and it was difficult to have a serious conversation wrapped up in nothing but bedsheets.

Ell had to decline any efforts to shake hands or hug his brother, but that had been easy enough to justify with the very clear lack of clothing. Neither he nor Fred was the best at smoothing over social situations, but they managed to end the visit on a happy note and agreed to come to the wedding.

Apparently, there was going to be a royal ceremony in Xenon first and then some kind of bachelor party and a less formal wedding at some restaurant in Archersville.

That was fine by Fred.

Traveling to another world didn't sound like his idea of fun, not to mention how risky it would be for Ell with zero stoneskin potion. Fred wondered if they should have asked King Grell for more scales since there were living Vulgora in Xenon, but he didn't want to have to explain why they needed them.

Ell seemed to be in really good spirits when the wedding day arrived, and Fred was glad. He had been so worried about his beloved boyfriend. He hadn't wanted to go to the big bachelor party at the Velvet Plank last night, but at least he was excited about the wedding.

"Hey," Fred called out. "Any idea where my phone charger is?"

"Uh, it should be by your side of the bed?" Ell replied from the bathroom. He was still getting dressed and trying to fix his hair.

"That's literally where I'm standing, and it ain't here."

"Maybe you left it in the living room? Look, just check my drawer." Ell paused. "Not the sexy stuff one, but the top one. I might have a spare."

"Thanks." Fred plopped down on Ell's side of the mattress and then reached in to dig around the indicated drawer.

The first thing he found was the novelization of *Legends of Darkness* he had given Ell so long ago. He picked it up with a smile, certain it was more worn now from Ell's obsessive reading. He flipped through it, and he paused when the pages caught on something. His first thought was that Ell had just stuck a bookmark in to keep his place.

But it wasn't a bookmark.

It was a scale.

Fred held it between his fingers and stared at it in shock.

"Hey!" Ell came out of the bathroom, ready to go in his pink tuxedo jacket and pants from the heist, though he wore the shirt buttoned up more modestly than how Lochlain had styled it. "Did you find…." He stopped short when he saw what Fred was holding. "Oh."

"You told me they were all gone?" Fred frowned. "You still had one squirreled away?"

"Uh, yes, and, uh, I can totally explain that." Ell wrung his hands. "I wanted to save it. You know, for something really, really special."

"Why not use it for your brother's wedding? What the fuck could be more special than that?"

"Well, uh, you know…." Ell smiled shyly. "Maybe *our* wedding."

Fred's heart thumped. "You've been saving this for… us?"

"Look." Ell took a deep breath and put his hands on his hips. "We've been dating for almost a year, we live together, we are very happy, if I do say so myself, so it's the next logical step! And I know we haven't talked about marriage, like, officially, but I got to thinking that if we did ever have a wedding, we'd want to invite our friends and stuff, and so, yeah. I took it upon myself to make an executive decision to hide one of the scales."

Fred had stood up from the bed, slowly approaching Ell as he rambled away. He smiled down at him, waiting for him to finish before he leaned down for a kiss.

"Is that a yes?" Ell asked.

"It depends. What's the question?"

"I don't know." Ell reached up, standing on his toes to hug Fred's neck. "What do you want me to ask you?"

"Hmm." Fred wrapped his arms around Ell's waist and picked him up from the floor. "What are you thinking about asking me?"

"Well." Ell bit his lips, gazing adoringly into Fred's eyes. "I was thinking about maybe asking you if you wanted to get married?"

"Huh. When exactly are you thinking about askin' me? 'Cause I got this thing to go to later. Might be kinda busy."

"How about tomorrow?"

Fred pretended to think about it, fighting not to smile. "I guess tomorrow could work."

"Tomorrow." Ell kissed him.

Fred cradled Ell close, and his heart was pounding away. He was overwhelmed with a rush of pure elation, and it made his eyes hot and his insides ache in the sweetest way. This was real. He could keep it.

He could be happy always—*forever*—with Ell.

This time last year he could have never imagined that he would be discussing marriage with such a beautiful and precious young man, and realizing that he was now holding his future husband in his arms made him want to weep with joy.

The kiss turned passionate quickly, and it wasn't long before Fred took Ell to bed and made sure to summon his cock tentacles at least twice. They had to rush to get ready again, but they were both smiling like big dopes the entire time. With the utmost care, Fred returned the scale to its hiding place inside the book.

Soon enough, Fred thought with a happy smile, Ell would need it.

They had another wedding to get through first before thinking about their own, so they loaded up into Fred's truck and headed over to the Angus Barn. The large building was built to resemble an actual barn, and it was even painted bright red. Despite the kitschy exterior, the inside was chic and polished with dark wooden floors and contrasting light brick walls. The sconces on the walls were lit with real candles, and the smell was absolutely heavenly.

Fred was really looking forward to tasting steak again.

Down to the private wine cellar they went, escorted by a well-dressed hostess, and it was a small and intimate space with a fireplace and dim lighting. Sloane and Azaethoth were here, plus a few others that Fred didn't immediately recognize. He was surprised to see Robert and Lochlain, and he was definitely going to ask how they'd managed to snag a royal invite.

"Hey! Ell! Fred!" Ted greeted them with a big smile. He was wearing a sharp suit in shades of gray with a green rose on his lapel.

Grell was in a richly detailed three-piece suit of the same green, and his sunglasses were dark emerald. He flashed a toothy smile. "Hello, darlings. Welcome."

Ted beamed at Ell. "You look great, bro." He stepped toward him as if to get a hug, but he hesitated.

Ell closed the distance between them, being very careful to shove his face directly into Ted's broad chest to avoid any skin-on-skin contact. "Hey! Thank you. So do you!"

Ted lit up when they embraced, and he rubbed Ell's back slowly. It was clear he'd missed his brother. "Mom and Dad are on their way. They're just running late."

"Oh? They're coming?" Ell gulped. "I mean, right, of course. They would be. Wedding. Got it."

"You'll be fine, bro. I promise." Ted pulled away to shake Fred's hand. "Hey, man. Good to see you again."

"Likewise." Fred grunted.

So far, so good.

"We'll finish the rest of the introductions shortly," Grell said with a smooth smile. "My son is currently occupied seeing to his date. Hopefully he'll be finished before your parents arrive."

"Probably not," Ted grumbled under his breath, laughing.

"But won't he miss the wedding?" Ell blinked. "If he's, uh, still occupied?"

"We're actually skipping the wedding deal, and this has turned into an all you can eat and drink sort of situation. After going through it once, I think I'm good. We'll do a lil' somethin' when Mom and Dad get here, but—"

"He's mad because I grabbed his ass at the closing of the court ceremony," Grell drawled. "Can you believe it?" He shook Fred's hand with a wink. "The suffering I must now endure."

Ell laughed. "Really? You did that in front of all those royal people?"

"He sure fuckin' did." Ted rolled his eyes. "Worse than Trip sittin' down in the presence of the goblin king when he got fuckin' crowned."

"Season two, episode four!" Ell gasped. "You remember that?"

It was Grell's turn to shake Ell's hand.

Even with gloves, Fred kept a close eye just in case.

"Of course I do," Ted was saying. "You only made us watch twenty million times."

Grell jerked as if he'd been stung, staring at Ell with wide eyes.

Ted made a face at Grell. "The fuck is wrong with you now?"

In a moment, Grell was no longer a man but a giant black feline monster with a long tentacled tail. His unnaturally arched back hit the low ceiling, and he snarled. He bared a mouth of pointed teeth, pushing himself in front of Ted and forcing him to back up into the room behind him.

Instinctively, Fred grabbed Ell and hugged him close, his heart pounding in fear as he retreated toward the stairs they'd taken down here. He didn't think there was much he could do against an Asra, but damn if he wouldn't try.

Although, it didn't seem like Grell wanted to harm Ell.

It was like….

Grell was afraid of him.

"Wha-what's wrong?" Ell stammered. "What did I do?"

"What the fuck?" Ted pushed angrily at Grell. "What's with kitty cat monster mode?"

"Your brother is the bloody Kindress!" Grell roared. "Stay away from him!"

"What? The star baby thing?" Ted snorted. "Shut the fuck up. You're fuckin' drunk."

"I'm what?" Ell's eyes widened. "No! No, that's not it. I'm part Eldress, maybe even part Asra—"

"Absolute bullshit," Grell cut in, continuing to back up and shield Ted. The room was narrow enough that he could keep Ted trapped behind the bulk of his giant body. "I don't know how I didn't recognize his scent before, but I sure as bloody fuck do now."

"Shut your cock holster!" Ted bellowed as he fought to work his way around from Grell's bulk. "That's my little brother you're talkin' about!"

Fred hugged Ell tighter, and he hated himself when he couldn't find a single thing to say in Ell's defense.

Ell's powers, his horns, his nightmares.

What Fred had seen that night in the alley last year.

Maybe he couldn't say anything because he knew….

While he struggled to speak up, Sloane and Azaethoth had come over to see what the commotion was about.

"Hey, what's going on?" Sloane demanded. "What's wrong?"

"The little brother of my beautifully sculpted fiancé is the Kindress, that's what's wrong!" Grell snapped. "Ha! And hiding as a ghoul doctor. Fancy that."

"What?" Sloane spat. "No way. We know Ell. He's not the Kindress."

"Yeah!" Ted glared. "Some of us are even fuckin' related to him!"

Azaethoth actually laughed. "You expect us to believe that little mortal is the firstborn of my great-great-great-grandfather?"

"Give me just a tiny moment. I need to speak to your dear grandpa, as a matter of fact." Grell looked up to the ceiling. "Dear Great Azaethoth, why am I surrounded by idiots in every world I travel to? Why do you see fit to punish me with this endless plague of stupidity?"

"Ell is our friend, Your Highness," Sloane said firmly, "and you have no proof."

"Go on and take a poke at the little fellow if you're so confident. Enjoy rotting."

That gave Sloane pause. "Rotting?"

"Where there is death, he brings life. Where there is life, he brings death." Grell rolled his bright eyes. "What the bloody hell do you think it means? If he touches you, you'll putrefy in what I imagine is a most unpleasant manner."

"But if he touches you and you're already dead…." Sloane looked at Fred and then Ell, and his expression was no longer as confident as it had once been. Something clicked, and he whispered, "Jeff."

Fred flinched.

"What, what about him?" Ell's voice was small. "That crazy cultist guy?"

"Have you met him?" Sloane pressed.

Ell's eyes widened, and he looked up at Fred for help.

"It's nothin'." Fred grunted. "Don't fuckin' worry about it." He took a deep breath. "I think it's time we fuckin' get the hell out of—"

"Jeff is the one who shot you," Lochlain realized out loud. Fred couldn't see him with Grell's giant body in the way, but he and everybody could sure as hell hear him. "Which means he's the one that—"

"Shut the fuck up!" Fred barked.

"He's the cultist that attacked you guys," Lochlain went on undeterred. "Back at Ell's old place in the country. Ell touched him, didn't he?"

"So what?" Ell demanded. "Yes! I did! I was trying to save Freddie, and—"

"Jeff said he'd been touched by the Kindress." Sloane was somber now, and his hand had dropped to his side, no doubt to summon his sword of starlight. "Was that really you, Ell?"

"What? Yes, but I'm not the Kindress!" Ell argued desperately. "Look!" He pulled off his scarf. "I have a scar! I can't be some ancient god! Only mortals scar!"

"You can scar if you believe yourself to be mortal." Grell narrowed his eyes. "You're the Kindress. You can pretend to be whatever you want to be."

"But I'm not pretending!"

Ted was pale. "What if he doesn't know that he is? Could that be a thing? That shit when we were kids—"

"You mean when he almost killed you," Grell cut in sharply.

"Look, fucker!" Ted remained indignant, despite how visibly upset he was. "That was a fuckin' accident. If he doesn't know that he's the damn star baby, then he can't hurt anybody, right? He can't be destined to try and destroy the world because of some bullshit corruption if he doesn't know he's corrupted!"

"Stop talking about me like I'm not here!" Ell groaned miserably. "Why don't any of you believe me?"

"Wait, wait!" Sloane raised his hands. "Loch touched Ell before. He gave him a blessing at Galmethas and nothing happened!"

"This is true," Loch confirmed. Then he paused. "I think."

"By the smell of it, he has access to Vulgoran scales." Grell sniffed the air. "Although he's not wearing one now, he could easily make a stoneskin potion. That would even shield a god from his power as long as he believes himself to be Eldress. He can literally manipulate his body to his every whim."

"Like Loch did when Bad Robert tried to read his aura," Sloane recalled with a frown. "He made himself appear silenced."

"Exactly so. Gods can manifest their will into reality."

"No, no, no!" Ell was on the edge of hysterical, and he shook Fred. "Freddie! Can we please just go? I wanna go home, please. Right now."

"We shouldn't let him leave," Grell warned.

"Hey! He's still our friend," Sloane argued. "Kindress or whatever—"

"I'm not the fucking Kindress!" Ell shouted, tears streaming down his cheeks. He looked up at Fred, begging, "Please. Freddie. Tell them!"

"Ell," Fred whispered, his chest growing tight.

"You...." Ell's lower lip quivered. "You don't think I'm the Kindress, do you?"

Fred hesitated.

That's all it took for Ell's eyes to fill with tears and for him to shove Fred away with a sob. "No, not you too... not you...."

"Ell." Fred tried to reach for him. "I'm sorry."

"No! Don't touch me!" Ell pushed him away. "Leave me alone!"

"Ell, please!"

"Don't you dare—!" Ell suddenly screamed, clutching his head as his entire body shook. He was being swallowed up by a blinding light, and his screams warped into a primal roar that made the entire building tremble.

Fred closed his eyes to shield them. He already knew what was going to happen anyway.

He'd seen it before.

When the light finally dimmed enough to look at Ell again, he stood before them with his majestic horns and his crown of stars—a crown given to him by his father, Great Azaethoth.

The very air seemed to shimmer around him from his power, and the sparks from his crown made the lamps flicker and buzz. The wooden floor beneath his feet was at once springing to life and sprouting saplings only to have them wilt and dry up into ash.

No one moved.

No one breathed.

Ell stared at his hands as if he didn't recognize them, and then he looked only at Fred, his expression one of utter heartbreak. His tear-filled eyes were now violet and so luminous it hurt for Fred to meet them.

Fred had to do something.

Anything.

Man or monster, Kindress or not, he loved Ell. He wanted to plan a wedding and marry him and be with him always and forever. Ell was his everything, and he had to save him. He had to stop this before it was too late.

"Ell, wait—" Fred begged as he reached for him again. His fingers swung through nothing but empty air.

Just like that....

Ell was gone.

Keep reading for an exclusive excerpt from
Suckers and All
by K.L. Hiers!

CHAPTER 1.

ELLIAM STURM was the Kindress.

The firstborn son of Great Azaethoth, a child of starlight trapped in an endless cycle of rebirth and death, who stories said would destroy the universe if Great Azaethoth did not drown him in his tears; the being that ancient Sages revered out of fear and modern witches considered a myth; a god whose incredible power was only rivaled by the Creator of All, Great Azaethoth himself.

And he'd just fled King Thiazi Grell and Tedward Sturm's wedding in a really, really bad mood.

Sloane Beaumont had battled old gods and madmen, solved many heinous crimes as a private investigator, but this was going to be his first time dealing with a literal legend.

"Can you track him?" Sloane asked Loch urgently.

"No." Loch shook his head, and his brow scrunched. "There's… nothing."

Loch was Sloane's husband, a gorgeous redhead, and also Azaethoth the Lesser, the ancient Sagittarian god of thieves, tricksters, and divine retribution.

Fred Wilder, a ghoul and Ell's boyfriend, was especially distraught. He punched the closest wall, shattering the brick and howling in rage. He was a huge man, and ghouls were very strong. No one dared approach him.

Lochlain Fields, a thief and Loch's twin, tried to comfort Fred in spite of the clear danger. He was also Fred's best friend. "Hey, hey, stop that. Come on."

"No." Fred pushed Lochlain away with a snarl, his eyes dark with anger. "This is because of you." His gaze traveled across the other occupants of the room with equal fury. "All of you. You did this to him. You pushed him! You all acted like he's some kind of a fuckin' monster!"

Lochlain stumbled back into Robert Edwards, his husband, and he argued, "Hey, no! We didn't—"

"Shut the fuck up!"

"Fred!" Sloane hurried over, though he stayed out of swinging range. "Hey, please listen to me. We didn't know! Okay? No one knew. We didn't mean for this to happen."

"The important thing now is to stay calm," Grell said quietly. He was in his true form of an Asra, a black cat monster with a mane of thick tentacles and more sprouting from the tip of his tail.

He'd been the one to identify Ell as the Kindress by his scent, and he had transformed to defend Ted and the other guests.

Not that it would have mattered.

Even the King of the Asra would not have been able to do anything against the Kindress.

"Stay calm?" Fred snarled. "Says the asshole who flipped out and turned into a giant fuckin' cat—"

"We need a plan," Grell continued, ignoring Fred's cursing, "or life as we know it is going to become very unpleasant for all of us. We have to stop him."

"Stop him?" Ted echoed.

Ted was human, Ell's older brother, and his large size suggested a former career in professional wrestling. It was said he had a rare gift of starsight that allowed him to speak to the dead. It would probably come in handy fairly soon, because he looked ready to murder Grell.

"I'm sorry, is there an echo in here?" Grell rolled his eyes. "Yes, stop him."

"You mean fuckin' kill him," Ted seethed.

"That's usually the general idea involved with stopping someone. It sounds nicer than saying 'let's go plot to viciously murder him—'"

"He's my baby brother!" Ted roared. "No fuckin' way! You don't even fuckin' know he's gonna do nothin'!"

Sloane retreated into Loch's arms for comfort, and he gazed up at him helplessly. He tried to ignore Ted and Grell fighting, asking quietly, "What the hell do we do now?"

"I don't know yet," Loch said, forcing a smile, "but we're going to do it together."

"All of this time, he's been right here with us. The whole damn time!"

"As Grell said, gods can hide themselves very well." Loch frowned. "If Ell truly believed himself to be human or the descendant of an everlasting race, then that is what he would appear to be even to other gods."

"He didn't know." Sloane's stomach twisted. "By all the gods, he didn't know."

"Well." Loch grimaced at the putrefied state of the wooden floor where Ell had been standing before he vanished. "He certainly does now."

Jay Tintenfisch came stumbling out of the bathroom with Prince Asta right behind him. Jay was an IT tech at the Archersville Police Department where Sloane had worked years ago. Asta, Grell's son and another Asra, was Jay's boyfriend.

The pair had been decidedly absent, though it didn't take a private investigator like Sloane to deduce what they'd been up to—especially since Jay had a fresh hickey on his neck.

"Whoa, buzzkill." Asta stared owlishly at them all through a pair of small round sunglasses. "What the fuck did we miss?"

"Ell is the Kindress," Sloane said, still having trouble believing it. "He, uh, just left."

"Very displeased," Loch added. "Did not want to stay for cake."

"Wait, what?" Asta actually laughed.

Jay paled. "Elliam Sturm is the Kindress?"

"And there isn't any damn cake," muttered Grell.

"No cake?" Loch gasped.

"No, no bloody damn cake." Grell sighed heavily as he transformed back into his human form. He was wearing a black on black suit, surprisingly drab for what Sloane had seen him wear before.

He grimly thought it looked like Grell was heading to a funeral—for the whole universe in fact, if the legends about the Kindress were true.

Sloane's thoughts ran wild, and he took a deep breath to sort them out.

The stories said that the Kindress was the first child of Great Azaethoth, but he sadly died before taking his first breath. Great Azaethoth cried so hard and for so long that a fountain had to be built to hold his tears. Great Azaethoth brought the child back to life, but his lingering pain was corruptive and drove the Kindress mad. The Kindress then tried to destroy the universe and to save it, Great Azaethoth drowned his own child in the fountain of his tears only to resurrect him once more and start the cycle all over.

Birth.

Impending destruction of the entire universe.

Death.

Again and again.

Something had to have changed. Something broke the cycle.

But what?

They knew that there was more to the story thanks to Oleander Logue's translation skills and that the Kindress's own tears might be involved. That was important somehow, that was—

"Hey, Asta!" Ted shouted angrily. "Know anything about Asran divorce? Because I think I'm gonna fuckin' need one!"

Sloane blinked, the thought lost for now.

"Nope, nope, nope." Asta shook his head. "Don't drag me into your gross domestic situation, step-kitty kicker. I don't want nada fuck all to do with it."

"Don't be dramatic," Grell scolded Ted. "We're going to—"

"Going to what?" Ted barked. "Talk about killing my brother some more? You bastard! You fucking scared the shit out of him! No wonder he took the fuck off!"

"He is literally capable of destroying this world with an errant fart and he was scared of me?" Grell scoffed. "Do you hear yourself right now, my love?"

"I was trying to talk to him, and you were too busy being a giant asshole!"

"And by giant asshole, you mean a loving husband who was trying to protect you—"

"Ell would never hurt anyone!"

"Are we so sure about that? What of this Jeff?"

Sloane cringed at the mere mention of the name, and a funny voice in his head said Je-fahfah.

Jeff Martin was a cultist who'd tried various schemes to awaken Salgumel, Loch's father, the god of dreams, who had gone mad in his divine slumber. He and likeminded followers wanted Salgumel to remake the world where Sages ruled once more. Although the old religion was having something of a revival due to the many strange events of the last few months, it was still widely regarded as an antiquated joke.

"He's dead." Sloane grimaced. "Jeff had a magical artifact that somehow kept the rot from taking him. Rot that he claimed was from being touched by the Kindress. Well, he took it out, and then…." He waved vaguely. "It wasn't very pretty."

"It was soupy," Loch recalled.

"Ugh."

"Well, it was."

"What you saw is what will happen to each and every one of us if we touch him," Grell said firmly. "Even gods."

Ted opened his mouth to speak, but he paused. "That's why he wouldn't touch nothin'? I thought he didn't know… I…." His brow wrinkled.

"Even if Ell didn't know he was the Kindress, he knew his touch was deadly," Robert said. He glanced to Lochlain for encouragement to keep going. "I almost touched him once, and he completely freaked out. I never knew why."

"We do now." Lochlain rubbed Robert's back.

"That's how he was healing ghouls," Jay said suddenly.

Everyone turned to stare at him, and he shrank back.

"Go on, babycakes," Asta urged. "Flash that big sexy brain of yours."

"Well, uh…." Jay fidgeted with his glasses and cleared his throat. "The Kindress brings death to where there's life, yes, but he also brings life where there's death. I'm not sure how he figured it out, but he had to know—"

"Of course he fuckin' knew." Fred growled. "He thought he had a gift from bein' part fuckin' Eldress. He used it to fuckin' help people! People like me! He is the best man I've ever known, and I'll be damned if I let any of you assholes touch a hair on his fuckin' head!"

Jay cowered behind Asta as much of Fred's wrath seemed aimed at him.

"Calm the fuck down, zombie boy," Asta warned, flashing his sharp teeth at Fred. "I will not hesitate to double tap your bitch ass."

Fred rose to his full height and stalked toward Asta. "Who are you callin' a bitch, bitch?"

"The bitch ass bitch walkin' this way!" Asta grinned.

Though Asta appeared to be a tall young man with the lean build of a scarecrow, hiding inside was another monster as formidable as his father's.

Sloane's heart ached for Fred, and he quickly left Loch to intervene. He pushed Fred back, soothing, "Hey, hey! I know you're hurting, but that is not the fight you want right now!"

"Fuck you!" Fred growled.

"We'll find Ell, I swear it! Okay? We will find a way to help him!" Sloane said earnestly. "He's my friend too!"

"But you… you don't…." Fred's rage wilted in a wave of grief, and his voice cracked. "I'm… I have to go find him. I have to tell him…." He hissed, fighting back a sob, and he suddenly wrapped Sloane up in a rib-crushing hug.

Loch was there next, his grayish-blue tentacles unfurling to wrap around them both. "We're here, my child," he said to Fred. "All will be well."

Fred looked at Loch, and his eyes were damp. "You told me that after Lochlain was murdered, and now he's standin' right there. I… I really wanna fuckin' believe you."

"Believe it," Ted said firmly. "We're getting Ell back, okay?" He cut his eyes at Grell. "Alive."

"What?" Grell pouted. "Oh, sure, suggest one little tiny murder and everyone thinks you're a monster."

"We'll find him," Sloane reaffirmed. "He was able to live this long without hurting anyone—"

"Except Jeff, who was a dillweed and absolutely deserved it," Loch chimed in.

"We can figure it out." Sloane smiled with what he hoped was confidence. "He probably didn't go far, all right? We should start checking familiar spots first. Your place, wherever you guys liked to hang out, okay?"

"Home," Fred grunted. "He probably went home. We…." He sighed. "We didn't go nowhere else."

"I'll go with Fred," Ted said immediately. "Probably best to see some friendly fuckin' faces and not assholes who wanna kill 'em."

Grell huffed.

Loch withdrew his tentacles, and Fred nodded slowly, much calmer now. The touch of a god could be quite comforting, and Fred appeared focused but not about to break anyone's arm anymore.

"I'll drive." Fred said.

"I'm going too," Grell announced as he fell into step behind Fred and Ted.

"The fuck you are!" Ted snapped. "Ell will flip the second he sees you!"

"So I'll make sure he doesn't." Grell narrowed his eyes. "Allow me to illuminate that thick shadowy skull of yours, darling. I love you.

You're a strong queen, you have an ass that won't quit, and I adore every moment I have the honor of spending in your delightful company. I know you're angry with me right now, but if you think I'm going to let you waltz off to go poke at one of the most powerful beings in all of creation, brother or not, with only a ghoul to defend you, you clearly have underestimated my affection for you."

Ted smiled as if deeply touched, but then he scowled. "Wait, did you just call me stupid?"

Asta snorted out a laugh.

"I would never." Grell quickly turned to Sloane and Loch. "Summon any other gods who are awake. Let them know what's happened. We need to gather our allies."

"Why?" Sloane frowned. "If Fred and Ted can calm Ell down—"

"Mighty big if to hang the fate of the universe on." Grell's bright eyes glittered. "We must be ready for the worst. We need the old gods to help us, as many as we can."

Sloane's stomach turned harder, but he nodded. "Okay. Well, as luck would have it, one of them is watching our daughter right now. We'll start there."

"May Great Azaethoth watch over us all."

"Good luck, guys." Sloane waved to Fred and Ted as they departed with Grell in tow.

"Be careful!" Asta called out after Grell. "I'll be real pissed off if you get turned into soup!"

"Love you too, my precious spawn." Grell winked, and then he vanished.

Sloane didn't know if Grell portaled or had gone invisible or what, but he now had much bigger problems to worry about. Everyone left in the room was looking to him for what to do next, and the resulting pressure weighed a ton.

"So." Sloane took a deep breath, grateful for Loch's lingering tentacle around his arm. "We let them go see if they can find Ell and reason with him. A small group is probably best for now since Ell's already upset, and his boyfriend and brother are our best shot at getting him to get himself under control."

"Then what?" Lochlain asked. "We have a welcoming party for the Kindress?"

"The Kindress is still Ell," Sloane said firmly. "We can talk to him. We can find a way to make this work. He lived his whole life without hurting anyone, but then…."

But then something changed.

"What is it, my love?" Loch asked. "Your nose is doing the wrinkle thing."

"We need to see Ollie. Right now."

"Would you like me to go fetch him?" Loch fidgeted. "It would certainly piss off Alexander, and oh, I would very much like to do it even more now."

"Can you go tell your uncle what's going on and bring Pandora here?" Sloane took Loch's hand. "I'd feel much better having her with us."

"Of course, my sweet husband." Loch kissed Sloane's brow. "I'll speak to my mother and sister as well, see who else we can rouse from their slumber in Zebulon."

"You know, we should probably call Stoker too."

Loch retched dramatically.

Sullivan Stoker was a local gangster who also happened to be Jake the Gladsome, the son of Zunnerath and the legendary Abigail, the first Starkiller—the first mortal to ever slay a god.

Sloane was the second.

"He's half god and very powerful," Sloane drawled. "I know you two don't get along, but we may need his help. He might even be able to help us find Ell."

"Anything that pinstriped slimeball can do, I can do better." Loch turned his nose up.

"He can hold a sword of starlight."

"I can make macarons."

"Yes, and they're delicious, but if Ell does something bad, well…." Sloane didn't want to think about it, but he knew Grell was right.

They had to prepare for the worst.

Ell had always been such a sweet young man, and it was hard to imagine him being a danger to anyone.

The Kindress, however, was the antithesis of life itself, and there was no telling what he might do. The vivid image of Jeff's face decomposing in seconds flashed in the front of Sloane's mind, sending a shiver down his spine.

He had fought and defeated vile murderers, deranged cultists, and old gods, but the Kindress was in a completely different league. He was a being of pure starlight, the most powerful magic known in the universe, and Sloane had no idea if the sword Great Azaethoth had given him would even be able to hurt Ell should the need arise.

After all, one touch from Ell would turn any one of them—even a god—into soup.

Shit.

Loch must have seen the worry painted all over Sloane's face because he said, "For you, my love, I will subject myself to his loathsome presence."

"Thank y—"

"Though I am reserving the right to decide how I deliver the message."

Sloane sighed, and he couldn't help but smile. "Thank you." He tilted his head to catch Loch's lips in a kiss. "I love you. So much."

"And I love you, my beautiful Starkiller." Loch's eyes turned black, filling with a quick flash of stars before he disappeared.

Sloane didn't miss a beat, addressing Asta, "Hey! Can I get a favor?"

"Yeah?" Asta peered over his sunglasses. "But if it involves whipped cream, I'm sorry but I will have to decline. I'm spoken for now, you know."

"Can you portal over and bring Oleander Logue here? Tell him that it's urgent. Oh, and that it's for me. If a guy named Alexander is there—"

"Yeah, yeah. I'll tell him you wanna make out with him again real bad." Asta grinned. "Consider it done, Starkiller."

"No, Asta—"

Asta was already gone, the portal popping so quick it sounded like a snap.

"Does he even know where Ollie lives?" Jay wondered out loud.

"I'm sure he'll figure it out." Sloane grinned sheepishly.

"What can we do to help?" Robert asked. "There has to be something."

"If you need something stolen, I'm happy to oblige." Lochlain offered a sly smile that didn't seem to have its usual charm. "Otherwise, it seems that we might just be in the way. I'd rather not die again, I'll be honest."

"It's okay." Sloane patted Lochlain's shoulder. "Look, let your sister and Milo know what's going on. I want all the members of the Super Secret Sages' Club to be on alert. While I hope this is an easy fix, well…."

"Best to be prepared for anything," Robert finished. "We know. I'll see if I have any leads on artifacts that may help us. Jeff had one, after all. So there's gotta be more out there."

"Thank you, guys. Seriously. We'll keep you updated."

Robert and Lochlain left, and Jay found his way back to the table he'd been sitting at with Asta. He had a glass of wine that was still full, and he grabbed it and chugged.

Sloane sat down across from Jay with a heavy sigh. Someone's wine glass had been left behind there, and he picked it up to steal a sip.

Fuck.

"What now?" Jay asked worriedly.

"We wait," Sloane replied with a wry smile. "Loch will bring Pandora, plus his uncle, Merrick, and Chase. Asta will pop back up with Ollie, hopefully soon, and I'm betting with Alexander and Rota following right behind once they realize we borrowed Ollie."

"How are you so calm?"

"I—" Sloane laughed. "I don't know. Practice?" He fidgeted with his glass. "Not my first crisis, you know."

"Right." Jay chuckled nervously. "I kinda slept through my first one."

"Yeah." Sloane thought over the question again, and he had a better answer now, adding, "I think part of why I'm so calm is because I know I don't have to do this alone. I have Loch, his family, and all my friends like you and Asta. Together we're powerful, and we're a force to be reckoned with." He held his head high. "Ell is one of us too. Kindress or not, we can help him."

Jay tipped his glass back. "I really, really hope you're right."

Asta popped back through a portal, and he had a very startled Ollie with him. "Found him!"

"Sloane?" Ollie's eyes were wide. He was a tall, muscular redhead known for his odd malapropisms and unusual stutter. "Why did the cat monster kittennap me? Because I'm pretty sure this is real."

"Hey Ollie!" Sloane grinned sheepishly. "I'm sorry, but it was the fastest way to get you here." He rose from the table to greet him and give him a hug. "We really, really need your help."

"Uh, sure. Nothing weird about this at all." Ollie purposefully turned away so he wouldn't have to look at Asta. "What's up?"

Ollie had a blessing of starsight like Ted did. Ollie's particular gift allowed him to see all that was hidden, so he could see what Asta truly was beneath his human form.

Asta didn't seem to notice, and he probably assumed Ollie was trying to avoid staring at him because he was naked now.

"Short version, uh, is that Elliam Sturm is the Kindress," Sloane said quickly, also averting his eyes from Asta's bare ass. "He just took off out of here pretty upset. Apparently he didn't know who he was, and we need to find him fast before anything bad happens."

"Kindress?" Ollie blinked slowly. "The… the firstborn of—"

"Yes, that one."

"Fuck, fuck, fuck." Ollie headed right for the nearest table to grab an abandoned drink. He chugged it. "Fuck, fuck, fuck—"

Sloane cringed. "Yeah, it's a little concerning. More than a little, I guess."

Asta sat back beside Jay and stretched his legs over Jay's lap. He nodded toward Ollie and magically refilled the glass he was trying to reach the bottom of. "There ya' go, Red. Enjoy."

Ollie paused long enough to say, "Thanks."

All at once, Loch, Pandora, Merrick, and Chase appeared. Merrick and Chase were shouting at Loch, Loch was shouting at them, and Pandora was giggling.

Pandora was Loch and Sloane's infant daughter, although, being a demigoddess, she was prone to growth spurts. She was the size of a one-year-old child though she had just turned four months. She had a big mop of curly red hair like Loch, Sloane's thick arched brows, and eight teeth that she enjoyed using frequently almost as much as she liked setting things on fire.

Merrick was a handsome black man in a sharp suit and Chase was an older pale ginger in a slightly less sharp ensemble. Merrick was Gordoth, the Sagittarian god of justice, and they were both detectives at the Archersville Police Department and partners off the clock. They were also both uncles, Merrick to Loch and Chase to Ollie.

Chase had his ever present fedora on, and it appeared to be smoking.

"—certain words that make her very excited!" Loch was saying. "You can't announce that you're going to B-U-R-N rubber!"

"It's a common expression!" Chase argued. "You know, hey, let's go! We're in a hurry! Let's burn some rub—"

"Don't say it!"

Pandora squealed excitedly and clapped her hands, and the tablecloths all ignited.

"Bad girl, bad!" Loch tutted. "No more fire!"

Merrick pinched the bridge of his nose, and the flames were quickly extinguished, including the last bit of smoke from Chase's hat. "If I am understanding what my very excitable nephew just told us, the Kindress is here on Aeon and left here in a very poor mood?"

"You got it," Sloane confirmed, walking over to smooch Pandora's cheeks. "Hey Panda Bear. We've talked about fires, young lady."

"Firahhh!" Pandora's eyes gleamed.

"No. No more fires."

"Hey, Daddy Ginger," Asta purred toward Chase. "Never did get a chance to thank you for the hookup. The dicking down has been awesome."

Jay turned a very unnatural shade of red and tried to hide his face in his hands. He and Asta had recently reconciled thanks to Chase.

Chase gave a quick salute. "Happy to help."

Merrick scoffed. "Can we focus, please?"

"Yeah, yeah. Focusing. Totally focused. It's the star baby, right?" Chase looked around for confirmation. "We're saying the big scary star baby is real? And it's Ell?"

Ollie took a break from drinking to reply, "Yup! It was Ell! Crazy, huh?"

Chase turned toward Ollie's voice. He laughed and headed over to give him a hug. "Hey! What are you doin' here?"

Ollie held up the cup. "I'm workin', Uncle Chase."

Loch wrapped his tentacles around Sloane and Pandora, saying, "We had a tiny mishap with a very small fire, but everything is all right. On a totally and completely unrelated note, we did not apparently fireproof the shower curtain."

"Oh, yes, totally unrelated." Sloane chuckled, appreciating the brief moment of levity. He knew there might not be many more to enjoy.

"What is happening now?" Merrick demanded. "Where are the others?"

"Robert and Lochlain are on the hunt for any less-than-legal items that might be able to help us. King Grell went with Fred and Ted to look for Ell at their place and a few other local spots, see if they can find him," Sloane replied. "There's a chance that Ell just needs a moment to calm down—"

"No, it is not that simple," Merrick cut in abruptly. "The Kindress is cursed to forever succumb to his corruption. I can only assume he has been able to resist this long because he was not aware of what he truly was."

"What are you saying, Uncle?" Loch frowned. "That now that he knows, he will be corrupted?"

"Yes."

"I would like to nominate placing the blame on King Grell."

"That does not matter," Merrick chided. "Whether it was King Grell or another or some other completely random act, this is destiny. The Kindress will always fail."

"Hey, but it ends too, right?" Chase squeezed Merrick's shoulder. "We just gotta wait for Big Azaethoth to come down and work up some tears, right?"

"That may also be a problem. Great Azaethoth remains in the dreaming and the fountain—"

Ollie swayed a little, and he sat in the closet chair with a loud belch. "Sorry, excuse me."

"How much have you had to drink?" Chase wrinkled his nose. "I can fuckin' smell you from here."

"My starsight thingie works better if I've had a few." Ollie stared long and hard at his cup. "This has been more than a few, so I'm thinking it's gonna work awesome."

"Can you see where Ell is?" Sloane asked gently. "Anything at all?"

"Sure! Totally. I've got this. I—" Ollie's head smacked into the table.

"I guess he don't drink like he used to." Chase made a face.

"It's all right." Sloane smiled patiently. "We'll wait. He's definitely our best hope for figuring out where Ell is now."

"So, let me get this straight because, you know, I'm slow at this Sage stuff." Chase pulled at his beard. "The star baby was Ell this whole fuckin' time and we didn't know? Why didn't he ever go all murdery like he's supposed to?"

"If he did not know he was the Kindress, it may have created a mental barrier against the corruption," Merrick replied. "Now that it has been removed, it is only a matter of time."

"And the corruption is from Daddy Azaethoth bein' all sad over murdering him a whole bunch?"

"Yes." Merrick sighed. "However, it may be more complicated than that."

"Oh. Fuck. Great." Chase hesitated before asking, "And why exactly?"

"Do not forget what the song said—"

"Ah, I got it!" Ollie whipped his head up. He hiccuped and glanced around the room in a drunken daze.

"Got what, kiddo?" Chase asked gently.

"The answer to your question."

"What question?"

Ollie's eyes fell on Sloane, and he pointed at him. "Your question."

Sloane blinked. "Me? You mean about Ell?"

"No, the other one." Ollie shook his head. "You wanted to know what changed. I can see it. I can see all the things, and they fit together like a neat li'l puzzle. No, like one of those machine thingies where a ball will go down a tube and hits a sock and then that fills up a tub with jam or something."

"I believe our starsight witch has had a little too much," Loch whispered loudly, "or he hit his head hard enough to sustain a brain injury."

Sloane eyed Asta, who shrugged and batted his eyes innocently. "What exactly was in that cup?"

"The Kindress," Ollie insisted, his words slurring faster now. "It's the Kindress. No, not that he's in my cup. That would be weird. Alcohol was in my cup. Is in my cup. But you! You wanted to know what changed the cycle."

"Yes." Sloane tried not to be alarmed that Ollie knew about a question he'd only thought about.

"Yup, that's the one." Ollie beamed.

Sloane cleared his throat. "Well, what was it?"

"Huh? What?"

"What broke the cycle, Ollie?"

"Oh! You did, Sloane."

K.L. "KAT" HIERS is an embalmer, restorative artist, and queer writer. Licensed in both funeral directing and funeral service, they worked in the death industry for nearly a decade. Their first love was always telling stories, and they have been writing for over twenty years, penning their very first book at just eight years old. Publishers generally do not accept manuscripts in Hello Kitty notebooks, however, but they never gave up.

Following the success of their first novel, Cold Hard Cash, they now enjoy writing professionally, focusing on spinning tales of sultry passion, exotic worlds, and emotional journeys. They love attending horror movie conventions and indulging in cosplay of their favorite characters. They live in Zebulon, NC, with their family, including their children, some of whom have paws and a few that only pretend to because they think it's cute.

Website: http://www.klhiers.com

Follow me on BookBub

A SUCKER FOR LOVE MYSTERY

ACSQUIDENTALLY
IN LOVE

K.L. HIERS

"A breezy and sensual LGBTQ paranormal romance."
—*Library Journal*

A Sucker For Love Mystery

Nothing brings two men—or one man and an ancient god—together like revenge.

Private investigator Sloane sacrificed his career in law enforcement in pursuit of his parents' murderer. Like them, he is a follower of long-forgotten gods, practicing their magic and offering them his prayers… not that he's ever gotten a response.

Until now.

Azaethoth the Lesser might be the patron of thieves and tricksters, but he takes care of his followers. He's come to earth to avenge the killing of one of his favorites, and maybe charm the pants off the cute detective Fate has placed in his path. If he has his way, they'll do much more than bring a killer to justice. In fact, he's sure he's found the man he'll spend his immortal life with.

Sloane's resolve is crumbling under Azaethoth's surprising sweetness, and the tentacles he sometimes glimpses escaping the god's mortal form set his imagination alight. But their investigation gets stranger and deadlier with every turn. To survive, they'll need a little faith… and a lot of mystical firepower.

www.dreamspinnerpress.com

A SUCKER FOR LOVE MYSTERY

KRAKEN MY
HEART

K.L. HIERS

A Sucker For Love Mystery

It's just Ted's luck that he meets the love of his life while covered in the blood of a murder victim.

Funeral worker Ted Sturm has a foul mouth, a big heart, and a knack for communicating with the dead. Unfortunately the dead don't make very good friends, and Ted's only living pal, his roommate, just rescued a strange cat who's determined to make his life even more miserable. This cat is more than he seems, and soon Ted finds himself in an alternate dimension… and on top of a dead body.

When Ted is accused of murder, his only ally in a strange world full of powerful magical beings calling for his head is King Grell, a sarcastic, randy, catlike immortal with impressive abilities… and anatomy. The two soon find themselves at the center of a cosmic conspiracy and surrounded by dangerous enemies. But with Ted's special skills and Grell's magic, they have a chance to get to the bottom of the mystery and save Ted. There's just one problem: Ted's got to resist Grell's aggressive advances… and he isn't sure he wants to.

www.dreamspinnerpress.com

A SUCKER FOR LOVE MYSTERY

Head Over
Tentacles

K.L. Hiers

A Sucker For Love Mystery

Private investigator Sloane Beaumont should be enjoying his recent engagement to eldritch god Azaethoth the Lesser, AKA Loch. Unfortunately, he doesn't have time for a pre-honeymoon period.

The trouble starts with a deceptively simple missing persons case. That leads to the discovery of mass kidnappings, nefarious secret experiments, and the revelation that another ancient god is trying to bring about the end of the world by twisting humans into an evil army.

Just another day at the office.

Sloane does his best to juggle wedding planning, stopping his fiancé from turning the mailman inside out, and meeting his future godly in-laws while working the case, but they're also being hunted by a strange young man with incredible abilities. With the wedding date looming closer, Sloane and Loch must combine their powers to discover the truth—because it's not just their own happy-ever-after at stake, but the fate of the world....

www.dreamspinnerpress.com

A SUCKER FOR LOVE MYSTERY

NAUTILUS THAN
PERFECT

K.L. HIERS

A Sucker For Love Mystery

Detective Elwood Q. Chase has ninety-nine problems, and the unexpected revelation that his partner is a god is only one of them.

Chase has been in love with Benjamin Merrick for years and has resigned himself to a life of unrequited pining. But when they run afoul of a strange cult, Merrick's secret identity as Gordoth the Untouched slips out… and so do Chase's feelings. The timing can't be helped, but now Merrick thinks Chase only cares about him because he's a god.

Even more unfortunately, it turns out the cultists want to perform a ritual to end the world. Chase's mission to convince Merrick his feelings predate any divine revelations takes a back seat to a case tangled with murder and lies, but Chase doesn't give up. Once he finds out there's a chance Merrick feels the same way, he digs in his heels. Suddenly he's trying to court a god and save the world at the same time. What could possibly go wrong?

www.dreamspinnerpress.com

A SUCKER FOR LOVE MYSTERY

JUST
CALAMARRIED

K.L. HIERS

A Sucker For Love Mystery

Newlyweds Sloane and Loch are eagerly expecting their first child, though for Sloane that excitement is tempered by pregnancy side effects. Carrying a god's baby would be enough to deal with, especially with the whole accelerated gestation thing, but it's not like Sloane can take maternity leave. He works for himself as a private investigator. Which leads him to his next case.

At least this strange new mystery distracts him from the stress of constant puking.

When two priests are murdered within hours of each other, a woman named Daphne hires Sloane and Loch to track down the prime suspect—her brother—before the police do. Between untangling a conspiracy of lies and greed, going toe-to-toe with a gangster, and stealing a cat, they hardly have time to decorate a nursery….

www.dreamspinnerpress.com